A Tail for
All seasons

Volume 3

A Tail for All Seasons

Volume 3

A collection of Manx stories

editor **Linda Mann**

Priory Press

Published by Priory Press Ltd
The Priory, Abbots Way, Abbotswood,
Ballasalla, Isle of Man IM9 3EQ
www.priory-press.co.uk

First published 2010
ISBN 978-0-9551510-7-1

Edited and typeset by
Frances Hackeson Freelance Publishing Services,
Brinscall, Lancs
Printed in Great Britain by
Bell and Bain Ltd, Glasgow

contents

Contents

preface

Many, many years ago I was lucky enough to be elected onto the Isle of Man Arts Council and was made Chairman of the Film and Literature Panel. It was a lot of fun and at times hard work but ultimately rewarding as I made a lot of new friends and discovered that just below the surface of our sleepy Island is a great deal of undiscovered talent.

However there was one award which recognised good writing and that was the Olive Lamming, set up to help and encourage authors and poets Island-wide whether they were penning fact or fiction. Last year I was asked to help judge the short stories and again I was surprised by how high the standard actually was. I was even more surprised to discover that the winners would remain unpublished and that is why if you read through this volume you will find stories by the top three finalists in the short story category and the winner of the story based on fact.

We also have a little treat and have included the winning entry to the Island's first junior CWA award. This little gem is hidden at the back and although it isn't set in the Island

and is very short, is nonetheless a cracking good, albeit dark, read.

This new collection is darker, scarier and twistier than the last and is I hope something that you will enjoy as the evenings draw in, the wind howls and the waves crash against the shore.

Happy reading

Linda Mann

foreword

It must be that time of the year again because there is another phone message from Linda Mann: 'Bob can you write a Foreword to another book?' What's the scribe of Ballasalla been up to now I ask myself, although I might have guessed as it's another volume of *A Tail for All Seasons* written by those industrious authors of Mann.

We have now had two launches of these excellent earlier volumes and I'm always surprised by what a pack animal authors can be. I'm not sure whether it's the wine, the company or the threats from Linda that gets them together, although I have heard the rumours of the small room with the padded walls and interesting ironmongery. After the readings they gather to talk to their fans – a growing number now –and each other alike. 'What's your new story about?' they ask, happy to share in the literary atmosphere.

It may be that writing is a solitary pursuit, sitting long hours by a guttering candle composing (with a sharpened quill full of dripping ink) another tale, although perhaps that is a slightly romantic view, but these writers take themselves off into their dream worlds so we can enjoy the product of these many, many hours of work.

Three things, I'm told are certain in life: death, taxes and another volume of *A Tail for All Seasons*, well at least you can now enjoy the third volume ... bother, somebody is knocking on the door ... it's the grim reaper with a tax demand. 'I won't be long Sir, I've just got this last story to finish reading. Perhaps you might like a copy of the new book in lieu of taxes?'

Enjoy this latest volume – after all, it's a certainty after death and taxes.

Bob Harrison
Evening Extra
www.manxradio.com

❄ January ❄

Colin Insole is a writer and part-time lecturer who lives in Lymington, on the south coast of England.

He has written occasional non-fiction articles for magazines on a variety of subjects, notably postal history. He contributed three short stories to a textbook for the British Sign Language Association and has written tales for the tribute anthologies dedicated to Gustav Meyrink and Mikhail Bulgakov, published by Ex Occidente Press of Bucharest, Romania. Recently Colin contributed to the short story collection *Back to the Middle of Nowhere*, published by Pill Hill Press, USA.

Colin has always had an interest in the history, language and folk stories of the Isle of Man.

The premonition

Colin Insole

On Friday 3rd December 1909, at twelve minutes past one in the morning, the Isle of Man steamer Ellan Vannin *left Ramsey Harbour for Liverpool, carrying mail, cargo and passengers. Although the weather was rough, she had negotiated far worse conditions in the past. But an hour and a half into the voyage, the winds increased to hurricane force and the ship finally sank in thirty feet of water on the Liverpool side of the Mersey Bar with the loss of all passengers and crew. Thirty-five victims were named but it is believed that others may have been on board.*

The January snows of 1909 on the Island were bitter and pro-longed. The railways were frozen, the steamers delayed and livestock perished in the remote farmsteads.

In her cottage, deep in Sulby Glen, as dusk fell, Lena Dowan was preparing her evening meal and banking the log fire high against the cold. She faced a dilemma. Her uncle, who kept sheep on an isolated farm near Rhendoo, had just left. He had brought bad news. His three best workers had fallen sick with influenza. The animals were dying in the

3

fields. He couldn't feed them or bring them to shelter on his own and he needed help. Lena agreed to stay the week with him, arriving the next day.

"If you know anyone else, they'd be most welcome – some big strong lad," he said as he closed the door, his face gaunt and worried.

At nineteen, Lena was the finest seamstress and dress-maker on the island. Aged only eleven, she'd first helped her bedridden mother earn shillings by mending the jackets and trousers of the lonely bachelor hill farmers. Her fingers were light and quick and the men grew to appreciate the little touches of luxury and comfort. Soon she began to make her own dresses with an elegance and taste that attracted the attentions of shrewd and wealthy women. Commissions followed and her reputation grew.

She knew many big strong lads but none she would feel comfortable working with alone. They would tease and bully her. But there was someone who might help. She made up her mind, quickly pulled on her coat and boots, and stepped outside. Already, she could see the light from his cottage, a quarter of a mile down into the Glen.

Gilrea Conill had always admired Lena but had been too shy to ask her to walk out with him. They both worshipped at St Stephen's in Sulby where he occasionally played the organ, supplementing his meagre earnings as a travelling school-master. At twenty, he was a careful and serious young man but was unpopular with the rough labourers. 'Limpy-Letty', the farmers' children had nicknamed him at school – a wet blanket, a dog in the manger – too weak and cowardly to join in their raiding parties on hen-houses or isolated orchards. But Lena liked his quiet ways. Both had lost their parents and lived alone. She would take the chance and ask for his help in feeding and sheltering the stricken animals.

Gilrea agreed immediately, blinking like a surprised owl in his cramped little kitchen. He even insisted on seeing her safely home, holding his box lantern high to find her the least slippery path in the ice and snow.

The week on her uncle's farm was a success. Despite their soft-handed fumbling, they managed to save most of the sheep. Busy with rare physical labour, they had no time to be embarrassed or coy and found they enjoyed each other's company. And every evening, exhausted and frostbitten, they fell asleep in the drowsy farm kitchen with its heavy sweet smells of peat fires, strong tea and fried bloaters.

When the snows thawed, they both bought bicycles and toured the Island together at weekends.

★ ★ ★

Paul Bellayne, showman, ventriloquist and master puppeteer, stepped off the ferry at Ramsey in early April 1909. Although assured and self-confident beyond his twenty-two years, an oppressive fear of his visit to the Island had grown over the past few days. The islanders called it 'monney-vaaish' – a death-warning – and last night, sleeping fitfully in a cheap Liverpool lodging-house, he'd had a disturbing premonition.

He dreamed of a body, broken and sea-battered, washed up on a dirty industrial beach, shadowed by grey wharves and warehouses. Rough prying hands tore at the man's clothing and clawed out a small money box, identical to the one he always carried, hidden deep in the lining of his overcoat pocket. The thieves were dividing and counting golden sovereigns but he could not remember the exact amount when he had woken, cold and shivering.

He had learned to trust his instincts. Two years ago, in Vilnius, he had turned his wagon back from a fair his family had attended for two centuries. He learned later that rioting had broken out and many caravans had been burned or smashed by the mob – the families now destitute. Throughout the ferry crossing, he watched the weather anxiously and viewed his fellow passengers with unaccustomed mistrust. The passage had been calm and uneventful but the faces of the crew puzzled and disturbed him. He felt he had seen them earlier in his dream but he could not quite recall the memory.

But now, safely ashore, he waited for the arrival of his caravan and prepared for the journey to Sulby Fair.

★ ★ ★

Lena loved the bustle of the fairground; the steam and farm-yard smells rising over the Claddagh from the animals' bodies and the familiar booths and drinking tents dotted over the green, with the farmers in their brown homespun, lazily smoking their pipes. The pair of them had walked up from the Glen to buy pullets' eggs and pick bunches of bluebells and primroses.

The fair was mainly livestock and farm produce. Entertainers were rare but sometimes fiddlers and pipers from Port Erin or Peel would play for pennies and the sour Punch and Judy man from Douglas with his hoarse voice and trembling hands would brave the crowd's mirth.

But on that bright April morning, with the smell of wild garlic filling the hedgerows, a long exotic caravan stood on the side of the Claddagh. The sign, in black and gold, read 'Bellayne's Puppet Theatre'. A varied cast of painted marionettes embellished all sides of the wagon whilst two huge plumed shire horses grazed by the roadside.

When the crowd of curious onlookers had swelled, the curtains on the theatre drew back to reveal a wide illuminated stage. The scene was instantly recognisable. It was Sulby Glen. A voice filled the arena.

"Ladies and gentlemen. Bellayne's Non Pareil, the most prestigious puppet theatre in Europe, presents for your entertainment and pleasure, the brutal murder of John Kewish, by his own son."

Both Gilrea and Lena grew tense and uncomfortable. The crime was still discussed locally in half-whispers and asides. In March 1872, unmarried John Kewish, aged 40, murdered his 69-year-old father at their cottage in Sulby Glen. Also living there was his mother, emotionally estranged from her husband and siding with her son in the many violent arguments that raged throughout the house, and a simple-minded daughter of about 30 years of age. Six wounds were found on the old man, also named John, consistent with stabbing by a pitchfork. John Kewish Jr was found guilty and hanged at Castletown and his body was buried in the grounds of Castle Rushen.

Although the murder had been committed nearly a generation before Lena and Gilrea were born, its figures stalked their childhood. Their families had known John Kewish. He had stolen their sheep and stormed drunken and violent outside their cottages in the small hours of the night until the dogs were set loose on him. Gilrea had an uncle who had liked to taunt him with ghost stories about the murderer.

"John Kewish is only sleeping – all cruddled up in his Castle Rushen grave. But he'll rise soon and he'll come looking for you. It'll take him three or four hours of slow walking and he'll stop on the way to collect and sharpen his little pitchfork."

Gilrea would lie awake until dawn, listening for the tap of the pitchfork or the roar of Kewish's voice in every gust of wind in the trees.

For Lena, it was the sister's story which troubled her. Her mother had seen the police wagon taking the deranged woman to the lunatic asylum – the same wagon that had hustled John Kewish to Castle Rushen the day before. She had seen the face staring out from the bars and heard the shrieking and cursing. Whenever Lena's fingers grew tired or slacked at her needlework, her mother snapped, "If you go bad, Lena Dowan, you'll end up like that poor nameless soul. Then the wagon will come for you and you'll die an old maid in the asylum. And your name too will be forgotten."

The puppets had an energy and character far beyond the skills of the Douglas Punch and Judy man. Each capered or staggered with a distinctive gait and only Lena's sharp eyes could see their strings, shadowed and green to blend with the scenery.

When John Kewish lunged at his father with the pitchfork, little gouts of blood spurted from the mannequin. During the execution, the hangman produced brandy from his pocket, uncorked the bottle and poured a draught down his victim's throat before swigging the remainder and hooding the prisoner. The spectators' mouths dropped, for the puppet had poured real liquid.

But it was their voices that unsettled Lena and Gilrea. These visiting showmen had captured exactly the dialect words and speech patterns of their grandfathers' generation. Half-remembered phrases from childhood returned as the voices rose over the Claddagh. When the sister was taken to the asylum, her screams echoed not from the stage but from the cart track that led to the Castletown road. Everyone stared and looked back as if expecting to see her face fading into the distance. The show ended and a girl of about ten edged shyly among the crowd collecting coins. Both Lena and Gilrea were deeply moved by the drama. Lena wanted to hurry away at once, away from the voices that had haunted her childhood and away from the gouts of blood and the dangling puppet.

But it was Gilrea, unusually brave, who urged her back. And every day since, he had regretted and cursed his curiosity.

"Let's peep behind the curtain and see how they do those tricks."

Propelling Lena forward, he pulled the curtain aside and started back, apologetic. Above his head, on a raised platform, exhausted from manipulating the puppets, was a young man, breathing in shallow gasps.

Momentarily angry at being discovered tired and vulnerable, Paul Bellayne then quickly judged the intruders, decided they were benevolent and impulsively invited them inside.

The caravan was cramped and richly furnished. It smelled of oils, varnish and spices. An old couple, their hands racked and swollen with arthritis, were preparing food for three young children, the oldest having just returned with the day's takings. Staring down from every shelf and alcove were hundreds of puppets, some yellow with the age of centuries. They had been modelled in the changing styles of lost generations: the forgotten pantomime favourites, the murderers and heroines only recalled now in folk stories and nursery rhymes.

Never had Lena seen such richness and delicacy of fabric that hung from their cork or papier-mâché bodies. There were purple satins, silk damasks with inlaid silver threading, gold brocade and intricate chinoiserie that swirled and shifted as the light changed. But even Gilrea noticed how dishevelled and threadbare their robes had become. They glared down in faded grandeur like a host of forlorn Miss Havishams.

Paul Bellayne noticed their glances.

"There is no one left skilled enough to dress our puppets and mend their clothes. Moths do their work and mice nibble unseen in the darkness. We lost our mother and two sisters to typhus in a Salzburg winter four years ago. My younger sister, Katya, is competent for the rough repairs of the clowns and villains you saw today but our true art is for the connoisseur. We entertain royalty in their palaces and the nobility in their salons. But their eyes would spot any flaws. The fabrics must shimmer and shift like gossamer."

Lena delicately lifted the frayed and faded clothing of an ancient female puppet.

"She is the Queen of Nineveh," said Paul. "Modelled and dressed in 1598. She danced before the court of Elizabeth. Shakespeare remarked on her form and beauty."

"May I?" asked Lena, and from her bag produced her sewing tools. Without pausing she matched the smoky gold of the costume with cotton thread and instantly threaded a needle so thin it reminded Gilrea of a tiny herring bone.

Paul Bellayne nodded and Lena set to work. There is a beauty and magic in watching an artist or craftsman at work and Lena held them silent and spellbound. Finally, the Queen of Nineveh was restored in all her finery.

"I had to turn and double the fabric where it was torn and faded but I think she'll do," said Lena, dismissing her work as if she'd simply reattached a farmer's jacket button.

"She is exquisite," said Bellayne. He pressed her to accept payment, which she refused. Finally the tension was broken when the old man unlocked a wooden cabinet and produced a bottle of brandy and glasses for them all.

"Tsar Nicholas presented us with a case of this five years ago when we performed at St Petersburg for the ninth birthday of the Princess Olga. Our play was preferred to the dances of the Ballet Russes. The wine comes from the court of Louis XV."

The drink cemented their friendship. Lena spent hours visiting the caravan, mending the puppets and teaching Katya the basics of her craft. Gilrea joined her when work allowed, bitterly resenting the time she spent with Paul. There were no arguments, no jealous quarrels, merely a brooding silent rage. But he smiled and simpered and all seemed well. For five months he became the showman's loblolly boy – an errand runner, fetching their food and passing the hat round for sixpences.

Summer passed. As the tide of daytrippers reduced to a trickle, by mid-September the puppet theatre was ready to return to the mainland. The caravan was manoeuvred onto the ferry. The old man bowed stiffly and handed a bottle of his Louis XV brandy to both Lena and Gilrea. Gilrea had not felt happier since April. Five months of smiling, of silent humiliations were over. He wished never to see them again. And then, as he mentally practised his faltering marriage proposal to Lena, he overheard Paul say to her, in an undertone, "I'll be back late November, early December, but I'll write first."

Cold and desolate, a broken despair and hardness entered Gilrea. He would employ whatever cunning and deceit he could muster to win her back. He would watch and spy on her.

He began by intercepting her mail. He knew the postmaster at Sulby well. It had been easy. His duplicity shamed and surprised him.

"I'm visiting Lena this morning. I'll drop her letters off – save John the extra journey."

Her cottage was a long detour and John the postman was grateful. And so it became a habit. Of course he had to endure the postmaster's sly jokes and innuendoes.

"I reckon in a month or two John'll need stop at only one cottage for the pair of you. And then your trouser buttons will be sewn on fine. She's a darling, that little one."

When he visited her she seemed preoccupied and hurried in her work. For the past two years she'd helped with the costumes for the late December production by the Douglas Choral Union. This year they were performing *HMS Pinafore* and Gilrea was playing the piano. Lena was making only Princess Buttercup's gaudy and extravagant dress and by late November the costume was already complete. To Gilrea it seemed as if she had rushed the work for something secret and more important.

On 26th November, a day of shadow and cold fogs, the letter arrived. He recognised Bellayne's ornate copperplate with the continental numbers. He had practised steaming open his own letters and re-sealing them with a thin colourless glue but still he scolded himself as his fingers shook uncontrollably. He read the letter.

My Dearest Lena
I will catch the early morning ferry to Ramsey on December 2nd and hire a dogcart for the trunk. I loathe deception and deceit but understand your reasons for concealing our plans from Gilrea.
I wish him well.
Yours ever,
Paul

Nothing could be clearer. She intended to leave the Island and dared not tell him. Paul was collecting her trunk and she would follow him soon after.

He began spying on her cottage for hours at a time, lying concealed and soaking wet in a rough ditch. He saw the trunk. It was hidden in her bedroom. Continually for three days she packed it, carefully placing objects wrapped in cloth, her body light and graceful, as when she'd danced so proudly with Bellayne at Douglas and Port Erin.

From mid-morning on 2nd December, Gilrea watched from his ditch. At midday Bellayne arrived, paler and thinner than in the summer. Unusually, Lena's lace curtains were drawn and all he could see were their silhouettes earnestly talking for nearly an hour. Finally the trunk was loaded on

the dogcart and Gilrea watched them embrace at the door of
the cottage. It was a lovers' parting, a kiss more fervent than
he had ever dared. As the horse started, Gilrea crawled from
ditch to gorse bush. He would cut across the Glen, follow him
and wait his chance.

* * *

Paul Bellayne had forgotten his dream of the previous April
throughout his summer stay on the Island. Yet a sense of fore-
boding returned as his dogcart climbed towards the Ramsey
road. Last night, in the same dingy Liverpool lodging-house,
the premonition had returned. The faces of the *Ellan Vannin*
crew, men he recognised and knew as friends, passed like
shadows while a storm raged. There was the body again, lying
in oil and tar on the beach. Hands ripped at the clothes and
coins were counted and divided.

And then he remembered. They had counted seventy-five
golden sovereigns – the exact sum he now carried, deep in his
overcoat, after giving Lena fifty pounds.

On a farm track, surrounded by strange twisted gorse
bushes, edged with flowers of fire, he was aware of a tension, an
ill-defined hostility. His horse sensed it too. He'd been made
welcome on the Island throughout the summer. Strangers
had warmed to him but he knew that malice flourished in
even the most benign and idyllic settings. Lena had told him
that a year or two back the farmers were in fear of wreckers
and incendiaries who came in stealth at night. He clasped his
knife and urged the pony forward.

Shivering and wet behind the furze bush, Gilrea watched
him and felt that his chance was gone. He returned to his
cottage and resolved to walk that night to Ramsey. He would
confront Paul in one of the town's inns or wait until the ferry
sailed. There, the matter would be decided.

★ ★ ★

At eleven o'clock that night, Gilrea locked the door of his cottage and began the six-mile walk to Ramsey. He knew it to be the most foolhardy and reckless act of his life. He sang softly to himself the lyrics of 'Mylecharaine', the solemn melancholy tune of his Jurby ancestors.

"And all alone she left me
Like a furze-bush in a flame of fire."

He stopped and spoke those lines in English, absorbed in his self-pity. In daylight, he always felt a part of this landscape, sensing the benign ghosts of his people in the rough pathways and shining gorse bushes. But tonight, indifferent or even hostile, they shut him out. The hills, black and massive, towered above him. There were no lights left in the isolated cottages and his box lantern seemed solitary and fragile.

In his darkest moments he'd imagined murdering Paul Bellayne. He could have bought a secondhand revolver and ammunition in Douglas for ten shillings and shot his rival in a secluded lane or bridleway. But he knew the futility of the act. He would become a nightmare figure like John Kewish for a new generation of children, or have his folly dramatised for a jerking penny-in-the-slot machine on Douglas sea front. No, his plan was more reckless, more romantic and true to his island forebears.

Lena had always teased him about his thrift. "You see every penny as big as a cartwheel," she said. "There are no pockets in a shroud." And she compared him to the miser, Mylecharaine, from the old song, who shamed his daughter by wearing odd shoes to church. She was wrong about Mylecharaine. His grandfather had told him the real story. Mylecharaine had deserved his sevenfold bad luck because he paid his daughter's dowry. Long ago, it had been the custom

for the bridegroom, if he really loved his girl, to pay hand-
somely for her. His grandfather had known a man, three
generations back, besotted with an Irish tinker girl, blown in
from Sligo during the hungry forties. A "scrawny wee skite
she was", but the man had paid her family twenty pounds and
a gold ring and they lived happily in Jurby still. And Gilrea,
who loved Lena, was going to pay Paul Bellayne to let her
go. He had beggared himself. All of his hard-earned savings
and inheritance had been withdrawn from the bank. He had
sold his mother's silver cross, kept in the family for centuries,
together with every keepsake and ornament. Nothing had been
spared. Only his cottage, cold and blank-walled remained.
"Lonely didst thou leave me," he repeated the words of the
song. Bellayne would understand. He acknowledged him as a
man of honour who respected the traditions and customs of
the old ways. Besides, with the money, Bellayne could afford
to restore his puppets. With these weasel words he reassured
himself and touched the metal money box deep in his overcoat pocket. He had raised seventy-five sovereigns.

As Gilrea entered the George at Ramsey at twenty minutes
to one, Lena Dowan awoke, a tiny doubt spoiling the success
of her day. Often, since the summer, she'd nearly spoken to
him about the trunk and her plans but every time she mentioned Bellayne, he'd grown taciturn and morose and changed
the subject.

Of course she'd imagined leaving the Island and joining
Paul. He'd asked her today, simply and guilelessly. And
she'd turned him down. She dreaded the confines of that
little caravan, the stories of violence and disease on lonely
European roads and the feeling that Bellayne was the last
romantic remnant of a lost tradition and time.

On hearing her refusal, Paul had bowed, hugged her and
wished her well. It was the same embrace Gilrea had witnessed

from his ditch.

"Will you marry Gilrea?" Paul had asked.

"Yes. If he wants me," she said.

"Sometimes a man needs help. Why not ask him yourself?"

And with those words he was gone.

Lena knew she would be successful at her work and her bicycle gave her the freedom to travel the Island she loved and visit customers, despite the mutterings of the hidebound old about young women tying up their skirts and showing their legs. Throughout the autumn, she had repaired and dressed a hundred puppets, the pride and pick of Bellayne's theatre, using original antique fabrics. Never again would she doubt her ability with fine expensive material. And she had been paid well. Fifty pounds was a fortune.

She regretted never discussing her work and finances with Gilrea. He worked long, gruelling hours and earned less than her. Recently he had become sullen and sensitive about money and Lena shied away from the subject. But no other man would have accepted or tolerated her solitary visits to the caravan. She'd fallen in love with him in the snows of January. His patience and tenderness with the farm animals had surprised and charmed her. She'd watched him asleep in front of the kitchen fire, wet and frost-bitten and imagined growing old together on the Island. She would speak to him tomorrow and propose. They could live in his house whilst her cottage could be her dressmaking shop. Relieved and settled in her mind, she turned over and fell asleep.

* * *

On Ramsey quayside at one o'clock, Paul Bellayne's unease grew. The storm was rising but he had known far worse weather at sea. His trunk was ready to load on board.

A woman spoke. "Good evening, Mr Bellayne. We'll need our sea legs tonight, I fear."

She worked in one of the Ramsey hotels. As she spoke her tiny pearl necklace moved and glinted in the gaslight. Thirty feet of water in Liverpool Bar, he had overheard a sailor say on the ferry that morning. Full fathom five. The words of *The Tempest* came to him: 'Those were the pearls that were his eyes.' He looked towards the *Ellan Vannin*, rising and falling gently in the harbour. 'The ship no stronger than a nut-shell.' And then he saw the wheel. In his mind, five men were gripping it, trying in vain to steer as the seas crashed over them. The same men now passed him in single file, mute and hunched. They were part of the crew of the *Ellan Vannin*, shuffling as if sleepwalking to the gangway. Each one solemnly nodded to him, distant and dreamlike. His premonition of the night before returned. The body of the drowned man, lying in the oil and tar of a Liverpool wharf, was turned over and the face revealed. He rushed to stop the ship from sailing.

Warm and snug inside the bar of the *Ellan Vannin*, Gilrea Conill ate greedily and self-absorbed. He would wait and speak with Paul Bellayne in a quiet corner of the ship. Somewhere on the quayside he could hear shouting. He thought of Mylecharaine and his own Jurby ancestors. Would Paul understand and accept his money? The shouting had increased. He hoped it wouldn't delay the boat. The wind was strong tonight. He never minded rough crossings. With a sigh of relief he felt the boat move from the harbour. Soon he would meet Bellayne. He joined a group of passengers. Amongst them was a member of the crew. He knew him well.

"What was the trouble on the quayside?" Gilrea asked.

"It was that showman Bellayne. Drunk, I suppose. Said we were sailing to our deaths into a hurricane." He laughed. "Refused to go on board and took his trunk back. It was filled to the brim with those puppets – all dressed up in fine new dolly-rags. He mentioned your name in particular. Wanted to speak to you desperately. I was coming to fetch you but then he said you had seventy-five gold sovereigns hidden in your pocket. I knew then he was drunk or raving."

✠ february ✠

Caroline Quaye was born on the Isle of Man and educated at Queen Elizabeth II High School, Peel and Isle of Man College. She is currently working as a civil servant and lives in Braddan with her husband and young son.

Caroline is a keen exponent of the art of hand analysis and graphology and has spent a lot of time researching the Island's wealth of history and folklore. Her other interests include reading, cooking and gardening.

This is Caroline's first published short story.

Traa-di-Liooar

Caroline Quaye

In the late afternoon, after another busy day, Ted dozed by the crackling fire. Dark snowclouds were gathering in the tutti-frutti sky. A rest by the fireside was just what he needed before his guest arrived. He snored intermittently. His white cat, with paws tucked neatly under its chest, watched the glowing coals through slit eyes.

★ ★ ★

The yellow-black sky over Douglas and Onchan had disappeared from view in the driver's mirror as Rebecca drove carefully along the dark country roads. She could feel herself relaxing as she headed to the west of the Island for a week at her dad's place. She was looking forward to a few quiet days in the countryside, though she was sure she'd be rolling up her sleeves to give her father a hand around the place.

She'd finished work early for a change, anxious to escape from town as soon as she could. There was little traffic on the meandering roads as she followed the hills and valleys. The sleet had stopped now and the clouds had cleared, giving glimpses of the sallow winter moon. Eventually, Rebecca turned into the familiar unlit lane. She smiled to herself at the creepiness of the rutted track which was lined with huge, skeletal trees arching to touch overhead so that she was driving through a surreal cobwebbed tunnel.

Then, there was the tiny house ahead. At the brightly-lit kitchen window she could see her dad with a tea towel slung jauntily across one shoulder. As she stopped the car she could see her father's grey head was bent slightly and he looked to be deep in conversation with someone.

Grabbing her rucksack from the back of the car she shuddered in the stillness as she sucked in the chill night air. There were no close neighbours here.

The cottage door was crowned with a plinth dated 1847 and her father was immensely proud that, in the five years since retiring, he'd turned a near-derelict old cottage into a welcoming home. Rebecca hurried inside, to the delicious smells of a home-cooked supper.

Ted beamed at her and cast a quick look towards the old chair. "Come on Spook! I've just been telling you your favourite young lady was coming. You'd better let her have a seat."

The handsome, pure white cat which was settled on the wooden rocking chair in the corner just blinked. His unusual turquoise eyes regarded both Ted and Rebecca nonchalantly before he stood, stretched and turned a few circles to settle himself again in a curl on his saggy old cushion.

Rebecca laughed as Ted grumbled, handing her a steaming mug of tea. "Guess I'll just stand then!" she said cheerily as she leaned back against the worktop and took a sip of her drink. "The roads were quiet."

Ted's mouth spread across his face good-naturedly in a wide smile.

"What? What!" asked Rebecca with high eyebrows and

the same wide grin.

"Aye! Friday four o'clock rush hour, eh?" Ted mused. "Which way did you come, anyway? It must have been nose to tail out past Chibannagh and the Eairy ..."

He whistled through his teeth at the mere thought of the non-existent traffic on the back roads and Rebecca knew he was teasing. Ted had a dry sense of humour and Rebecca just pulled a cross-eyed face and laughed, shaking her head, knowing he wasn't really expecting an answer to his question.

They settled to play cards at the small kitchen table, taking it in turns to baste the chicken Ted was cooking for their evening meal. The scrumptious smells of the roast merited Spook's attention and he loitered around cunningly, trying to look inconspicuous. Rebecca beamed as Ted announced he'd made her favourite cherry pie for pudding.

"Well, tinned filling but homemade pastry. Just hope it's not like cardboard! We'll just lash on some custard and it'll be fine."

The chicken was moist and delicious and Rebecca was thoughtful as Ted fussed at the oven after removing their plates. Her father was always so busy planning this and that. He'd relished the challenge of taking on the old crofter's cottage when a pal who owned the nearby farm had suggested it. The cottage, though, had proved to be a considerable project for a man of advancing years. "Go on into the sitting-room, Rebecca. I'll fetch the pudding in a minute."

Rebecca went through and Ted followed. The room was already warm as Ted poked at the coals and jammed another log on the fire.

"Saw a few good things at the Mart in Ramsey this after-noon. I got a smashing old captain's chair that just needs a sand down and a coat of lacquer. There was a big old fancy picture frame that I thought maybe you'd like, love. I'll show you tomorrow – it'd look smashing with a mirror behind it."

Rebecca was pleased. Her dad really had an eye for nice pieces of furniture.

She sat close beside the fire, enjoying the scorching heat and the forest scent of the log and its quiet cracks and hisses. She stared, transfixed by the caverns in the coals, daydreaming of the old lamp-lit Manx mineshafts of Glen Rushen, Foxdale and Laxey and the harsh lives of the people who had gone before.

Ted appeared again in the doorway. He placed a very deep bowl in front of Rebecca which was almost full to the brim with buttercup-yellow custard.

Ted saw Rebecca's eyebrows shoot up.

"I thought we were having pie?" she asked, anticipating a tale of disaster about the pastry.

Ted was already delving his spoon into the bowl "It's in there somewhere … Let's just say it needed the custard."

As they ate Spook skulked away up the stairs and when Rebecca went up to bed at eleven thirty he was sleeping near her pillow.

Looking out of the small bedroom window, Rebecca stared across the undulating countryside towards Peel Hill in the distance, its little toothpaste-cap shape of Corrin's Folly outlined clear and strong in the moonlight.

The spare bedroom was cold and Rebecca knew she wouldn't be able to sleep. She headed back down the steep stairs to see if her father had a hot water bottle. Ted was in the kitchen, rummaging in a tatty cardboard box.

"Thought you were doing your crossword?" she asked. Ted's glasses were perched on the top of his head.

"Traa-di-liooar! I just thought I'd have a look at this stuff before heading for bed. Timmy at the mart said old Doris Kewley's estate left some items for auction, and this box of old bits."

"So, what's in there? You didn't pay good money for an old box of rubbish, did you Dad? Without even knowing what was in it!"

Ted pretended he hadn't heard and continued his gossip about the old woman who had died.

"Her family had been farmers for generations – she was the last of the line. But she hadn't been right since she was a girl. She lived to a good old age though." Ted stood up, nodding at Rebecca to head into the sitting-room.

"The story goes that her father had upset some gypsies many years ago, when Doris was just a toddler and the angry travelling folk had cursed his family. Don't know whether there was any truth in it, probably just a load of old nonsense. We all know how superstitious the Manx were all those years ago."

They carried the box to the sitting-room.

"Sounds intriguing, Dad. What kind of curse?" Rebecca pulled a cushion from the sofa and settled on the floor as Ted placed the box down lightly on the mat.

"Well, the gypsies departed, leaving a 'gift' for Kewley's family, only the gift turned out to bring menace and evil into the home and the family were never the same after that." Ted sniggered. "Oh, the story's been exaggerated over the years, no doubt, by all the island's story-tellers. Apparently they were cursed if they kept the thing and cursed if they tried to get rid of it."

Rebecca rolled her eyes as Ted carried on.

"Years ago, gypsies would call around to the farms on the Island offering labour. Well, they were expected really, and they would be given shelter and food for their work. No right-minded farmer would turn them away, for the gypsies had many old ways, passed down the generations and the locals believed it was bad luck not to offer them work."

"So what had the farmer done to upset the travellers, then?" Rebecca was smirking, relishing the conspiratorial way her dad shared a bit of gossip.

"Timmy said that one day Kewley had accused a gypsy of stealing some little thing from his cottage and he openly declared that he didn't trust the lot of them, said they were a bunch of thieves. Folk far and wide were amazed at his brazenness but Kewley sent the gypsies packing. According to the story they left him something one of them had crafted, and told him it would protect his family if he kept faith with the travelling folk and stopped berating their kind. But farmer Kewley was reckless and poured scorn on the travellers and their ancient traditions and beliefs."

"So what about the gypsies? Did they call looking for work each year after that?" Rebecca wondered how people could have been so superstitious.

"No. The travellers never called there again. The other farmers knew the gypsies were hardworking, decent folk. And most of the Manx respected the gypsy traditions. Kewley actually boasted how he'd shown the gypsies the door. But, back then folk would never intentionally cross a gypsy. Even the locals gave Kewley a wide berth after that. The story goes that Kewley's crops failed and Doris grew and became a simple child, not the full shilling as they used to say. Whether she'd have been that way anyway we'll never know. I remember my mother telling me about her, how when Doris was a little 'un, living in the old farmhouse she'd rise at dawn to polish the slate floor for hours with milk, only to then fetch the muddy-hooved goat inside to feed and milk it. She supposedly used to talk to people no one else could see. Poor old Doris died a spinster, and reached nearly a hundred."

Rebecca smiled wryly at Ted's tale. Her father, being a real old Manxie, loved a good story.

"So this stuff belonged to Doris?"

"Yes. Timmy didn't want to touch it – said he just wanted shut of it!"

Ted's mysterious air made Rebecca smile.

The box contained an odd mix of items. An old bone-handled penknife, a pocket-sized hard-backed book of manx folklore, a small canvas wrap containing shoe-polishing brushes, two large stiff-bound books full of very old photographs. There were several rainbow-ribboned war medals and an old bumbee cage encasing two pure white pebbles. Finally, across the bottom of the box was a curious scattering of fircones and a large number of fat conkers.

Ted seemed disappointed by his 'wild card' buy but Rebecca was fascinated by the photograph albums.

"Well," sighed Ted. "It's true what they say. A fool and his money are easily parted."

Rebecca pored over the photographs, which gave no clue to the identities of the solemn sitters. Some of the pictures were marked as having been taken at a photography studio on Douglas Head but others were of unknown origin.

"Who were all these people, Dad? This is part of a family history. The same faces at different ages. It's so sad that they've ended up in the hands of strangers."

But Ted was rooting again, in the bottom of the box, counting out the conkers fondly, marvelling at their size, perhaps remembering his own happy conker-gathering days in his youth.

Spook mooched about, then stepped delicately into the box to sit on top of the remaining fircones. Ted shooed Spook away and as the cat leapt indignantly from the box Ted reached for something shiny and gave a whistle as he turned it in the firelight.

"Well, well. Who's this grand little fella then?"

Ted and Rebecca's eyes met and held each other's gaze for an instant.

It looked like a large conker in the palm of Ted's hand but as it shimmered in the fire's glow Rebecca could see that it was actually a finely carved wooden figure, smooth and gleaming.

Ted was smiling triumphantly as he handed it to Rebecca.

The detail was quite incredible. It was a tiny hooded man, one hand behind his back. His knees were bent, with one foot forward as if he'd just risen from a deep regal bow. In one hand he held a penny whistle and his long face was tilted, chin up, frozen in a leering grin. Rebecca turned the little carving in her hand, unable to resist stroking its surface. It was as smooth as flint.

"Oo! I don't know if I like him or not, Dad! You don't think that could be ...?" Her eyes were narrowed with uncertainty as she passed it back to her father.

"No! It would be long gone." Ted smiled at her supposition. "There's some skill gone into that though, Rebecca. I can't think what kind of wood that is."

Ted slipped the carving into his pocket and put the fireguard around the grate.

"I'm going up, love. See you in the morning. I'll pop a hot water bottle in your bed on the way past. Goodnight."

"Mmm. Goodnight Dad!" Rebecca sighed and moved to curl up in the corner of the sofa to have a good look at the photograph albums. She loved staying over at her dad's, always feeling totally relaxed and at peace the second she put her toe through the door. Spook came to settle beside her as she picked over the portraits; she lifted some only to find the pencil inscriptions on the reverse so frustratingly faded that she was unable to decipher anything meaningful.

Spook purred quietly as they lay together and soon

Rebecca's heavy eyes closed on the day. She lay cocooned in the warmth from the dying fire as its smoky smells lingered in her dreams, conjuring wood sprites and faeries and deep, leafy glens.

* * *

Rebecca awoke with a start in the near dark room. Spook sprang with a hiss over her chest and face at the very same instant, clawing her unintentionally in his panic to get away. The noise was deafening and Rebecca was on her feet immediately she realized where she was. She was frozen with disbelief, disorientated in the small room. She realized with horror that something terrible was happening in the room directly above her. There was an incredibly loud thumping. It sounded as if something or someone was banging clumsily about the room, crashing on the floor and knocking into heavy furniture. Then, realizing it was coming from her dad's room she groped her way, breathlessly through to the kitchen towards the staircase. The banging was getting louder and louder and in her panic she knew her dad must have been taken ill or at the very least be in the throes of some terrible nightmare. Why hadn't he called out to her?

As Rebecca reached the curtained door at the bottom of the staircase the thumping stopped. She felt dizzy now, scared.

"Dad? Are you okay up there?" In her terror she could barely recognise her own voice. As she stretched out a shaking hand for the light switch there was an almighty crash from above as if an enormous cupboard had been pushed over.

Frantically, she bounded up the old wooden stairs to the landing, dreading to open the door of the room where her father lay. With a throbbing heart she lifted the old latch, and lurched awkwardly into Ted's room.

Darkness. Total darkness. And silence. Unexpected

silence.

Then a long, low-toned snore.

Rebecca flicked on the light.

Ted slept. His glasses, a book of short stories and the little carved, grinning man were on his bedside table. Nothing in the room was out of place.

Rebecca backed out. Her mouth was terribly dry. Rebecca did not turn off her bedside lamp that night. Hours later she heard Spook meowing and scratching desperately at her door as the room's dark shadows melted in the weak light of the dawn. She crept out of bed to let Spook into the room and as he settled beside her she finally fell asleep, grateful for his presence, comforted by his loud purrs.

★ ★ ★

The chopping sounds from outside the cottage seemed to be keeping time with Rebecca's pounding headache as she squinted to see the time. She rose and took all her bits and pieces to the neat bathroom for a shower. After dressing, she headed across the landing to go downstairs. Her dad's bedroom door was wide open and, for some reason, her eyes were drawn to the bedside table. The wooden figure was not there and as she carefully negotiated the steep, dimly lit stairs she found herself wondering where the strange little thing could be.

Ted was in the fresh air, clearing thick-stemmed gorse from the patch of land beside the cottage. It was a beautiful morning and a pick up truck was parked at the top of the lane. Jack Cashin, whose family lived nearby, was piling some of the woody roots into a small mound in a clearing. Jack and Rebecca had known each other since school.

"All right, Rebecca? Come to give us a hand?"

"Well, I thought I'd make some coffees first!"

"Ted's done a good job up here. He's pretty much got the whole field cleared on his own in a week. I told him to wait till the weekend and I'd be up to give him a hand but he's gone at it hammer and tongs!"

Ted, stooping near the hedge, bellowed over good-naturedly, "Orchards don't sort themselves you know!"

By noon, the field was part rotivated. Ted suggested lunch so they headed to the house for chicken sandwiches. Spook shot off the chair and out through the door as soon as the trio entered the kitchen.

Rebecca stared after him. "Well, that's a first! Normally Spook won't leave the kitchen for three days if Dad's cooked chicken."

Ted produced the little carving from his trouser pocket and told Jack the tale of Doris Kewley's belongings. Spook watched them sulkily from the kitchen windowledge, his warm, pink nose touching the cold glass so that a little dribble of liquid formed a line on the window pane.

It was dusk when Jack headed off home after covering the garden rubbish with a large tarpaulin to keep it all dry.

★ ★ ★

Much later, Ted and Rebecca made a good chicken stock and chopped vegetables. A thick broth was bubbling away in no time. After they'd eaten Rebecca made herself a coffee and poured Ted a Guinness before they settled down by the fire. Rebecca watched television whilst Ted did crosswords and looked through the old photo albums.

Ted had placed his carving on the mantlepiece beside the sturdy clock.

"Where's Spook? I've hardly seen him at all today." Rebecca was puzzled. The cat was usually never too far from Ted's roaring fire, often giving little yelps as his fur became hotter and hotter. Ted glanced around over the rim of his spectacles; he hadn't noticed Spook's absence.

"Oh, he'll be chasing the long fellas out in the field. Clearing all that ground today will have the longies on the move!"

Rebecca smiled at her dad's quaint avoidance of using the word 'rat' but shuddered as she thought it was probably true. Living in the country Spook had a big playground!

Rebecca looked over again at the figurine.

"Dad, is it just me or does that carved thing give you the creeps too?"

Ted didn't look up. "It's a piece of wood, Rebecca."

Rebecca sat quietly, watching the fire. She remembered waking up on the sofa the previous night and wondered if she should tell her Dad. Would he just laugh?

She stared over at the carving, noticing that it appeared to be a musical performer. He was somewhat hunched, his head and hands overly large.

Ted rose from his chair. "I'll take this upstairs if it's scaring you!"

"Put the kettle on!" Rebecca shouted, cheekily as Ted passed through the kitchen. She heard him climbing the steep stairs.

Bless him! He didn't like the idea that Rebecca wouldn't want to stay if she felt the old cottage was creepy, but after all who could blame her for having an active imagination? The cottage was well over a hundred and fifty years old.

She closed her eyes in the warmth of the fire. Had she imagined those noises the previous night? It had all seemed so real. Had the carving and the photograph albums just unsettled her with their history and imaginings of things gone before?

The mantle clock chimed eleven as Rebecca yawned and stretched out her pink-socked feet to the hearth. Ted came back in with a sudoku book he'd fetched from his bedroom.

"You and your puzzles!" Rebecca laughed.

"I'll do some dishes and head up, Dad. Don't you be too late, you must be shattered after all that work today. Goodnight."

After washing the few dishes Rebecca opened the back door and stepped out into the freezing air, calling to Spook urgently.

There was no sign of the cat as the black trees waved. The night moaned ghoulishly in the strengthening wind which was the only sound, the subtle breath of nature, huffing and sighing as ragged scraps of cloud streaked the disc of the moon.

Shivering, she dipped back inside. Upstairs, her bedroom was cold as she turned on the bedside lamp and pulled the curtains together at the window, jangling the little curtain rings. She pressed her face to the glass to stare out across the countryside, noticing the occasional dots of house lights and the starry night sky. As her eyes looked at the land around the house she spotted something strange glowing out in the yard, just within the puddle of light cast from the kitchen window. As she looked she saw that the florescent white and red-slashed shape looked like an old Manx flag, torn from a pole and blown into the yard like a disused cloth.

Rebecca undid the metal window hook and leaned out into the night, transfixed now, wondering why she hadn't noticed the odd thing when she'd called to Spook some moments before.

Then she knew.

She dashed to the landing where the only light was the golden glow from the bedroom. Reaching the top of the stairs she heard a strange laugh-like sound from behind her. She turned sharply in the lamplight. She surely hadn't imagined *that*?

Then, her balance compromised, she plunged. As she fell, her whole body twisted in the narrow stairwell. In weird slow motion she grasped desperately for the hand rail, not realizing until she hit the bottom wall with a thud that her sudden journey was already over.

Ted heard the clatter and was at the bottom of the stairs almost as soon as her body crashed to a halt. She was too shocked to cry. Shocked, too, at her father's pallor as he found her there, crumpled on the bottom step.

"Did you just trip? What happened?" Ted had helped her to Spook's chair. "Those damned stairs are so steep. You'll be black and blue tomorrow."

But Rebecca had struggled to her feet, and was already unbolting the back door.

"Becky?"

She walked outside until she disappeared into the darkness. Ted stood open-mouthed, hearing her scuffling about on the dirt track. She stepped back, puzzled, into the light cast from the kitchen.

"Rebecca, do you mind telling me what's going on?" Ted wanted to add *because you're beginning to scare me,* but stopped himself.

"It was Spook, Dad! Lying there on the track, battered and bloodied as if he'd been in some ghastly accident! He must have dragged himself off somewhere. We need a torch!"

"Come on inside." Ted reached out to take Rebecca's arm but she pulled away fiercely.

"We can't just leave him, Dad! He was in a terrible state. I thought he was dead for sure. Please! We can't just wait until morning."

Ted headed inside and, agitated, Rebecca hurried after him in search of a torch.

"Rebecca!" Ted called quietly from the sitting-room,

sounding only slightly bothered about the cat's predicament. Angrily, Rebecca marched into the room to find her dad standing beside the fire shaking his head at her.

Rebecca stopped in her tracks, a sick feeling washing over her as she immediately saw, at Ted's feet, the handsome cat calmly washing his whiskers in the firelight.

Her mind whirled as she stared at them both. Whatever this mind-trickery was, she didn't like it. Not one bit.

"Come on Rebecca. Let's put the kettle on ..."

Standing side by side with Ted at the sink Rebecca felt very uneasy.

Unnoticed, a monstrous, hooded silhouette slanted down the staircase wall behind them. The shadow dipped and danced, with wicked abandon, silently lurching a mischievous jig before it crept back into Ted's bedroom.

* * *

Later, in the living-room, Ted looked up from his sudoku puzzle to watch Rebecca's troubled face as she dozed on the sofa. It was late now, the room was peaceful.

He wondered what it was. He had been carrying his empty coffee cup from the sitting-room when he distinctly heard the sound, similar to the satisfying clip-clopping of horse hooves on hard gravel. He couldn't think what it could be. The moon was full, and the yard and lane were chalky and surreal. Ted's curiosity drew him to the kitchen window.

As he leaned forward at the sink he gave a little shout of astonishment.

Right outside, as if it was perfectly normal, in Ted's back yard stood a huge black mare. It was close to the house. Steamy breath escaped the horse's nostrils in the cold air as it looked right in at Ted, bold as brass. Curiously the creature's mane was tightly plaited, as if it were a fabulous show-horse.

"What the …?" Ted whispered in a half-laugh.

Then the horse dipped its head and moved unhurriedly, its hooves thudding softly as it headed towards the lane. Ted watched, noticing to his surprise that the horse was pulling a low cart.

Its load, too, was clearly visible. And to Ted's horror he saw that on the long wooden cart, was a long wooden coffin.

Ted's senses prickled with a sudden icy sweat.

"Dad, are you okay?" Ted jumped. Rebecca was standing, sleepy-faced, at the sitting-room doorway. Ted was at the window, staring out across the yard. She walked over to him.

"Do you know, as I woke up on the sofa just then I could have sworn I heard the sound of horses hooves, in the yard." She stared up at the bright moon. "It's such a still night out there. This full moon is playing tricks on us!"

But Ted was distracted, not even turning to Rebecca. "There was a horse." he said quietly. "Out there. I saw it. It was the strangest thing!"

"When? Did you go out, Dad? Where could it have come from? Does anyone around here have horses? Maybe we should phone someone."

But Ted didn't seem to hear the questions. He continued staring at the yard, a haunted expression on his grey face.

"Leave it, love. Traa-di-liooar! I think it will be all right." He seemed quiet. Rebecca knew, from the falter in his voice, that he hadn't told her everything. Reflected in the kitchen window she saw his face crumple in the half light. Thinking she hadn't noticed, Ted cleared his throat awkwardly and made himself busy moving cups about on the draining board.

"You go up to bed, Rebecca. I just want to check we're all locked up."

He kept his back to her as he moved towards the back door. Rebecca bid her father goodnight and headed slowly upstairs.

Ted unbolted the back door and took a few steps out into the yard, surprised at the mildness of the night. His eyes searched the track for something. From behind the stair curtain a silent Rebecca saw Ted raise his hand to his face and put his knuckle into his mouth like an upset toddler. What else had he seen? Could he have heard or seen something horrible, as she had the previous night?

Ted was standing, pensive under the milky moon. Rebecca noticed Ted crouch suddenly to the ground. His gasp echoed in the still air as he stretched out and lightly touched the rough ground with searching fingertips, tracing the crescent shapes of the hoofprints.

★ ★ ★

When Rebecca emerged for breakfast the next morning she knew Ted had visitors. There were serious voices coming from the kitchen.

Jack Cashin and his mother Mary, known to Ted for many years, were sitting at the kitchen table. They all fell silent as Rebecca walked in, still aching and stiff after her fall the previous night.

"We've been hearing about your eventful night. How are you this morning, Rebecca?" Mary was smiling kindly as she poured Rebecca a cup of tea from the brown-bellied teapot.

"I'm fine, just wrenched my back muscles a little. I gave Dad a fright too, though!"

Ted laughed and Rebecca noticed that the small carved man was in the middle of the table beside the sugar bowl.

"It's either the full moon or that awful little thing that's upsetting things around here. Spook won't even be in the same room as it!"

Ted nodded. "Rebecca's right, you know. I've only just realized, but it's true."

Looking suddenly serious, Mary continued.

"Do you believe it's the gypsy gift from all that time ago? Wood whittling's an ancient craft, the travelling folk passed those skills down the generations. If it's a real worry you should just throw the thing away. Don't harbour evil and you mustn't delay!"

Ted interrupted with a loud guffaw. "An old block of wood can't be evil! Talk sense, woman! You sound like the simple, uneducated people who truly believed in hexes and the like. I'm not throwing out that bit of skilled craftsmanship because my friends and neighbours are the most superstitious folk in the entire west of the Isle of Man!"

Mary was pink-faced now and haughty. "If I hadn't known you so long, Ted, I would have taken offence at that remark! Why did old Doris Kewley keep the thing for so long, then? It's not exactly nice to look at!"

"I think you should throw it out, Dad! You just don't know!"

"Pah!" Ted almost spat in disgust.

"Are you afraid of what might happen if you try to get rid of it?"

Three pairs of eyes looked at Ted, waiting for an answer.

"Traa-di-liooar. Load of superstitious nonsense!"

Pushing his chair noisily away from the table, Ted headed out into the yard.

Jack smirked awkwardly and followed, pulling on his heavy Wellington boots at the back door.

"He makes my blood boil! There's just no hurry about him. Typical Manxman! Thinks he's always right."

Mary was agitated as she lifted the carving and stared at its carefully chiselled, mocking face. Rebecca spoke. "There's something else. I had a weird experience on Friday night after Dad had gone up to bed. There were all sorts of crashing and banging sounds from upstairs but when I went up everything was quiet. I was really spooked."

Rebecca couldn't stop a little smile turning up the corners of her mouth at Mary's truly appalled expression.

Thoughts of the wooden man crept into all of their minds throughout the rest of the day.

★ ★ ★

"I won't be too late, Dad!" Rebecca wrapped a scarf around her neck as she noticed Jack's headlights in the lane.

"I'll leave the door unlocked for you. Have a good time, Rebecca!"

It was one of those nights unique to Peel. From the promenade a dense sea mist crept into every little street in the old town. The sea whispered softly as it moved pebbles up the shore. Chimney-smoke smells hung in the night air as Jack and Rebecca strolled between pubs.

"Let's get chips and eat them on the promenade," suggested Rebecca quietly. She preferred the stillness of the night air to another crowded bar.

They sat with their portions of chips on the promenade feeling strange in the hush of the foggy night, whispering like children who'd stepped outside into the wonder of freshly fallen snow.

The familiar town seemed unusual and mysterious as the fog cocooned them.

"I used to imagine ghostly horse-drawn coaches trotting through the streets on nights like this," Rebecca confided with a daft smile on her face. Unwrapping the hot vinegary chips, Jack gave a muffled laugh before they tucked in hungrily, agreeing that chips always taste better in the fresh air.

A scraping sound approached and suddenly, beside them, there appeared a huge black hound. The dog sniffed about loudly as Rebecca realized she was practically holding her breath. She had jumped when the dog had loomed up to them from the bleakness. A tiny orange glow emerged, and the dog's owner, smoking a cigarette, came close by.

"Evening! Come on Jet, leave the good people to their supper." Jet had already scuffled by and the owner followed silently.

"That hound almost made me tip the tray of chips and run! I thought it was the damned Moddey Dhoo!" snorted Jack dramatically. Rebecca's heart was still hammering and somehow the spell of the night had been broken.

They finished their chips and ambled along the quayside, lost in their own thoughts as the sea lapped the harbour walls and the boats creaked and pulled at their moorings.

"I always thought I'd like to do a night in Peel Castle for a bet, you know, in weather like this, when it's really creepy. That old mutt was just like the Moddey Dhoo, the black dog that's supposed to haunt the castle. I'd never been that scared about stories of the big black dog, well not since I was about seven years old anyway – but Jet really put the wind up me!"

They laughed, each well aware of the castle's old legends.

After a pause Jack spoke quietly. "My mum's not happy about Ted hanging onto that carved figure, you know. Is there anything else you haven't told us?"

Rebecca shrugged.

"Oh well, we'll just have to keep a close eye on him."

★ ★ ★

There was a chilly drizzle later when Rebecca dashed from the car to the cottage. Spook was sulking again on the window-sill and arched his back in a stretch as Rebecca approached. He eventually followed her inside and slinked into the sitting-room.

She crept up to bed, falling into a deep, restful sleep.

In his room, Ted slept fitfully. He could hear a faint scratching sound and suspected a mouse. He just couldn't settle.

There it was again, the subtle scraping. It was coming from somewhere in his bedroom. Where was that damned cat when it was needed? Ted sat up in the darkness, wondering if Rebecca was hearing any mice in her room or if Spook was tucking into a mousey midnight feast in there. It was no good worrying about the situation, it would have to wait until morning.

He tried to settle back under the covers, when he heard a noise shockingly close. Ted's heart thumped and he raised himself up on one elbow, very slowly.

Pale moonlight glowed through the thin curtains as Ted listened.

There! He heard it again, right in front of him.

Ted was unable to move, quite horrified. Something shifted, super quick, and as his eyes became accustomed to the dimness, he could make out the shape of it at the end of the bed.

But that was no mouse!

At first Ted thought he was surely dreaming. But incredibly, as he strained to see, he knew beyond doubt that somehow the wooden figure was there. Ted's mouth hung slack-jawed in surprise. The figure flipped and flicked in an acrobatic display of great agility from one corner of the bed end to the other.

It pretended a boxing bout, with no opponent. Ted was transfixed. The figure was no bigger than the palm of Ted's hand and its bluster was ridiculous. It could do little harm to Ted. He reasoned that even if this were not just an astonishing dream, the worst it could do would be a mere bop on the tip of his nose!

It stopped moving with a flourish, and swept low in a bow

so that Ted knew that the acrobatics, the performance had been for him.

Rising dreadfully slowly the imp tilted its face towards Ted with a jerk. Ted felt cornered, vulnerable as it fixed him with its lecherous grin.

His throat horribly dry, Ted swallowed painfully as to his horror the figure lifted its massive hand and drew a skinny index finger maliciously across its throat from one side to the other.

Pointing at Ted, it nodded and slashed a finger across its windpipe again, still with its sinister grin. Ted could only stare, aghast.

Suddenly it flipped a somersault, landed again squatly and bent forward, clutching its stomach as it began a laugh. In a sickening silence it rocked to and fro with shaking shoulders, laughing at its captive audience.

Ted found himself screaming. Screaming with all his might, a soundless frantic scream in the darkness. As the clouds in the night sky cleared the face of the bright, full moon Ted saw his shocked, grey-haired, white-faced reflection in the wardrobe mirror opposite the foot of his bed. The mischief maker had vanished.

His hypnotism unlocked at the sight of something real, Ted groaned and curled under the covers. His sleep, when it finally came, was ravaged with images of the devilish creature and the sight of his own hollow-eyed reflection in the gloom.

★ ★ ★

At breakfast, Ted decided to break the spell. He could no longer keep quiet about what he'd seen.

Rebecca was appalled and when Jack and Mary dropped in, mid-morning, to see if Ted and Rebecca fancied a walk over the hills, there was much conversation.

It was a fine morning and in the fresh, still air, Mary loudly voiced her consternation. "There's a gypsy curse on it, that's for sure. A clever one at that! Mind mischief, the worst kind. There can't be any more of this 'traa-di-liooar' now Ted! You've got to get rid of it!"

"I'm not just going to throw it out!"

Ted was agitated and immediately Rebecca lost patience.

"Dad, you know how weird things have been this week. In all the years you've lived in that cottage I've never experienced anything like it – so if you say traa-di-liooar again I'll go beserk!"

Jack flashed a look at Rebecca in surprise at her sharpness, though he knew she had Ted's wellbeing at heart.

"I wasn't going to say traa-di-liooar!" Ted said sheepishly, looking drawn and worried. "I was going to say we can't just throw the thing away. We'll have to destroy it somehow."

As they marched higher through the muddy, gorse-edged fields, they formed a plan and later they returned to Ted's cottage in thoughtful silence.

By dusk they had built a good bonfire. It took some time to get the fire started but, as the blancmange sky darkened the flames began to lick at the stalks and roots and branches.

Rebecca watched the blaze, its centre resembling a burning dense forest, the stuff of a nightmarish fairytale. Dark orange embers floated from the pyre to swarm like frantic goldfish above the searing heat, up, up into the darkening sky. Only the hissing and crackles of the burning wood broke the silence.

"Are you ready, Ted?" Mary meant business and Rebecca wondered if they were doing the right thing, if the carving would still cause its mischief to its owner even if it were destroyed. Ted hadn't answered and Rebecca suspected he had changed his mind about burning it.

But, slowly, Ted pulled the ugly thing from deep in his

anorak pocket and turned it one last time to wonder at it's tawny richness in the firelight.

As he bowled it, suddenly, into the belly if the bonfire a theatrical cry from Mary "*Devil be gone!*" brought a reluctant smile to Rebecca's lips in the darkness.

The fire popped and blazed, showering out burning embers. It was done.

★ ★ ★

Ted slept late the following morning.

Rebecca was up at the crack of dawn, feeling relieved and a little foolish at their serious actions of the previous day. They'd certainly look back and laugh at their memories of this week for some time to come.

Spook slinked out of the cottage as soon as he'd eaten. Rebecca watched from the kitchen window as he scoured the land outside. Light-hearted, she busied herself cleaning.

In the drizzle Spook nosed about at the back of the charred bonfire remains. At its edge he spotted the conker-hued thing, badly burned but intact. The cat cuffed at it with its paws courageously, sensing any danger had gone. Spook was merciless, dabbing and jumping at it until he had moved it across the dirt towards the rough lane. As it rolled the cat followed, leaping playfully, as the figure bounced along the rutted track, miraculously missing any troughs in the dirt so it was soon out on the open road where its journey was over. A car whizzed past as Spook nearly bounded onto the road, causing the cat to twist sideways and pelt back up the lane, back to its own territory and safety.

Flashes of bright colour appeared two hundred yards up the high-hedged road and as yellows, reds and oranges neared Ted's lane one of the cyclists pulled over to adjust his helmet and glug some water. The others rode on.

He spotted the wood, meaning to kick the lump out of the road in case a motorbike rider or other cyclist came upon it. He couldn't help but pick it up, as he was astonished to see that it was an ugly carved figure.

"Well, well! What have we here then?"

Amazed to find the thing there, in the middle of nowhere, he popped it into his backpack so he could have a really good look at it later.

He rode off, but in the darkness of the small black bag the nasty imp was still grinning mischievously.

❀ march ❀

Peter Carlé was born in London. Peter has travelled extensively and has worked as a police officer with both the Hong Kong and Metropolitan Police. He then worked as a solicitor's clerk in the East End of London before qualifying as a barrister. Finally he moved to the Island where he became a Manx Advocate and worked in the Attorney General's Chambers.

Peter is now retired and has moved back to the UK where he lives on a canal barge. His hobbies include fishing, drinking real ale, travelling and writing. He has had two other short stories published by Priory Press entitled 'Ghost Walk' and 'Manx Molehills' and is currently in the process of writing a full-length crime novel.

ꜰɑuʟk ʟɑw

Peter Carlé

This sealed document is to remain in a locked safe at the Manx Museum in Douglas, Isle of Man. Not to be opened and read for one hundred years from this date – 31st March 2010.

I write this document as a true and accurate record of the most horrendous and chilling events that I witnessed on 30th March 2010. I have not stated anything false nor stated anything that I do not believe to be true.

Pulling a heavy wheeled bag back to the Attorney General's chambers after a busy morning in court, I was exhausted. It had been a long and tiring session in the Staff of Government Division, the appeal court of the Isle of Man. After three frantic weeks of preparation plus four-and-a-half days standing in court arguing the law I wanted to get to my room, then enjoy a cup of tea and a sandwich before tackling the paperwork.

On my desk was the morning post – letters, memos and new files that required advice. Nine voicemail messages and twenty-seven new e-mails had arrived during the morning.

I groaned. There would be a similar host of messages when I turned my mobile phone back on after being switched off in court. Oh for the old days, when people wrote letters and waited a week for a reply. The phone rang as I sat down. Had I known what extraordinary and terrible events the phone call was going to lead to I would not have answered it.

It was the secretary for a senior partner in one of the most prestigious firms of Manx advocates. She spoke briskly.

"Your appointment for three o'clock this afternoon. Mr Selby cannot make three o'clock; he has to see an important client who is flying in to sort out some urgent tax matters – being the end of the tax year. We've rescheduled your appointment for two o'clock."

I was too tired to argue.

At two o'clock that afternoon I sat in Mr Selby's office, in Arbory Street, Douglas. The walls were lined with legal books and also with old photographs of Mr Selby's father and grandfather when they had been in charge of the firm.

"Coffee, biscuits?"

I accepted the offer. There had been no time for a drink or a sandwich in my chambers. Mr Selby organized things with his secretary, a lady who was the very model of efficiency.

Mr Selby, a small, very elderly man with receding grey hair, had large bristling eyebrows that he raised dramatically to emphasize a point.

"It is vital that we have advice from the Attorney General's chambers within the next twenty-four hours on this very sensitive matter."

I put on the most helpful smile I could manage.

"I appreciate you say this matter is vital and sensitive. But, your request for advice only went to the AG two days ago. He is over on the adjoining isle with the Chief Minister trying to sort out a major tax problem with the UK Treasury. I will do my best. Usually the law relating to trusts and charities moves rather slowly ..."

"Well, normally, but – " Selby moaned and complained as he pushed a large cardboard box over to my side of the desk. He muttered something about it being the end of the tax year and how the accountants wanted to settle matters urgently. I ignored him and studied the box. Inscribed across the top were the words *Archibold Stamford Faulk deceased 1910. Trust documents.*

"Does this relate to something one hundred years old?" I asked incredulously. "If so, what is the urgency?"

He shifted nervously in his seat and coughed,

"It is a secret trust that this firm administers. I am a trustee. I have become aware that perhaps we might have allowed the trust to go on for far too long ...", he faltered, "past the legally permitted time for such things ..."

Now it was my turn to raise my eyebrows with exasperation. "Also," he continued, "the trust property recently had to have emergency roof repairs – the cost was far greater than we had imagined. The trust fund now owes us money. We had to cover the bill for the roof repairs. A most unsatisfactory set of affairs. So the question is – what do we do?"

The reply came to my lips but fortunately I did not say the words out loud or I might have been facing a complaint to the Manx Law Society. It was annoying that I was being asked to sort out someone else's mess. The firm had been doing very nicely out of this trust fund for one hundred years and now the money had run out they wanted someone else to sort out their problem. I demanded an empty interview room to work in and some tea. Selby told his secretary to arrange things. How I wished that I had a secretary to sort out my mountains of paperwork, answer the phone, deal with appointments, take messages, then serve excellent cups of tea and coffee.

I sat in the quiet interview room reading through the old documents: the will of Mr Archibold Stamford Faulk and an extraordinarily worded document that created a secret trust after his death. The trust was to maintain a house in Port St. Mary. The house was 'to remain empty for the benefit of the Manx people as a whole and for the particular benefit of the residents of Port St. Mary.' Finally, there was a red leather-bound notebook that was tied up in thick black cotton tape.

It was much easier dealing with the well-organized secretary than with old Selby. I was intrigued by this secret trust and made arrangements to drive down to see the house, taking along the Faulk documents plus a car boot load of my own files to look at when I got home.

It was half past three that afternoon when I arrived at the promenade in Port St. Mary. I drove slowly along the road. On my right was the sea and the harbour, on the left a magnificent row of Victorian terraced houses. In the middle of the row, looking immaculate, was Faulk House. I stopped and got out of the car. A man in his sixties, with powerful shoulders and close-cropped grey hair was waiting for me.

"Hello pal. I'm Alan Tankersley, the caretaker."

He walked briskly, holding his head and shoulders erect. I was curious,

"Are you ex-forces?" He grinned slowly and nodded. "Yes pal. Marines. Did fifteen years with them then took a bullet in my back – Northern Ireland. I loved the Marines – it was my whole life. But invalided out … came back to the Island, did building work. Took over as caretaker here when my old man died." He stopped at the front door and turned to me. "My father, and my grandfather were the caretakers before me."

Amazing! Firstly, I discover that Selby, his father and his grandfather before him had administered the trust. Secondly, I discover that Alan Tankersley, his father and grandfather,

52

had looked after the house. It was freakish. I stared at the property: a magnificent set of thirteen large steps swept up to the front door.

He opened the front door. We stepped into a large vestibule with a beautifully tiled floor. Then we went through a second heavy door to a hallway dominated by a huge staircase with a magnificent carved oak balustrade. The front room was breathtaking. Large windows gave a wide elevated view over the sea. A grand piano sat proudly in the corner of the room and the windows were adorned with plush purple drapes. Underfoot the carpet was burgundy red and felt amazingly thick.

We toured the house. The rooms were decorated with rich wallpapers, enormous mirrors and large tapestries. The house was massive with high ceilings and lots of rooms. I counted thirteen steps up to the next floor. There was a large bedroom with adjacent dressing rooms, a big bathroom with a Victorian bath, a study lined with old books and photographs. Another thirteen steps up to more rooms filled with small beds and Victorian children's toys. Then another set of stairs to the rooms under the eaves, sparsely furnished as servants' quarters.

The whole place was perfect – as if the Victorian inhabitants had just cleaned it and left five minutes ago. "How old is this building?" I asked in amazement as we walked down to the hallway.

Alan Tankersley took a deep breath and paused. "This row of terraced houses was built in eighteen eighty by Mr Archibold Faulk. My great-grandfather worked for him as his foreman and later as his agent. All the houses were sold off except for this one – Faulk House. Mr Faulk kept it as the family home for him and his family until the tragedies happened."

"What tragedies?" I could feel a cold chill in the house and shivered. Tankersley's face looked grim as he continued his account.

"Well pal, these houses were built on a piece of land that the local people said was haunted by old mysterious figures, appearing at night, moaning and screaming. Local people blamed Mr Faulk for disturbing things ..." He tailed off.

"He had a beautiful wife and two children when he moved in. But one day the youngest child, a boy, was found in the cellar with his neck broken – must have fallen down the stairs. Later, the remaining child, a daughter, appeared to suffer some kind of brain fever; she was talking some strange language. Mrs Faulk nursed her for several days. One night the child disappeared. Her body was found washed up on the shore directly in front of the house.

I shivered again. "You mentioned the cellar. I've lost count of all the floors and all the rooms in this house. Where is the cellar entrance?"

He hesitated for several seconds then shrugged his shoulders. We went to a small wooden door built under the stairs. I had taken it for a cupboard. He opened the door and led me down a steep narrow wooden staircase of thirteen steps. I realized we were directly underneath the magnificent stone steps at the front of the house that led up to the front door. At the bottom of the wooden steps were four doors. Three of the doors were open. One was a glass door that led out onto the front garden. A second door led to a room with windows overlooking the front garden. The third door led to a scullery with sink, mangle, clothes lines and windows at the back of the property. No doubt this was where the servants washed clothes.

The fourth door was made of magnificent black oak and remained stubbornly shut. I pushed and heaved at it and asked Alan Tankersley if he had a key but he shook his head vigorously.

"A cupboard?" I asked.

He hesitated then nodded slightly. Suddenly he burst out, "And finally the beautiful Mrs Faulk. She was found, hanging in the scullery. Must have been suicide they said, brought about when her mind was unhinged after the death of her two children."

I felt cold and clammy. Shivering, I asked Tankersley, "Is there any heating? And how is the house lit?"

He hesitated. "No pal. No modern central heating or anything like that. No gas or electricity in these houses in eighteen eighty. They would have used open fires to keep warm, candles and lamps to light the place. Nothing added since then. It never gets freezing cold though – the houses on either side have modern central heating and the warmth permeates through. In the wintertime I come in, mornings and afternoons, to keep the kitchen range burning."

We went up to the kitchen at the back of the house. It felt warm and cosy. The huge black iron range generated a lot of heat. Instantly I felt more relaxed. "So how do you light the house at night?"

He shivered, "I never come here at night! There's a torch though by the front door for emergencies." He looked at his watch. "I'm sorry but I have to go now, I have an urgent family appointment."

He handed me a card with his address on it. "Don't stay too long. Leave before it gets dark." He also gave me the keys. "You can hold on to these. Lock up when you leave the house. Drop them in to my house this afternoon or first thing tomorrow morning."

I sat in the warm kitchen and opened the cardboard box containing the trust documents. Again, a shiver ran through me. I moved a wooden chair next to the range and propped myself against the warm black ironwork. I untied the black cotton tape, opened the red leather notebook, and began to read the contents.

The opening words of the notebook read:

My name is Archibold Stamford Faulk. I am a Yorkshireman by birth. God has granted me a special gift. I am equipped with the wonderful and amazing ability to make money. It seems that all I touch turns to gold.

I read with fascination how he had made a small fortune as a young man in Yorkshire. When he came to the Isle of Man for a holiday with his young family he instantly saw the possibilities of building hotels and houses on the island. He bought parcels of land in Douglas and down in the south. His last purchase was a thin strip of land running along the bay in Port St. Mary. In the centre of the piece of land was a small hump of earth. He got this piece of land very cheaply from a farmer. Locals said the land was cursed. Faulk laughed at them and drew plans for a row of magnificent houses to be built along the strip, facing out to sea.

All of my other building projects went well. The building of boarding houses, guesthouses, and hotels were completed quickly and cheaply. The local Manx men were good hard workers and I paid them cheap. But the project to build a grand sweep of houses along Chapel Bay in Port St. Mary was not so easy. Local men grumbled and rumours spread amongst the workmen about the land having a curse on it. I had to increase their wages to keep the men working there.

My foreman was no milksop, a Yorkshireman like me; he could use his fists to put down any one who challenged his orders. He had spent fifteen years in the service of his Queen and country as a sergeant. Yet even he struggled to get the Manxmen to complete some of their work on the Port St. Mary site. They refused to tackle the old hump of earth in the middle of the strip.

I yawned suddenly. I was exhausted. The court case had taken all the energy out of me. Taking a deep breath to clear my head I continued reading.

Therefore, I sent my foreman, Mr Tankersley, back to Yorkshire. His job was to recruit a tough gang of workers who would do what they were told in return for good money. He returned with six men, all hardened by years in the army, men who did what they were told and kept their mouths shut when necessary.

This gang of Yorkshiremen led by Mr Tankersley set to work to clear the hump of earth. On the afternoon of the third day Mr Tankersley came to speak to me. He said me that he had sent the Yorkshiremen away early – with some extra money in their pockets – telling them to celebrate because it was his birthday. I knew he had lied to them. I also knew he was no fool. I waited for his explanation. He told me that they had been digging very deep into the earth below where the hump had been. They were preparing the foundations and cellars of the houses. He saw something that seemed man-made. He cleaned it and realized it was a large golden cup. He quickly dropped it as if it were nothing valuable, covered it over with earth then sent the men away.

I was excited by his story and planned the next move carefully. That night he and I went back to the place. We carried a heavy canvas tent, two shovels, a crowbar, sacks and a lantern. We erected the tent over the place where he had been working, lit the lantern, made sure it was carefully screened, then set to work digging. Soon we had uncovered the large gold cup. We placed it in a sack. Then we slowly revealed a skeleton. There was a huge rusted sword, what remained of a shield, some small pieces of leather and delicate white material with gold thread, even a lump of reddish hair on the skull. We dug all night finding many chains, crosses, coins, jewellery – all made of gold and silver. Around the neck of the skeleton hung a beautiful large cross and on the ring finger of the right hand was a huge gold ring.

The account continued. He wrote of the secret nightly visits to the place and the accumulation of a vast hoard of precious items. He and the foreman swore to keep the find a secret between them. After three nights they had cleared the place of everything – even the skeleton was put into a long wooden box and removed.

Faulk then dressed himself in his smartest clothes and set off to England. He made enquiries at the British Museum and found the names of several English and Irish noblemen who collected antiquities. He sold some of the gold and silver items to these members of the aristocracy for their private collections. He was very well paid.

The work continued on the Port St. Mary site. The Manxmen still refused to work at the place where the hump of earth had stood, so the gang of tough Yorkshiremen worked there. The sweep of terraced houses was completed except for the middle house – where the hump of earth had been. The small team of Yorkshiremen was not as fast as the large gangs of Manxmen working on the other houses. The other houses were sold off one by one as the middle house was still being finished.

One morning the foreman rushed to see me. Two men were trapped in the cellar of the middle house. A wall had collapsed in the cellar and they were buried under stone and earth. I joined the foreman and the four members of the gang as they tried to shore up the wall and dig down to find the missing men. We found the two bodies and I arranged for them to be sent back in coffins to their families in Yorkshire. Mr Tankersley escorted them and handed over a heavy purse from me to each of the families.

The remaining four members of the gang became uneasy and unhappy about working in the house. I told them they were fools to let their imaginations run wild. They said they could sometimes hear the yells and screams of their dead friends in the cellar. I paid them extra money and they stayed on. The house was virtually finished when one of the men fell when doing some work on the roof. He lay dying on the ground uttering strange words. The remaining three men refused to stay any longer. They took the body of the man back to his family and never returned. Mr Tankersley alone finished the remaining work on the house.

I kept the bones, the artefacts, and the treasure hidden in a locked storeroom where I was staying. I was not afraid of what I had done. I laughed at superstition. These things had brought me much money. I was now a very wealthy man.

I decided to take the middle house for my own use. I had it furnished with the best drapes, mirrors and furniture to please my wife. In the basement Mr Tankersley and I built special cabinets to house the skeleton, the sword, the jewellery and other items. Meanwhile, I wanted, for the sake of my wife and children, to become a celebrated member of society on the Island. I supported my wife when she organized charitable events and made generous donations to the local charities. I was keen to discover what I could about the idea that was growing on the Island – the idea of building a Manx Museum to house Manx historical items and to research the history of Mann.

But I wanted to know whose skeleton was hidden in the cellar. I asked questions of the experts in order to try and identify the secret treasure trove. Could it be the grave of Godred Crovan the legendary Viking who subdued large parts of Ireland and Scotland and became known as King Orry of Mann in the eleventh century?

In 1865 I was honoured to be appointed a member of the Archaeological Commission by Governor Loch. I bestowed money on the temporary museum of artefacts in Castle Rushen and asked many questions of the curator. I was drunk with power. I was a respected member of society and held in high esteem amongst the antiquarians. If only they knew I had been a grave robber and had priceless items in my cellar. At night I spent countless hours touching and gloating over my collection. Sometimes Mr Tankersley joined me. We drank wine from the gold flagons and chalices and boasted of our success. I paid him well and appointed him as my agent for all my business affairs. I felt distaste for my business matters; I wanted to concentrate solely on my collection.

One day I attended a dinner in Castle Rushen – where a great academic who was famous for his knowledge of the Irish, Manx, and Vikings gave a speech. I drank too much, my tongue was loosened and I said much to him that should have remained unsaid. He became excited and wanted to view my collection. I finally agreed. I made him promise to come late at night to my house and not to tell a soul. He was due to catch the ferry in the morning so I told him to bring his bag and I would put him up for the night.

I checked that my family and servants were asleep. I opened the front door to his quiet tapping and led him down to the basement. He examined my collection with growing excitement. He spent a long time looking at the coins, the pieces of jewellery, and the skeleton, all the time becoming more excited. "This is a bishop's ring. This large cross round the neck of the body, this is a particular type of cross worn by early bishops. These must be taken to the British Museum to be looked at by experts. A marvellous find."

I was furious with him. My gold in his hand. My silver pieces. My artefacts. He wanted to take them away from me. His voice got louder and louder as he told me his theory. "These are not early Viking objects. They come from the middle of the twelfth century. That was when the Isle of Man had its first bishop – Bishop Wilmund. A giant red-headed man. He became corrupted by the power and the gold given to him. It is said he became a worshipper of the devil. He murdered, he robbed, he looted – he was a notorious bandit just like the Vikings of old. He took a small army of men with him and attacked parts of Scotland and Ireland. He seized gold and silver, looted and burnt, tortured and murdered. No one knows when he died or where he is buried. Legend is that he was buried in the south of Mann, his wealth buried with him.

Suddenly there was a crash that came from below me in the house. I pulled myself up from the chair, confused and tired. It was getting dark. I ought to go home. What was happening downstairs though? Had the caretaker come back to look for me, or had someone or some animal wandered in through the unlocked front door and started exploring the house?

I walked to the small door in the hall that led to the cellar. On opening it I realized that the stairs going down were very dark. I remembered the torch by the front door, fetched it and switched it on, then went down.

I discovered something extremely important. Both the caretaker and Archibold Faulk in his notebook mentioned 'the cellar'. But I was not walking down to a cellar. It was just the ground floor of the house. Outside the house the steps led up to the front door on the first floor of the house. I was going down the internal stairs from the first floor of the house – they led to down to the ground floor. I looked round. Yes I was right. It was the ground floor – it had windows front and back. So where was the cellar?

At the foot of the stairs were the four doors. I realised that the heavy oak door that had been so solidly closed before was now open. It was not a cupboard door – for behind it I could see an alcove then a flight of stone steps. I went down, the torch just about giving me enough light to see. The damp walls were made of rough-hewn stone. Had someone or something come down here and caused the loud crash? I called out and received a chilly echo.

There were thirteen narrow steps down into a low cellar. Along one wall were some wooden cabinets. I walked slowly alongside, shining the torchlight down on them as I went. The cabinets were made of black oak fronted with thick sheets of glass and they had gorgeous displays of old gold and silver coins, jewellery and artefacts. The last cabinet was a shock. I looked down at a skeleton. Some red hair was attached to the skull. A chain with a large cross was arranged around its neck. A huge ring sat on the ring finger of the right hand. Next to the bones of the right hand was a huge rusty sword. The skeleton was long: he must have been quite a tall man when he was alive.

I stared at the bones for a long time. Finally, I reached out with a trembling hand to see if I could open the glass lid. It lifted easily. I touched the cross and chain, then carefully lifted it and placed it around my own neck. The large ring I slid gingerly on my finger. A wonderful feeling of warmth spread through my body. I was powerful, strong and capable of anything. I lifted the great sword. It felt good in my hands.

And then I saw him. Dressed in the best Victorian clothes he was touching the coins, lifting up the large gold chalice, fingering the beautiful fine jewellery. His voice pierced my brain.

"Such a wonderful collection. It must be the skeleton and treasure of Bishop Wilmund. The world has to be told of this great discovery."

What! Lose my gold! Lose my fabulous collection so that mindless morons could gawp at it? No! No! No! The sword swung three times and he lay on the floor. I chuckled. No one knew of his visit here. I would dispose of the body. Then my collection would be safe. In a corner of the cellar were the two shovels that had been used to dig up the treasure. I grabbed one and went to work at a place where the flat stones making up the floor of the cellar were loose. Placing the torch on the ground, I prised up several stones and began digging. It was hard work. The sweat was running off me. The torch was fading and I was struggling to see. Finally I decided the hole was large enough to put the body in. I lifted up the body and stood before the hole.

"Father, father, what are you doing?" I turned to see who was calling. It was a young boy dressed in old-fashioned nightclothes. He was standing with a lighted candle at the foot of the stairs. He stared at me and then at the bloody body in my arms. The boy threw up his arms, dropped the candle, and ran up the stone steps. I could hear his footsteps but could not see him in the darkness. There was a crash and a series of bumps. I put the man's body down, picked up the torch and ran to the steps. Lying at the bottom, with his neck hanging at a horrible angle, was the young boy. He was dead! I felt a huge sense of loss.

I went back to the man's body. My mind was in turmoil. The collection of gold and silver must be kept secret at all costs. I had murdered the man so I must hide his body to evade detection. I buried him in the hole and pulled the stones back into place over the top. Then went over to the body of the boy, picked it up and carried it up to the ground floor. I shut and locked the heavy oak door leading to the cellar and placed the boy's body at the bottom of the wooden stairs that went up to the main hallway of the house. To anyone finding him there it would look as though he had fallen and broken his neck on the stairs that went down from the main hall to the ground floor.

After dealing with those two dead bodies I remember no more. Slowly, in a mist of terror, pain and confusion I became aware that I was back in the cellar. It seemed that much time had passed since the death of the little boy. I was drinking deeply from the beautiful shiny gold cup. I stared at it. A large face with red hair stared back at me from inside the cup. Was it my reflection or a glimpse of something reaching out to me from the past? A mixture of despair and sadness hung over me. The wine helped confuse the brain and blot out some of the horrors. I sat in a chair next to the cabinets fingering the gold and silvery finery.

More time passed. I slowly became aware of a little girl standing next to my chair. A lovely child with golden hair. Had I forgotten to lock the cellar door? My mind was so confused. I felt happiness and love but also a great fear. She was trembling and crying. "Father I followed you down here, what are you doing? What are these things?"

I removed the cross and chain from my neck and the large gold ring from my finger. Clumsily I placed them on her. She was still crying. I wanted to shut her up. Her cries got louder. They were echoing through my head. Somehow I managed to lift her up to the big cabinet so she could see, by the flickering light of a candle, the magnificent skeleton. That would please her, that would surely make her shut up. She screamed and jumped from my arms, falling into the open cabinet next to the skeleton. She went limp. I was able to pull her out with no serious damage to the skeleton. After removing the jewellery from her I carried her up the cellar steps shaking her to try and wake her. Suddenly she screamed then jumped out of my arms before running away. I went back down to the cellar.

Pain. A searing headache. It seemed a long time later that a woman came in to the cellar. She seemed strangely familiar to me. Attractive, blonde, yet with an air of great sorrow, she approached me as I sat drinking wine from the gold cup. "What are you doing here?" I asked.

Her answer made no sense to me. "Archibold, I know you have always ordered me and the servants not to come down to this cellar of yours but I have to see what keeps you down here for hours and hours every night. Please do not be angry with me."

I was annoyed by this unknown woman who had invaded my sanctuary and who spoke nonsense to me. "Leave me alone woman. It is not a place for you." But she was fingering the big cross and chain hanging around my neck, touching the large gold ring on my finger, asking me stupid questions. I seized her by the neck and shook her till she went quiet and limp. She stopped breathing. What to do with this meddling creature? I must get her away from the cellar. I carried her body up the steps and went into the ground floor scullery, the room used by the servants to do the washing. Empty washing lines hung across the room. I undid one of the lines, made a clumsy loop in it and placed it round the neck of the woman, hiding the marks on her neck. I took her body and lifted it up against the wall, tying the loop of rope to a hook in the wall. Her feet were now suspended several inches above the floor. Then I placed an upturned chair on the ground by her feet. "Anyone finding her will think she hung herself." I cackled loudly.

I returned to the cellar. Everything became blurred and confused. In my head were terrible worries – no one must disturb my wonderful collection of gold, no one must touch it. How could I preserve the wonderful skeleton and the beautiful objects? I must find a lawyer, someone who would follow my instructions without question."

★ ★ ★

I was waking from a deep sleep. My head was throbbing. Into my mind came my desire to see Mr Selby and give instructions about a will, and some kind of secret trust to preserve the wonderful collection. "Very important that I see Mr Selby." I shouted.

Someone spoke. I opened my eyes and saw a man in a white coat. "You must rest. You are in hospital. You are safe now."

"What happened?" My voice was weak and croaking. I tried to sit up from a lying position but was barely able to move. The man, who I realized now was a doctor, took my pulse as he spoke to me. "Do you remember being in a house in Port St. Mary?" I nodded. "You were slumped against the kitchen range. The caretaker found you. You were barely alive. The kitchen smelt of fumes. The caretaker said that there was work done on the roof recently. Some debris had fallen into the chimney and blocked the flue. The noxious fumes from the kitchen range were slowly killing you."

Later, Alan Tankersley the caretaker visited me. I gave him specific instructions. "Get the chimney cleared. Then you personally must brick up the doorway to the cellar. Make it look as if it was always blocked off."

He shivered then slowly nodded in agreement. "Yes, yes, that would be best." He hesitated and spoke quietly, "My great-grandfather used to spend a lot of time in that cellar with Mr Archibold Faulk, both of them drinking heavily. One night they drank far too much. When Mr Faulk woke up in the morning he found my great-grandfather stretched out on the cellar floor lifeless. He carried him up to a bedroom and got a doctor but my great-grandfather was dead. Not long afterwards Mr Faulk took his own life. My family has had plenty of money from its association with that house – but I wish we had never had anything to do with it. I know about the cellar but never go down there." He went off, promising to seal up the cellar straight away.

Mr Selby visited. I asked him point blank, "What happened between your grandfather and Mr Faulk?" He looked sheepish. I was angry. "It's your fault that I nearly died. You should have warned me about that house. Also, you have knowingly continued to administer a trust that was in breach of the Manx law. Now tell me the truth!"

Mr Selby stared into space and spoke in a level tone without emotion. "My grandfather was a young, penniless, newly-qualified lawyer when Mr Archibold Faulk asked him to visit the house in Port St. Mary. He was paid a large sum of money by Mr Faulk to set up a secret trust to ensure the house was to remain empty forever. It may be that my grandfather let his greed run away with him – he seemed to follow Mr Faulk's instructions rather than obeying the Manx law. With the money given to him by Mr Faulk he was able to set up the best law firm on the Island. After Mr Faulk took his own life in 1910 my grandfather used to visit Faulk house regularly. My grandfather became morose and short-tempered. Eventually he suffered terrible delusions and had to be certified. He died in hospital."

The legal advice I gave him was forceful. "Now look here, Selby, your family and your firm have acted badly. You must do exactly as I tell you. Arrange for Faulk House to be given free to Manx Heritage, the house to be open to the public as a Victorian museum but no one is to live there and nothing is to be done to change the physical state of the house. Then, I need you to witness a document that I will draw up. The document must be given to the Manx Museum and left sealed with them for the next one hundred years." Selby agreed.

When Selby was gone I gave a huge sigh. The nightmare was over. In a hundred years' time, when my statement was opened, someone else could decide what to do with the house and the contents of the cellar.

I was pleased when I got a message from Tankersley.

The cellar (and contents) is completely sealed.
No one would know that it ever existed.

When I was packing up my things and preparing to leave, I was visited by the hospital administrator. "When you were brought in to the hospital unconscious we took possession of all your valuables for safe keeping. Here they are."

Inside a clear plastic bag was my wallet, some loose change, wristwatch, and also a big cross on a chain and a huge gold ring. Absentmindedly, I put them on. It felt good to wear them. If only I could shake off this nagging headache and strange feeling of terror.

April

Angie Greenhalgh lived in Africa, Germany, the Far East and mainland UK before settling on the Isle of Man with her husband and two sons. She graduated from London University with a BSc in Economics and Geography and in 1973 was awarded a scholarship to study for her MA in Canada where she worked afterwards with the Ojibway people and the Innuit.

Angie enjoys many country pursuits including fishing. She is a keen walker, amateur artist and is interested in the archaeology, mythology and folklore of the British Isles. She is also the author of various published works in the UK and abroad and her book *Forgotten Magic of an Enchanted Isle* is published by Shearwater Press.

Her short stories 'Laa'l Breeshey' and 'Home Run' have been published in previous volumes of *A Tail for All Seasons*.

can you tell me?

Angie Greenhalgh

"So … why do you scream?"

"I just have to … to stop it happening. But it only works for a moment before it starts again."

"What does it feel like?

"I don't know how to say it."

"Just say how it feels to you at the time."

"I've tried to explain before. But it doesn't make sense."

"It might make sense to me. Just think about when it's happened to you before. Think how it makes you feel. And just say it."

"I don't like to think about it too much in case it starts it off."

"Faith, it's important that you tell me. Don't worry. You're safe here. "

"At first it's quiet, like. Very small and soft, like white feathers in the corner of a room before it gets bold again and starts slithering around and making patterns of noise so tiny and delicate it's almost pretty. And you think, 'Oh well, perhaps this time it will be nicer, so I'll let it happen just to see if it will be' … because sometimes it is. And when that happens it's almost perfect and everything fits together except for one sound, that one piece which waves like a strand of seaweed in the water making ugly shadows·and then you know that's the turning point and it will be bad again. Then it grows until the colours change and gets bigger like the shadows of trees in the wind and the noise grows so it's like a storm of raindrops in my head. But not water, no that would be better … but it's the same noise as the feeling of sand scratching my eyes as the wind whips across my face on the beach when the skies are grey and there is no sun. And I want to scream again to stop it … so I can think. But I know that if I do there will be too much trouble, so I start to growl, deep in my chest to chase it out of my head. I try to keep it low, so that people won't hear, but then it won't work properly and there will be too much water dripping from my mouth onto my chin. So it's better to be more open, like, and shut it up with a sudden roar … and then it's quiet again and I can breathe without it telling me its stupid things."

"And what do you think other people think about this?"

"They get nasty."

"Do you understand why?"

"Why what?"

"Why they get nasty toward you?"

"No."

"But you say that if you scream there will be too much trouble … so sometimes you growl and try to keep it low … so I do think you know that it upsets people around you."

"But if they knew what it was like they would understand."

"What do you think is more important? What is happening to you or the people around you?"

"I dunno. It all hurts. It's so bad sometimes I just wish I

didn't have to be me any more."

"Is that why you cut yourself?"

"I don't do it."

"So who does?"

"I dunno."

"If it's not you, it must be somebody you know … Faith, do you want to tell me who it is?"

"No. I don't know who it is."

"It must hurt. Don't you feel any pain when you are cut?"

"No … It all stops for a while and it's a better place to be."

"Can you tell me about that place?"

"It's quiet and white. Sometimes, I'm in a tall building, like, with pillars but no roof and there's stars and a silver web, but no spider in it, and the web pulls at the pillars when you breathe and then you see everything and it's so beautiful because suddenly you know everything … and the whole universe breathes with you and there's a huge heartbeat that connects you with everything and you feel whole and the voices and rushing noises have stopped … they don't matter any more …"

"That sounds a good place. Is that the only place you go to?"

"Sometimes there's a dark cave with a circle of light in the roof and water drips into a black pool in a stone well, making a beautiful noise that goes on forever and it feels like velvet and I'm not alone anymore."

"Who's with you, Faith?"

"The others."

"What others?"

"Just others."

"Tell me about them."

"I can't see them. I just know they're there."

"Do they speak to you?"

"No, not in the normal way."

"What do you mean? How do they talk to you?"

"They don't talk. It's just a feeling. Like breathing. It's the same."

"So how do you know what they are saying?"

"I just know."

"What do you talk about?"

"We don't talk."

"Well, what do they say?"

"It's not what you would understand."

"Try telling me … I want to understand."

"It's like not being alive. But still being alive, some place else. Like floating in water with your eyes closed. Like not being you but part of something else that just is and always will be and you're just part of it and you're only really your proper self when you are there."

"Mmm … If you could describe the others, how would you? Are they like anybody you know?"

"No."

"Anybody at school?"

"No."

"In your family?"

"No."

"Like any of your friends?"

"I don't have any friends."

"Could I meet them?"

"I don't think so. You're not a girl."

"Oh. So the others are girls?"

"I don't know how old they are. But we are not men."

"No men?"

"No."

"You say 'we'. Why?"

"Because when I'm with them, I'm part of them. We are together."

"Tell me what that means."

"It's like being joined up with yourself, but it's not really me any more even though it is."

"You mean the others are all like you?"

"Yes. Something like that."

"But are they parts of you that we don't normally see?"

"I dunno."

"Are they more like your mother or your sister ... or your grandmother?"

"No. Not really."

"Have you ever met anybody like them?"

She laughs. It's the first time he's heard her laugh.

"What's so funny?"

"Met them? Where? Here? On the Isle of Man?"

"No. I'm just trying to understand ... trying to help you."

He realises his mistake immediately as he sees her lips tighten. She drops her head, and gazes at the floor in silence. He senses her withdrawing into herself again.

"Look. Forget what I just said about help. It won't ever be like that for you again. I know it must have been awful, Faith. I want you to know that I am not going to treat you the way you've been treated before. But I have to assess the situation, to know what's best for you. There have been too many ... er ... things happening that makes it necessary. Can you remember what you do that upsets people?"

"You mean the screaming, growling and not letting people touch me?"

"Why don't you let people touch you?"

"Because I can see things."

"What things?"

"The bad things that are going to happen."

"What bad things?"

She twists her hands in her lap. Biting her bottom lip she looks up, her ten-year-old eyes full of tears.

"They don't like it when I tell them I know how they are going to die."

"How do you know?"

"When they touch me I see it, like in pictures. It's horrible."

"What about animals? Is it the same with them?"

"Dogs don't come near me. They whine and keep away. Cats are different. I like cats and they are the only ones who like me."

"Have you got a cat?"

Her lower lip trembles.

"Not any more. The last doctor said Pookie should be taken away from me. He said I could have her back only when I behaved and stopped having tantrums."

"And how do you feel about that?"

"I miss her so much ... I want her back and try so hard not to have the tantrums ... but I can't stop them ... except for the cutting ... that helps keep me quiet when the bad things start inside me. The cutting stops them. Please will you help me get my Pookie back?"

"Yes ... If you can tell me ... help me understand. Why do you call them bad things?"

"Because that's what everybody else says they are."

"Do you think they are bad?"

"It's just what's going to happen."

"Do you see anything good?"

"It depends ..."

"On what?"

"I dunno."

"Okay. Can you give me an example?"

"What do you mean?"

"Something that could happen to me. That you can see. Show me."

"Please … it's not like that."

She dropped her head again and became silent. She lifted her left hand to her mouth and seemed to be sucking her thumb for comfort. He sensed that she was withdrawing.

"Well, I think that's enough for today. You've done very well, Faith. We'll meet again next week for another talk."

Suddenly her head jerked violently upwards. Her blue eyes glazed, almost sightless, staring at a point above his head. The eyelids seemed to have disappeared and two glassy orbs rolled almost backwards into her skull.

"*Te kiune as aalin nish, agh bee sterryn cheet dy-gherrid.*"

His jaw dropped.

"What?"

Her thumb slipped from her mouth as she lifted her head. The eyes slowly refocused upon his.

He studied her pale face.

"What did you say?"

"I can't say it again."

"Why not? "

"I just can't."

"Can you write it down for me?"

"I don't know how to spell those words."

"Can you say it again?"

"I can't remember it any more."

"What did it mean?"

"I'm not sure. But we might not have the meeting next week."

"Why not?"

"It's fine and calm now, but there's a storm coming soon."

"Will that stop you from coming to the meeting?"

"Perhaps."

"Do you often speak like that, Faith?"

"I don't know. I can't hear what I say."

"But do you know what you are saying?"

"I feel what it means."

Her shoulders hunched. She looked very tired.

"Okay. Time to stop. If you remember what those words mean, write it down and tell me next week. Linda, our nurse, will take you into another room now, to be weighed and have a little blood test whilst I have a chat with your mother."

The nurse rose from where she had been sitting at the back of the room and guided the thin little girl towards the door.

Faith stopped and turned. She looked at him gravely.

"Don't go to the Chicken Rock on Saturday."

Then she turned and before he could say anything, had left the room.

Puzzled, he scribbled a few notes in the file then picked up the small tape recorder from his desk.

"Consultation with Faith MacGrigor concluded at 10.35 a.m. Monday 11th April. Follow-up appointment for her next week to be arranged a.s.a.p."

He took out the used tape and inserted a new one, glancing at the name on the top of the open file.

"Initial interview with Mrs Susan MacGrigor, mother of patient Faith MacGrigor."

A tentative knock at the door.

"Come in."

A neatly dressed woman entered, possibly in her late thirties or early forties. Her curly red hair was in total contrast to her daughter's long locks of straight, jet-black hair.

He stood up and shook her hand, indicating the chair opposite his desk.

"Please take a seat, Mrs MacGrigor. I'm Dr O'Hara, Martin

O'Hara. Thank you for coming to see me. I realise how difficult and deeply distressing all this must be and from the case notes that you have seen a lot of different people over the past few weeks, so please bear with me as I expect you've had to answer all these questions before. I'll be taping our conversation – if that's all right with you?"

"Yes, that's fine." Her voice had a sing-song lilt which was hard to place – not the usual Scottish accent.

"Well, as you probably know I'm a consultant psychologist and your daughter has been referred to me for assessment for psychotherapy – we generally don't like to use medication-based solutions on children if it can be avoided. I'm in communication with her social worker and have already spoken with Mr Pickering who was the psychiatrist you met last week. So, let's begin. I see that you are a widow?"

"Yes, four years now. But we'd been separated for two years beforehand. Davy was an alcoholic. Things got pretty bad. I couldn't take it any more – his terrible mood swings, the constant shouting and when he started hitting me, I walked out. Left Glasgow and got a job in London as a housekeeper for an elderly couple who didn't mind having my two girls around. Sally was nearly seven and Faith was four."

"You don't come from Glasgow originally though?"

"No I'm an Islander, from Lewis in the Outer Hebrides. My father came from the Isle of Skye to work in Stornoway, met my mother and we lived in a small village called Callanish. My mother's family have always lived there. Davy was from Wales, a place called Pentregethen in Pembrokeshire; a one-horse place, he called it. We met in Glasgow, both worked in the same hotel. I was a cook, he was a professional bartender. A good one. But that was only his sideline. He was really a professional gambler and was very good at that too. He made a fortune on cards and horses. His luck seemed to run out when he hit the bottle, though, and then it was a downhill spiral all the way."

"You moved to the Island last October?"

"Yes After Mr Harper died I stayed on to look after Mrs Harper but she was taken into a nursing home last August and the house had to be put on the market. So I fancied a change from being in the city, applied for the job at the new big hotel on the promenade. I thought Island life would be good for the girls." She sighed. "But how wrong could I be? Things seem to have gone from bad to worse since we arrived."

"So you live in a flat in Douglas?"

"Yes. I'm renting at the moment. On Senna Street. It's convenient. I can walk to work and it's easy for the girls for schools."

"And it's just you and the girls still?"

"If you mean is there any other man in my life – no there isn't! And hasn't been since I left Davy. Now, such long hours in catering ... any free time is taken up with looking after the girls. It seems that I've not spent as much time with Faith as I should anyway ... look what's happened ... I blame myself for not spotting it sooner. Just so busy and tired with the new job. Don't understand how she's got so out of control."

"When did you first notice anything?"

"Well looking back on it now, it all seems so obvious ... but at the time I didn't think anything awful was happening. Put her change in behaviour down to the move and thought she'd snap out of it when she made some new friends. But she'd just stay in her room doing bits of things and go for walks sometimes on the Prom with her sister, until Sally mentioned about how Faith was frightening all her friends away with new, strange talk. In the end Sal wouldn't go out with her. So Faith just stayed in her room a lot more, making things. And to be truthful I'd rather her be there than walking around the streets of Douglas on her own."

"What sort of things did she make?"

"Oh, you know, craft things, like macramé with string and rope, lots of knotting and I just thought it was a project from school – didn't find out until I talked to her teacher at the first parents' evening that it wasn't anything to do with school."

"Were there any other changes in her behaviour?"

"She, she ..." Susan MacGrigor's voice cracked as she pulled a tissue from her bag and dabbed at her eyes. "She wouldn't let me touch her any more. She'd pull away almost hysterical and scream. I didn't know what to think and she wouldn't say why ... so I tried to put it out of my mind ... went along with it and thought if I didn't make a big deal, it would go away ... but it didn't. And I had so much to do, no back-up or anybody to talk to ... and now I've lost my little girl ... Dr O'Hara, she was so loving to everyone before and now she's like a stranger and hardly speaks."

Susan MacGrigor was unable to stifle her sobs.

"How long has she been self-harming?"

"I don't really know when it began ... but looking back there were little bits of screwed up blood-covered tissue in the wastepaper basket in her room and as she'd had a lot of nosebleeds in London, I thought it was that ... because she's not started ... well you know, she's not old enough to have her periods. It would have been at the end of October I think, when she first started doing the rope stuff. Then when I asked her about the cuts on her hands, she said she'd broken a light bulb. There was always a good reason for the cuts on her hands and feet so I didn't give it a second thought at the time. It was such a shock when I got the phone call from school and the social worker came round to see me. I'd not seen her in the shower for a long time ..."

"And that was when?"

"February. Her class had been swimming and her teacher noticed all the scars. What kind of a mother am I, that I didn't spot it?" She began to cry again.

"Susan, may I call you, Susan?"

She nodded.

"Susan, you are not alone in this. It is quite common that parents are often the last to know. There is one very important aspect in Faith's case, and that is that we have found out about this relatively soon. Self-harming is symptomatic of mental health imbalance and often begins around adolescence. It is for many a way of dealing with family problems, bullying, personal difficulties and so on. The move to the Island may have triggered a revisiting of the stress in her early years when you were having problems in your relationship with her father. I suggest that Faith comes to see me again soon."

He noted that Susan had regained her composure.

"Do the girls ever mention their father?"

"Sal was old enough to have seen some of the bad things and I think she was relieved when we left for London, but Faith was a real daddy's girl and she took it hard. She was generally in bed, a sound sleeper, when things were at their worst. She kept asking for him for a long time though. She looks like him with her black hair. He was very Welsh. He used to say that there was a lot of the 'black Irish' in his family as well on his mother's side. She acts a lot like him too. Also she's started sucking her left thumb when she's concentrating. Never did as a baby, just this past year. She has his eyes. But she never talks of him. But it's odd, you know." She gave a little laugh. "He was always a one for going on about the wind and now she does too! Must be living close to the sea!"

"Well, Susan. Thank you, this has been very useful. I think that's enough for today. Please will you speak to my secretary and make Faith's appointment for next week and here's a number to contact if you need to speak to me at all before then."

* * *

Dr O'Hara contemplated the rain lashing against the window of the Port St Mary Yacht Club, "Never thought it would blow up like this when we set out this morning. There was just no sign of a storm."

Alan Christian lifted his glass of whisky and smiled grimly. "Joys of the Irish Sea, Martin me boy. Them Met fellers don't always get it spot on, yer know. Can't be too careful. The sea's a cruel mistress especially if yer not prepared. So ... ready to tell me what happened?"

"Well I was one of the four boats that had put up at Ramsey last weekend and I wasn't going to move *Quest* back to her mooring until next week. But on Thursday I got a phone call from Eddie asking me if I wanted to have a bit of a tester, just for fun before the 'Round the Island' race next month. So, on the spur of the moment I decided to join them. The forecast had been for a south-east Force 6 for the morning, dropping to Force 3 to 4 south-west for the afternoon. Things were going fine rounding the Point of Ayre and I used my new sail, that kite, which took full advantage of the following wind. And I was well ahead. But as I beat down the west coast *Quest*'s speed dropped and I realised she'd picked up something on the prop. After struggling for a while I managed to release it by turning the shaft with pipe grips until it spun freely, but I still couldn't get up much above 5 knots. The rigging wasn't set up properly and I really could have done with having you there as the mast was pumping a bit alarmingly. By then the others had left me for standing and were just distant spots on the horizon.

"Shortly after passing Peel the fog rolled in ... that Island

'Mannanan Mist' you always joke about, Alan. It reduced visibility to about two hundred feet. I tacked slowly down in about 16 knots of wind toward the Calf.

"When we set out we'd all decided to take the passage between Chicken rock and the Calf, rather than do the extra three to four miles going out past the Chicken. Just off Port Erin the fog began to clear, and as it was only an hour after slack, I decided to go for the faster option and take on the Chicken.

"But then all of a sudden the wind speed started to increase to about twenty knots. And the wave- reach from the southern Irish Sea was hitting the shallower water around the cliffs and piling it up into some really big waves. There were some randomly huge ones, like pyramids, pushing me everywhere and the sky was closing in. It was then I remembered what one of my patients had said earlier in the week. On Monday, long before I even knew I'd be out today with *Quest*."

Martin hesitated, taking a long swig of his drink.

"The patient told me not to go to the Chicken Rock on Saturday. She was quite emphatic when she gave me the warning. And there was another thing … I'd taped our conversation, as per normal, and she also told me 'It's fine and calm now, but there's a storm coming soon.' She said it to me twice. First in a language I couldn't understand at the time. But my nurse recognised it. She'd been sitting in on the consultation and told me afterwards that she thought it was Manx Gaelic. So we got it translated by Wednesday and it was exactly the same as what the patient said later in the interview in English, 'It's fine and calm now, but there's a storm coming soon.' There was a veiled implication as well that our next appointment might not happen, possibly as a result of this.

"And I must admit, being out there, alone, with the weather changing so fast, her warning came back to me and to be honest I felt a bit spooked. I could have pressed on and probably normally would have done. But in light of what she'd said on Monday, when even I didn't know that I'd be out sailing on Saturday I made my decision ... I turned back. And this is the really scary thing – I only just made it into Port Erin before my prop went completely. Only just managed to get in without smashing *Quest* up on the breakwater."

Martin looked at Alan gravely.

"So you'll know what the outcome could have been if I'd carried on?"

Alan nodded.

"Yes. Not a pretty scenario. Forty-odd years of sailing these waters ... safe to say with the wind speed and the currents pulling towards the Chicken you'd have been dragged onto it ... even with yer prop working, it would have been a hairy passage on your own. Glad I didn't get yer telephone message or I'd have been with yer, and I'd probably have talked yer into making a run for it and then ... well we would have got more than our feet wet."

He gave Martin a wry grin.

"Not worth thinking about what could have happened, eh? It didn't. Lucky for you that yer patient is obviously a sound Manx gal and knows the weather better than the Met boys. Must be a woman who sails? Speaks Manx pretty well? Not so many of us around. Wonder if I know her?"

"No, that's the weird thing, Alan. Not a woman. She's a ten-year-old girl, who moved to the Island just six months ago."

"My God! Yessir, that's strange. And the warning in Manx? Do her parents speak it?"

"Not as far as I know, but I'll be meeting her mother again next week. I'll ask. "

"Without breaching patient confidentiality, does she live

in the west of the Island? You know, watch the weather out here. Got a feeling fer the place?"

"No. She lives in Douglas. Some street off the Prom ... called Senna, I think."

"Senna Street? Yes, I know it – name rings a bell for something – memory's not what it used to be. She can hardly predict weather patterns on the west coast from there! Well, young feller, lucky for you to have had the warnin' and even better that you heeded it! Now, about that prop, do you think we'll have it fixed in time for the 'Round the Island'?"

★ ★ ★

Dr O'Hara smiled at the little girl as she entered the room.

"Hello Faith. It's nice to see you again. Please sit down. Now, I have to thank you for warning me about not going to the Chicken Rock last Saturday. Otherwise, as you probably know, I might not have been able to be at the meeting today."

Her expression remained blank. He waited for a response, carefully observing her for any hint that she understood, but there was no change, if anything only a growing look of suspicion.

"Do you remember what you told me last time?"

"No."

"Never mind ... now I know you've not been to school for a few weeks, so how is the home tuition going with Mrs Parker?"

She fiddled with the hem of her jumper, looking down at the floor.

"'S' all right, I suppose."

"And how do you like learning the Manx language?"

"What language?"

"Haven't you been learning some Manx?"

"No."

She looked up, confused.

"Okay, it doesn't matter, don't worry about it … I just thought you had. Anyway, how are things going? I believe you do a lot of craft work at home, with string and ropes – what are you making at the moment?"

She looked sideways and seemed to be studying the skirting board on the far side of the room.

"Nothing much. The same things as usual."

"And what are they? I haven't seen them. What are they like? Can you tell me about them?"

"Just rope stuff that I make into knots."

"I see. Does it make you feel better when you make them?"

"Yes."

"Can you tell me why?"

"Just does. That's all."

"When you make the knots does it help you? The way you feel inside?"

"Yes."

"Does it stop the cutting?"

"It's a different thing."

"What do you mean?"

"Another feeling. A different story."

"Oh, so the ropes tell a story?"

"Not the ropes. The knots!"

"Ah, so tell me about the story the knots tell."

"It's a story about the wind."

"Can you tell me the story, please Faith?"

"No. It's the knots' story, only the knots can tell the story."

"So how do you know how to tell the story to the knots?"

"I just know, that's all."

"Is it a good story?"

"I dunno."

He took a deep breath and thought for a moment.

"If I gave you some rope now would you be able to show me how you make the knots, please Faith? I use knots a lot when I'm sailing. I like knots. It would be good to see how you make your knots. And I'll show you some of mine and tell you their story … how I use them."

She sat a little straighter in her chair and seemed to perk up a bit.

"All right then."

He reached for the length of rope that he'd brought in that morning.

She sniffed.

"Is that the only piece you've got? I usually need three pieces. It's better that way."

"I can get some more if you want."

Her face became animated.

"Yes please."

He reached into his desk drawer again and pulled out several small lengths of assorted rope.

"Here we go. See what knots you can show me with these."

She smiled as he handed them to her.

"Thank you. It feels nice rope. It already holds a story of the sea in it, doesn't it?"

"Well … yes, I suppose you could say that. It's been knocking about on board my boat for a while. It's handy, you know, if I need little bits for jobs like splicing and whipping rounds. It must have picked up the sea story when it was there."

He watched intently as her small fingers fumbled with the various pieces. She looked up.

"It's no good."

"Why?"

"I can't do it here. I can't feel anything. I need the feeling to tell me what knots to make."

"Well just show me how you normally do it. You don't have to tell a story this time. "

She started to become distressed.

"It's no good. I can't do it by myself. I have to be at home."

"So does somebody help you at home?"

"Well, in a way they do."

"Who?"

"The others. I told you about them last week!"

"Oh yes, I remember, they're all girls aren't they?"

"Yes."

"Did I ask you how many others there are?"

"There are eight of them. Now we are nine. They said they'd been waiting a long time for somebody like me."

"Eight of them? Are you sure?

"Yes, and it only works properly if there are nine of us."

"Are they there all the time?"

"I think so. But we only meet when I'm on my own."

"Do they come to your house?"

"No, they were already there."

"What do you mean?"

"They've always been there. But they also are in the place with pillars and the cave place I told you about before."

"Do they help you with the cutting?"

She looked horrified.

"No! I don't know about the cutting. I told you. It just happens when the other things, the bad things start up in my head and I can't think properly and the pictures inside my head get strange and frightening."

She became flushed, agitated and anxious.

"I don't want to talk any more now. Can I go?"

"Faith, if you tell me what's happening to you, I can make things better and we can get Pookie back."

Her little face lit up with hope.

"Really?"

"Yes. I promise."

"All right then. I'll try."

"Okay, okay, Faith. That's good. So it's not the same thing as the knots then, when these bad things come?"

"No. Concentrating on the wind helps to keep those pictures away ... most of the time. It gets worse if people touch me. I get their story then. Sometimes they are very bad stories."

He remembered the problems Linda mentioned they'd had with her last week when they tried to take her bloods.

"The eight others. Are they the same age as you?"

"No. I don't think so. They seem to have been around a long time. But they help me."

"How do they do that, Faith?"

"I can't explain it."

"Try."

"I can't."

"Why not?"

"I'm not supposed to. It's secret. If I do they will be angry. It's secret."

"Are the bad things anything to do with the eight others?"

"Perhaps. I'm not sure."

"When you told me about the storm coming last week, how did you do it?"

"I don't know. Sometimes when I put my thumb in my mouth I can see things ... but that makes it easier for the bad things to come through later. They get stronger."

"I think that's enough for now, Faith. I don't want you to get too tired. I'll find out where Pookie is and next week I'll let you know when she can come home."

Her eyes beamed with happiness.

"Oh. Thank you, thank you, thank you."

He waited for her to leave and then switched off the tape recorder, gazing thoughtfully into space before writing a few notes in the file. His phone rang.

"Thanks for letting me know Linda … Yes … Tell Mrs MacGrigor I understand. Yes, whenever she's ready. That's okay."

He put down the receiver and scrolled through his emails and then the phone rang again.

"Oh yes, that's fine Linda, put him through … Alan, you old rascal … Yeah fine … how are you? Still going and grumbling, as they say? What? No … I've not been able to speak with the mother … What? That sounds interesting. No I'm not doing anything then. Okay, a quick drink then, at 6.30 … Oh yes, the parts for the prop were dispatched today. Yes of course I checked … sent out today … should be on the Island in a couple of days … Yes … See you later then."

* * *

The interior of the Quayside pub in Douglas left a lot to be desired, but the beer was good. Martin spotted his crew mate sitting at a table under one of the only working lights.

"Sorry I'm late Alan, last patient was too … suffering from the 'knock on effect!' Now what have you pulled out of the library? Must be interesting woodworm to get you so excited! Great, thanks for having ordered my drink. Well, crack on – tell me what you've discovered whilst I slake my thirst!"

"Well, fella, you got me thinkin' when you told me about that gel and how she warned yer. Now yer know I'm a bit of a divil for the old Manxie stuff, folkore, heritage and all that. Well, I've forgot more than I remember – showin' me age, lad, showin' me age ... so I've been goin' through a lot of me old books and got into a right good hunt. Scent's still hot, lad, if yer know where to look in the first place, and now the internet is a great thing to crack on with. Anyways, getting right to the point. There's a lot more that meets the eye than what yer think ... psychology is one thing, but I don't think it's just that in this case. Now fasten yer seat belt, open your mind and I'll take yer on a quick trip through years of knowledge, boy, years and years of it! Ha. Up to the task? Well yer might need to be gettin' another order in to keep me whistle wet. Thirsty work, eh?

"Well lad, it's like this. When yer talked about Senna Street it rang a ruddy great bell ... couldn't place the facts right away, but here we go. I've photocopied the relevant bits so that yer can take 'em back with yer.

"First stop was that good Manx scholar J.J. Kneen. He died in 1938 but his *Place-names of the Isle of Man* is still a classic. See what he says about Senna Street:

Senna Road: The meaning of Senna or Sena is doubtful and we have no early records. It may be Manx Shennagh, 'old land' which possibly applied to a small piece of land before it was built on.

"Fair enough, lad, but I knew somewhere I'd read something else and went through me papers drivin' the missus mad with the mess until I found a photocopy I took years ago at the Manx Museum Library.

"Now listen to this, lad, just listen to this. Train, in his *History of the Isle of Man* published in 1845, page 366:

that it is a singular circumstance, that down to the year 1808, the streets of Douglas were without names; and the houses unnumbered to 1843. All went by the general name of Douglas, with the exception of the northern suburb called Sena, which signifies old; and the place called the 'Fairy Ground' near the Quay. My friend, Dr Oswald, asks if this Sena can be the site of the Druidical nunnery mentioned by Mela.

"And in his footnotes he quotes Oswald's *Guide*, page 84:

Pomponius Mela speaks of an Island called Sena in the British sea celebrated for the oracle of the Gaelic divinity whose priestesses, nine in number, enjoyed the faculty of raising the wind and the sea by verses, of predicting the future and of changing themselves into animals. Mela de Situ Orbis lib.iii.

"Now where's that pint? Hmm, thanks lad. Now don't say anything yet, Martin, there's more to come. Ssshh ... just listen a bit longer.

"Sir George Laurence Gomme – how's about going through life with that mouthful? Yer'd want to gum something up, eh? He was President of the British Folklore Society, a mighty learned academic feller, published a classic, the *Ethnology in Folklore*, in 1892, been reprinted recently, damned good read!

"Anyway ... listen to what he says in Chapter Three, page 49:

In the Isle of Man, Higden say the women 'selle to shipmen wynde, as it were closed under three knots of threde, so that the more wynde he wold have the more knots he must undo'. These practices may be compared with the performances of the priestesses of Sena, who, as described by Pomponius Mela were capable of rousing up the seas and wind by incantations. In Wales there was the 'cunning man of Pentregethen' who sold wind to sailors and who was revered in the neighbourhood in which he dwelt more than the divines; he could ascertain the state of absent friends.

"Still hot on the trail, I found the Higden reference, *Higden Polychronicon* by Trevisa, published in London in 1482 – getting back in time now, boy, aren't we? 1482! But it'll get a lot older yet ...

"At the same time I followed up *Dalyells Darker Superstitions*, page 250, Mallett's *Antiquities* Volume I, where they talk about this art of wind knotting:

the knots were cast on a leathern thong, moderate breezes attended the loosening of one, stronger gales the next and the vehement tempest even with thunders with the loosening of the third. These knotted thongs were sold to navigators.

"Now look at this map, Martin. It's 'Europa' by Pomponius Mela, drawn in the first century AD. Mela was supposed to have died around 50 AD. He lived in Spain."

"Wait! Wait a minute Al ... You're going too fast for me. This is a bloody avalanche of quotes but what you're telling me about Senna Street is that it was originally the site of some sort of oracle where there were nine priestesses who could control the weather ... selling knots to sailors, predicting the future and changing into animals? Interesting superstitions – don't forget my family was from Mayo and even though my parents have lived in Liverpool for the last fifty years my mother spouts all sorts of rubbish from the Old Country."

"But listen to what I'm saying, Martin ... I'm as cynical as anybody, you of all peoples should know that! But look at this gel, what she told yer! What she knew! How? I don't know what else yer've picked up from her ... but has she said anything else that ties in with all this?"

"I have to be circumspect here with regard to confidentiality of my patient. But I can tell you that we're dealing with a very disturbed pre-pubescent girl whose behaviour verges on a constant state of hysteria ... However there are certain elements I've gleaned that do strike a chord with what you say ... Today she mentioned that these 'others' are eight in number and have waited a long time for her to come. But equally this could be symptomatic of multiple personality syndrome or schizophrenia ...

"I've only just started gaining her confidence. She doesn't like doctors – she's had one or two bad experiences recently with other doctors who touched her and she went into a frenzy and had to be medicated. She doesn't like to be touched in any way, even by her mother. I'm not sure if there has been any abuse in the past yet and this behaviour is a result. She says it's because she sees how people will die as well as seeing their 'stories', as she puts it.

"Her behaviour at school has been so disruptive that she hasn't been allowed back. Since Social Services took on her case she's been at home most of the time and the situation is becoming worse rather than better. She's withdrawing into herself more and more. All symptoms of a very disturbed mental state.

"But the wind knots are interesting ... she's been knotting ropes for the past few months in her bedroom ... says it's to do with the wind. But she couldn't do it in my surgery today. So this story really seems to be a fabrication."

"But, Martin, how do yer explain her predictions last Saturday?"

"I can't. She put her thumb in her mouth, eyes rolled back and she came out with a load of Manx and today she couldn't remember any of it, nor has she learned any Manx language."

"What did yer say then about her thumb?"

"She put her left thumb in her mouth and today she says when she does this she can see things but is frightened by how it makes 'the bad things come through later'."

"My God Martin! Yer talking about the Seer's Thumb!"

"What the hell? Alan, what else is in that pint?"

"Listen Martin, don't mock me. I'm serious ... yer in my realm now, laddo. I've been interested in Gaelic tradition all me life. What yer described is textbook Second Sight or

95

Seership – the eyelids turning back upon themselves, staring eyes, sucking of the thumb, well recorded in the Highlands and Islands, Ireland and Wales. The Isle of Man has had its fair share of folk with the Sight.

"The Seer's Thumb was something that the Irish poet Finn did, and the Welsh poet Taliesin; their stories are too long to bore yer with but they centre around them accidentally acquiring a great wisdom and almost supernatural knowledge when they burned their thumbs and sucked the burning drops from them. Irish Finn Mac Cumaill, originally a warrior, became a poet and seer after scalding his finger with three drops of liquid from a pot cooking the salmon of wisdom, Taliesin from scalding his finger with three drops from Ceridwen's cauldron where she was cooking up another wisdom dish, and then we have the same Scandinavian tradition of Sigurd who did pretty much the same thing burning his thumb on Fafnir, the dragon's, heart when it was being roasted – and incidentally, the Isle of Man has probably more Sigurd stones than anywhere in the world. Go and look at the early Christian crosses on the Island, you'll see pagan carvings of Sigurd and his thumb.

"Hell, even Shakespeare talks about it when one of the witches knows Macbeth is approaching by the feeling in her thumbs: 'By the pricking in my thumbs, something wicked this way comes.'"

"Okay, all very interesting, Alan, but –"

"Martin, one question … Was she like this before she came to live at Senna Street?"

"No … Not from what I've been told so far. But we might have only just picked it up. We don't know what was happening prior to them moving here. I need to get reports from the family's London GP and her previous school."

"Do yer know where the parents were from originally?"

"Yes, the father came from some isolated village in Wales and the mother's background was the Scottish Islands."

"Classic Seer Country! Perhaps it's in the genes? And now she's in a place which is a time bomb! Poor kid ... if what I think is happening, really ... must be a bloody nightmare. For her and everybody around her. They should move before it's too late. Perhaps it is already. What's her father like?"

"He died from alcoholism four years ago."

"Any mention of ..."

"Wait a minute ... The mother said he used to be a very successful gambler and always chewed his thumb when he was concentrating on his betting. And that the daughter was taking after him and there was something about wind as well."

"Perhaps he drank because like his daughter he saw things and found it hard to cope?" O'Hara laughed.

"Alan, we could go on all night and I respect your views and appreciate your research but I think if I don't get home soon I'll be lynched and the dog will be given my dinner. The same will probably apply to you as well and no doubt you'll tell Aalish it's my fault again! Let's talk some more when we're fixing the prop at the weekend. Always good to have a sounding board, however wacky, and I'll read your photocopies. Thanks a lot for doing them."

* * *

The following Sunday Alan Christian climbed on board *Quest*.

"Shouldn't take us too long to get this fixed. But I've to be back for 4.30 to go to one of the grandchildren's birthday parties. Martin, be the good doctor, remind me to take some painkillers before I leave!"

O'Hara laughed and looked at the horizon.

"No probs, Alan. Judging by what seems to be blowing in from the south-west we should try and get it done before we get hit by rain. Pass me that oil, please, this thing's a bit tight … Thanks. That's better. Oh, by the way, read your photocopies and I must admit I've had time to think about what you said in the meantime … it is an unusual perspective and I'll admit not one that I'd easily be persuaded by – the medical approach moved on from Mumbo Jumbo magic a long time ago – but there were some things that surprised me. Can you pass those grips again please?

"Now … what was I saying? Yes. That place in Wales that the girl's father came from in Pembrokeshire. Well, it's the same place Gomme mentioned, Pentregethen, where the cunning man lived, the one who sold wind to sailors. And later after speaking with the girl's mother on the phone, because she'd missed her last appointment and I needed to check on one or two things anyway, I found out her father's family were originally from Skye. She still uses that surname because she never married my patient's father and it's actually quite an unusual spelling of a well-known clan. So without breaching confidentiality of the name I can tell you that I was able to discover quite easily that this branch had provided the Laird's Seers for generations. And the place where she comes from on her mother's side in Lewis is considered to be one of the most important megalithic sites in the world. On a par with Stonehenge."

"Callanish!"

"How did you know that, Alan?"

"Come on now fella … If you're interested in prehistory it's a real Mecca – an incredibly special place. Been there twice. Once in me own boat, with me Manx flag's three legs flying proud!"

"There … do you think that's okay now?"

"Fittin's tight and the spins good ... Yeah, should be right enough ... Now all we need is a good wind and some luck and who knows ... we might win the 'Round the Island' yet!"

"Doubt it Alan! You're world class I'll grant, but the boat's not in the same league as most."

"It's skill and luck that sometimes make all the difference between winnin'and losin' ... But it'll be great crack all the same. Now let's have a quick coffee in that nice little caf' yonder and yer can finish telling me what yer think."

★ ★ ★

O'Hara pushed his mug of Italian coffee to one side of the table and placed the photocopy of the map in front of them.

"Never make these tables big enough, do they? Now if you place so much faith in Senna being located on the Isle of Man I'm afraid this is where your argument falls down. Giving me this map, Alan, you shot yourself in the foot! Senna is marked as south of Britannia off the western tip of Gallia where Brittany would be!"

O'Hara gave his crewmate a triumphant grin which began to fade as Alan burst into laughter.

"I was waitin' fer that ... wondered how long it would be before yer navigatin' skills tried to chop that one out of the water! Now don't be so smug, remember what yer see is all relative. Yer've got to look at who was was drawin' the map and when. What information Mela had and all the stories that went with them. It was word of mouth as much as anything. Let me show yer. Look at the Med ... All of the countries, islands and mountain ranges are pretty good considering. The Greek islands are very good and even up into the Black Sea. But this was the known world, Martin, very well-known to sailors and Greek geographers, but the further west and north yer go the knowledge of places becomes hazy and their relative placing spatially inaccurate. I've spent a lot of time studying the early maps."

O'Hara groaned. "Oh no … Here we go … Alan just cut to the chase, then. Tell me why you think it's the Isle of Man."

"Look, Where the Isle of Man should be there's nothing at all. No Scillies, no Channel Islands either. No islands off the west coast of Brittania except for a big blob that's called Jvverna, obviously Irish – excuse the dig! But everything to the east is pretty well recorded, suggesting that the western passage wasn't used as much. Look at the shape of Brittania – just a triangle. Wales doesn't figure, nor Cumbria and elsewhere in Europa lots of details of bays and river mouths are included … Can't figure out the Cassiterides – means the Tin Isles – off the north-west of Spain, but then sea traders would probably want to keep the origins of tin secret: not wanting others to find where they got the stuff from and flood the market, so to speak. So reckon it's a code for Cornish tin mines. The Orkneys and Shetland are pretty much in the right place, which supports me theory about the major sea routes being off the eastern seabord of Britain and well, mentioning Callanish, look past the British Ocean, Brittanicus Oceanus and way over here, due north of the Black Sea is a place called Hyperborei, the Land behind the North Winds.

"Diodorus Siculus was a Greek geographer of the first century AD and gives a better description of the place as an Island roughly the same size as Sicily with a huge temple where the God comes down to visit every nineteen years – he was talking about the lunar standstill at Callanish, an awesome event even today. It's now accepted scientifically that this is the only possible location for the Hyperborei. But it's a long way off from where Mela drew it!

"Also, I don't know if yer realise it, but the Isle of Man has only relatively recently been called that. In the past it had many other names. It may have been the Tir n'Bham – the Isle of Women, where there was an oracle. But think, Martin, what we now all accept as the Isle of Man being Manannan's Island – Manannan – the major Gaelic Divinity of the Brythonic people. Important in Irish and Welsh mythology, a sea god who controlled the wind and the weather, when sea travel was so vital. Keeper of the Crane Bag of knowledge? Were these priestesses part of his cult? Was there a special oracle here that was also a secret place originally, its location a place hidden, like the Island often is, by mist? Perhaps the mist was also an allegorical one? Symbolic ... like the tales of the Irish and Welsh heroes to the Isle of Manannan in search of knowledge?

"So Senna, renowned as an oracle, like Delphi, would be known of perhaps only vaguely in legend and not a place visited by many. Like most oracles only the top boys were allowed, and the priestesses had to be virgins married to their vocation, like nuns, pure and unsullied. No wonder they didn't want too many seafarers popping by. But who knows, over time maybe it was just a bunch of wise women selling their strange knowledge on land where Senna Street is now? All that incredible history condensed into one streetname? Makes yer wonder, doesn't it?"

Alan glanced down at his watch.

"Christ, is that the time? I'll be drawn, quartered and hung from the yard arm if I don't get me skates on! See yer next week when we sail her back. Not much time left now before the race."

Punchdrunk with the storm force of facts, O'Hara stared after him with an open mouth.

★ ★ ★

Two days later O'Hara sat staring at the little girl. She'd lost even more weight and looked so weak and fragile that he had to stop himself from putting his hand on her shoulder. It might bring more horror than comfort if she really could see some of the things he'd seen, or what his end might be.

"I've some good news for you, Faith. Pookie will be home tomorrow."

Her face brightened with an incredible smile of pure joy.

"I saw him yesterday at the Cat Sanctuary. He's as fat as butter and looks very sleek and happy, but I'm sure he will be very pleased to be back with you."

Her head dropped, the smile vanishing instantly.

"It's not my Pookie."

"What do you mean?"

He began to worry that he'd been shown the wrong cat, or even worse a replacement, and perhaps she'd sensed it.

"It can't be my Pookie … Pookie's not a boy!"

He laughed with relief. Alan's approach was getting to him – he was starting to think irrationally.

"Oh, no, sorry Faith, my mistake. I got told off yesterday as well, by the lady at the Cat Sanctuary for calling her 'him'! All cats look the same to me."

She looked defiantly up at him. She obviously had lost trust. It would be a difficult session now and probably not in anyone's interest to labour through the next thirty minutes. And then another twenty minutes with the mother.

"Tell you what, Faith. Your mum's outside, let's ask her if we can go in my car and pick Pookie up right now."

She looked up in shock.

"Really?"

"Yes. Come on."

★ ★ ★

102

O'Hara kept glancing in the mirror at the happy little girl on the back seat of his car cuddling the small black cat that was lying contented upon her lap.

She caught his eye in the mirror and smiled with gratitude.

"This has been the best thing ever. Thank you Dr O'Hara!"

He smiled back and winked at her mother in the passenger seat.

"It near broke my heart too when they said it was necessary for Pookie to go away ... but what could I do? Thank you from me as well. Would you like to come in for a cup of tea?"

"Thank you, Susan, that would be appreciated."

The interior of the house on Senna Street was rather dark, but apart from that quite homely. Faith sat on the sofa with her cat, but the grin had gone now and she seemed rather nervous as they waited for their tea.

"Well, Faith. I've kept my word. You've got Pookie back. So would you try and show me how you do the knots again, please?"

"I only do it in my bedroom. It's only girls allowed in there ... but you could watch outside from the hall."

He followed the child out of the living-room and tried to contain his surprise when they didn't turn left and go up the flight of old wooden stairs; instead she opened a small warped door, part of the panelling underneath them and they made their way down ancient narrow stone steps slanted and worn by countless generations. There was an overpowering smell of damp which increased as they descended. At the bottom was a small passageway.

She glanced at him nervously, indicating two doors at the end.

"That's mine. You'll have to wait here Dr O'Hara, quietly.

I'm sorry, but you can't come in. The others won't like it. But if I sit on the bed you should be able to see me make the knots for you."

O'Hara nodded and stood silently in the doorway, stooping slightly due to its lack of height.

The bedroom was quite dark, obviously converted from a cellar. He could make out the light well of a basement window, which meant that they were well below the level of the pavement outside.

The room seemed quite small and cell-like with just a little single bed in the middle. But then as his eyes became accustomed to the gloom he almost choked. The room was actually quite large, but it was stacked from floor to ceiling with hundreds, if not thousands, of pieces of rope coiled into rolls. Stacked upon each other, not randomly but neatly, like a filing system, according to the thickness of the rope.

"My God," he breathed, wondering who else from the Department had actually been to see this.

The questions flew like a storm around his head but he kept quiet as she'd requested.

Faith sat on the end of the bed. The cat stiffened, arching its back as though electrified, holding its tail at an abnormal angle to its body. She picked up three pieces of rope and began to mutter something low and unintelligible. She turned her head towards him and her eyes were once again white glassy orbs shining sightlessly in the darkness. He could see her small fingers working quickly amongst the rope in frenzy.

And then for a moment, he couldn't be sure, perhaps it was his imagination ... but the musty smell of damp seemed to be replaced by that salty sweetness which he loved. The wind off the sea.

"Dr O'Hara! What are you doing down there?"

"Just came down to see Faith's bedroom, Susan."

"Oh no! Oh no!"

He turned to see her slump down and sit as if defeated upon the top step. A shaft of light illuminated her face, creased with anxiety.

"Please don't tell anybody that's where she sleeps, Dr O'Hara. I'm sure they'll take her from me if they know. I can't keep her upstairs in her room. She won't stay. I know it's bad down there ... the air's terrible, and it's so damp, but she won't be told. Screamed and screamed, foaming at the mouth like a mad thing until I let her have her way. There's nae stopping her. What am I to do, Dr O' Hara? What am I to do?"

She broke down, sobbing, tea spilling from the cup into the saucer she still clutched in her trembling hands.

"Don't worry, Susan. I think under the circumstances you had no choice. I won't say anything ... but this puts another dimension on the problem. It's good that I've seen this today. I'll consider what we have to do and we'll discuss it next week. Don't worry, we will work this out."

Faith walked out of her bedroom, in her hands some knotted rope.

"This is for you. You'll need it some time soon."

Her voice was flat, cold, without emotion.

"Thank you, Faith."

O'Hara shoved it quickly into his pocket as he climbed the stairs, his immediate concern for the distraught woman above.

★ ★ ★

Alan Christian squinted at the sea in front. They'd just made it safely through and past Chicken Rock, and the hard part of the course was over.

"Well Martin, the props held up. Yessir, so far so good. And now here we are no wind, absolutely nothing, just drifting along the south coast of the Island hoping for that occasional puff of wind to help us around Langness point. At least all the craft are in the same predicament."

"Alan. Do you want to put your theory to the test?"

"Now which particular one would that be, young fella?"

"The one about Senna Street being an ancient oracular site where women sold wind to the sailors in the form of knotted ropes?"

"Now how in Mannanan's name am I goin' to do that?"

"Go below Alan, and in the pocket of my Helly Hansen jacket you'll find a knotted rope. Please fetch it and we'll try it out."

Alan stared at him, gave a lopsided smile and went below. Within a couple of minutes he was back, examining the complex knotwork as he walked toward O'Hara.

"Mighty queer stuff going on here. Never seen such work before! Looks almost too intricate to have been done by human hand and yet too irregular for any machine. Where did yer get it?"

"You're only allowed one guess."

"Off of yer little patient at Senna Street?"

Martin nodded and smiled.

"Well let's see how this works. You can do it, Alan, it's your baby. Just undo the first one … I don't really expect anything to happen anyway, but better not start a hurricane!"

They both laughed as Alan undid the first knot.

"I don't know what I'm supposed to do … but I suppose if I shake it at the sails?"

"Search me, Alan. I'll leave it to you to do."

"All right then, young fella, here goes!"

Alan shook the first unkotted rope at the limp sails. Nothing happened.

O'Hara gave a wicked wink at his crewmate. "See, just

superstitious bunkum."

"Now just a minute, lad, just a minute. This is not from the era of push-button technology ... But do yer see that, Martin? There's wind coming in. Look the sails are filling. I'll be damned ..."

Alan swung round to look at the other boats. Their sails were still slack and empty.

Quest shuddered slightly and began to glide forwards slowly through the flat glass-like expanse of water.

Alan chortled.

"Could be a fluke, like. Let's really test the theory. And it's not cheating – we just found wind – that's true, isn't it?"

O'Hara was shaking his head and chuckling. "Nobody would believe us anyway. Go on then, Alan, test it a bit more ... I know you're dying to. Undo the second one!"

Alan struggled with the bigger knots until the rope was free of them and waved it at the sails.

"Go boyos, go!"

"Now, I've been wanting to say this forever ... since watching Gregory Peck in *Hornblower* ... Forgive me, Alan."

As the wind filled the sails with increasing force O'Hara threw his head back, laughing like a schoolboy and shouted, "Let the wind take her, Mr Christian!"

Soon the other boats were just mere specks on the horizon behind them and *Quest* sped up to Laxey, past Maughold Head and into Ramsey to cross the finish line.

O'Hara slapped Alan on the back.

"That was bloody unbelievable, Mr Christian. It's going to be hours till the others get here. The champagne can wait, I've got something that needs doing urgently."

"What's that, skipper?"

"There's the matter of a very frightened little girl, her mother, her sister and a small black cat who need to be picked up immediately and taken to stay at my house, until we can find alternative accommodation. Oh, and you might like to follow me in your van ... there's an awful lot of knotted rope you might like to store in your shed!"

MAY

Vivienne Higgins is Manx born and lives in Douglas with her husband and young daughter. After leaving the Isle of Man College in 1985 with a BTEC National Diploma she worked as a manager for the Isle of Man Treasury.

Vivienne now works as a freelance writer with a specific interest in Manx history, herbalism and the flora and fauna of the Island. She has written various pieces published in Manx Life and her short story 'Voices' was published in the first volume of *A Tail for All Seasons*.

An ill wind

Vivienne Higgins

Peel Beach, May 1720

Two bunched fists were in front of the child's face, the knuckles knotty and rough. William Qualtrough watched his daughter keenly.

"Choose, my pretty."

Katherine jumped up and down, almost slipping on the seaweed beneath her feet, squeaking like a young gull in her excitement.

"Can't!" she laughed, clutching her bonnet and spinning round.

"And may ye' pick the right one ..."

The child bobbed forward, tapping the left hand with a feathery touch. She held her breath as he slowly unfurled each finger and counted.

"*Nane, jees, tree, kiare, queig.*"

Finally her prize was visible.

"Ooh! What is it, Dadda?"

"Treasure, my love. Washed ashore or brought in by a mermaid from some wreck I shouldn't wonder. A gem, as rare

111

as rare can be."

Her eyes twinkled at the deep purple piece of beach glass in his hand. It caught the rays of the cold winter sun just a little, being a well-worn scrap, its edges worn smooth as a pebble.

"If you turn it this way," said William, "it looks like a star."

"It does Daddy, *gura my ed!*"

In the parlour later, her mother turned the little lump of glass about in the firelight.

"What a pretty colour! Purple. Purple for power, so they say. Yes, a good find, and rare, mind ye. 'Tis an unusual colour for glass. I think Dadda's more of a magpie than you, my sweet!"

William smiled sheepishly. It was true. He liked nothing better than to scour the shore for treasures with Katherine.

"Will Daddy make me a necklace, Mammy?" the little girl yawned later, climbing into bed.

"I'm sure he shall, child," said her mother, tucking her in tight. "*Oie vie,*" and kissed her goodnight.

As she slept, her father crafted a necklace in a pentagon design, twisting copper wire round and round the glass. He looped a strong cord of fine leather through the back, knotting it tight, then laid it high on the mantel shelf until morning. When Katherine stirred at first light, William was fastening his boots near the door.

"Daddy, are you going to the fishin'?"

"*Moghrey mei,* Katherine. Aye, but I have something for you." He came to her and drew the necklace down over her head.

"May this always keep you safe for me till I come home." The glass shone at her throat. "I love you, *Katreeney.*"

"I love you too, Daddy, *gura my ed.*"

He kissed her cheek, sweet with sleep, and she settled back

down to slumber.

William and Annie walked to the boats and the Peel women kissed their menfolk farewell. When the fleet had taken to sea, the women watched, singing their traditional Peel songs and murmuring prayers to keep their men safe. The stormy weather was a worry, the wind already tearing at skirts and bonnets.

Katherine was waiting anxiously at the fire when the gathering gale blew her mother in through the door.

"Don't fret, my love," whispered Annie, hugging her little daughter's troubles away. "We are his guiding light, Katherine, remember that. Our love will be a beacon until he returns."

"Aye, I know, Mammy."

But Katherine always worried, and always would worry, just like her Mammy and her Mammy's Mammy before her. The wind screeched through the thatch.

"Right ... let's get busy."

Katherine lingered a moment to admire her necklace, fingering the neat, tight wirework. It was important, this little piece of treasure, and she meant to keep it forever.

Peel Hill, late summer, 1743

The breeze was bracing as Katherine, grown to womanhood, her husband Roddy and their small daughter Kitty, climbed upwards. Church was over and little Kitty felt light as air as her Daddy swung her onto his broad shoulders. Her coppery hair was loose now and soft as thistledown, blowing in his eyes and hers. The fishing fleet was at rest below, with the town of Peel, small and smoky, tucked in behind it.

"Where's the *Peel Lass* Daddy? Which one is she?"

Roddy pointed out the lugger.

"I wish I could sail on a boat like that," sighed Kitty. "One day I will be a fine lady and I shall watch all my ships come in, by one, by two, by three!"

"So you'll own a whole fleet, will you?" chuckled Roddy.

"P'raps! And I'll choose myself a handsome husband from one of the fishermen – just like Mammy did!"

"Aye ... but he'll be terrible busy at the herring, like your Daddy," laughed Katherine, tickling Kitty playfully.

"No Mammy ... he won't be fishing for herring. He'll be helping the mermaids fish for treasure, far, far away."

"Well, I'll miss you when you're on your travels."

"We'll *always* come back to you," said Kitty.

"We?"

"Aye, Daddy *has* to come with me to fight off the pirates!"

Katherine smiled, proud of her little daughter's spirit and vivid imagination.

★ ★ ★

At suppertime Katherine ladled out broth at the fire. She passed a dish to Roddy, then filled her own.

"I dreamt of my father last night," she said.

"He's watching over you, my love," said Roddy, dunking his bread into the steaming broth.

"Aye, I know it. And as my dream closes, he holds me tight. It warms me through." Her voice faltered.

Roddy saw Katherine's chin was wobbling behind the bowl of her spoon. He gently stroked her pale cheek before placing his warm hand over hers.

"You're tired, lovey."

"I am. But I do miss him Roddy, his talk and his tales. But it's so long ago ..."

"Aye, it is. Remember him, but don't be forgettin' how to live yerself. We've children of our own to think of and fend for." He tenderly squeezed her hand. Katherine touched her still-flat stomach, smiling about the new baby that would come.

"He's watching over you. Life's for the living Katherine – he'd not want you to be a-grieving."

A tear landed in her bowl.

"Aye. You're a good, wise man, Roddy Mylchreest. I thank the Lord for you."

She smiled, curled her fingers round his, and ate her broth.

★ ★ ★

October 1743

Galen McKay cared for no one. He never had and he never would. At twenty-nine he was handsome in a disarming way, and tall, with thick brown hair that flopped into his eyes in a rakish manner. His nose was crooked, due to an altercation with an angry husband in his youth, and somehow it enhanced his air of mystery. He had a reputation as a no-good and a scoundrel, a reputation he fully deserved. He revelled in his notoriety. And he could play the game with the ladies, any game he liked. With the flighty ones, he would pick and choose. With the married or the more respectable maidens *he* decided if and when they warranted his attention. He had lost count of the girls he had ruined, and, caring not one jot, was unable to remember more than a dozen by name. The Isle of Man was a fresh hunting ground for Galen McKay. The lassies were long-haired, bonny and rather shy compared to the louder, coarser Scottish girls he was used to.

When he turned up in Peel on the morning of 13th October 1743, he had no plans, no work and no idea where his next hot meal was coming from. But with a leather purse full of ill-gotten coins, and an idea where the alehouses were, he knew he'd find some work – anything would do – with his usual banter. Thieving was often his next step, but this little town seemed too hard-up for that. Well, he'd bide his time until his luck was in.

Watching the fleet that bleak morning, Katherine Mylchreest had flitted past him like a moth near a candle, taking his breath away. She was not the most beautiful girl he had ever set his eyes upon, but she was pretty enough, with the look of a fairy about her and, somehow, he felt he was bewitched. He had no idea who she was, where she lived or what her circumstances were, but he was certain of one thing – he meant to find out. And in the wrong place at the wrong time, Katherine Mylchreest had no way of knowing that the stranger was already making plans for her.

★ ★ ★

"Brr ... but it's cold out there. That wind's been slicing me up all day!" Roddy turned round to warm his backside at the fire as Katherine fussed with his boots.

"These are soaked through!" she chided.

Kitty ran over, carrying her little dolly, and he swung her off her feet, her laughter pealing round the room. Katherine hung up his socks.

"You'll catch your death, Roddy Mylchreest! And these boots need mendin' good and quick, too!"

She placed them as close to the fire as she dared. Soon the smell of warm, damp leather and his wet woollen socks mingled with the peat smoke. "Now sit on that settle and stay there! Don't be trampin' and drippin' and droolin' all over my floor ... the meal will be ready presently."

He did as he was bid, tapping his clay pipe on the fireside wall.

"Old Widow Kinvig had better watch out." He winked

at Kitty. "You'll be turning into an old scold just like her, Katherine Mylchreest!" he chuckled.

"Mammy, what's an old scold?" chirped Kitty from the table.

"Never you mind, Kitty Mylchreest!" spluttered Katherine, brandishing the ladle at her husband. "I've not fed you yet, hold your tongue if you're hungry!" But her eyes twinkled.

They settled down once Kitty was asleep, Katherine at her spinning wheel and Roddy to his mending, chatting, until the fire was low.

"There's a Scotsman blown in on an ill wind this morning," Roddy said softly.

"Why do you say that?" his wife asked.

"I've just got a feeling he'll bring trouble with him. He's a queer one. Says nothin' but listens all the while, just watchin' us all. He's looking for work on the fleet. Can't give much account of himself so Juan Clague won't have him on the *Peel Lass*. Aye, he's a shifty one all right, and men say he'll bring bad luck, what with the wind changing to the east. If no one wants him he'll have to take himself home."

"Home to Scotland," murmured Katherine. "Well, don't worry yerself. He'll be gone soon enough if he has a family to feed."

"That's just it, he has no family to speak of, no roots at all. Men like that are no good. They care nothing for their crewmates and chase women as casual as you like. No, I don't like him comin' here."

"Don't be daft, Roddy, you barely know him."

"Aye, and that's how I plan to keep it. He's got no respect for anyone and as coarse and foulmouthed a body you've never met. He's fond of the drink too! Keep clear if you see him!"

"Roddy! As if I'd even pass the time of day with a man of his sort. Dear me, no. I've no wish to talk to the likes of him."

Roddy sucked on his pipe and soon began to doze in the warmth of the fire. Katherine looked up later and saw his pipe-bowl resting on his chin. He was fast asleep, but his face looked troubled. Was the Scotsman really so bad?

* * *

In Market Place next morning, under a sullen sky, Galen McKay watched the Peel women going about their business. One had caught his eye, her shawl drawn tightly round her shoulders.

She went from woman to woman, murmuring a message which was quickly passed along.

"*Gura my'ed, Katreeney,*" the women called after her.

When she approached the well, Galen slipped unnoticed behind a cart. Up close, she was the pretty maid from yesterday, fine-boned and wispish, yet with a certain confidence about her. Elfin-faced, her head was held high, her cheeks flushed from her hurrying, quick and busy like a little harvest mouse.

She skirted the grounds of St Peter's church. The Scotsman, keen for a bit of fun, moved swiftly to cut her off at the top of Church Lane.

"*Moghrey mei,* my sweet *Katreeney.*"

His gravelly, heavily accented voice wrapped round the Manx moniker of her name, making it sound almost sinful. Her gasp crackled in the air. She stepped back, clutching her shawl and her bonnet, both of which were coming loose. A gust of wind wrenched at her bonnet. The Scotsman reached out to it. Her hair, caught in a haphazard knot at the nape of her neck, escaped its pins and fell in a caramel cloud round her shoulders. She gave a cry as though she had been struck.

"Leave me be, sir!" she stormed, her eyes flinty and dangerous. "And I am not your 'Sweet *Katreeney!*'"

He roared with laughter at her vinegary response, and dipped into a deep, mocking bow. "I beg your pardon, Madam. But you do indeed look sweet enough to eat."

She caught her breath at his unforgivable insolence, pursing her lips whilst attempting to re-tie her flapping bonnet strings under his amused scrutiny. The stranger refused to remove himself from her path, so she was forced to dodge past him.

"Miss *Katreeney* ..." he called after her.

She paid him no heed. He called louder and louder still, until she had to stop. "I'm hoping *all* the Manx girls aren't so unwelcoming. Can we not be friends, you and I?"

His eyes flickered over her. Her face grew flushed as she felt herself scorched under his gaze. But she knew better than to throw a mad dog a bone and, refusing to answer, she held her head high, gathered her skirts and marched away.

She was furious that he had managed to waylay her. Her heart hammered still! Now she could well understand Roddy's raging last evening. Yes, the Scotsman was indeed all her husband had said he was. And if her current uneasiness was anything to go by, perhaps he was worse.

★ ★ ★

Peel Beach, November 1743

Dusk was falling on Peel Hill. The moon was bald and the air crisp with winter's chill as Katherine scurried home across the shore. The Corlett family in Charles Street were better after having one of Annie's mixtures. Katherine had banked up their fire with the gorse sticks and peat, cut bread, warmed broth and taken her leave, promising to call again at daybreak.

The rain was heavier than ever, and, stroking her stomach fondly, she reminded herself that a soaking wouldn't do her any good. Kitty would be fretting, too, if she didn't hurry back. Clutching her shawl tighter round her slim shoulders, something moved ahead and to her right. Stretching lazily, a dark figure leaning against the wall of one of the inns was watching her move across the beach. She caught her breath, his height was unmistakeable. It was Galen McKay.

As a shudder rippled through her, a rumble of thunder made her grip her basket tighter. She stumbled on, glancing once again towards the inn. But he had gone back to the fireside, no doubt, and his jug of ale.

Flustered, she caught her foot on a hank of seaweed and toppled forwards with a cry, landing heavily on her knees, scraping her face on her basket. She tasted blood on her lip, at the same time hearing the crunch of heavy boots on pebbles. The Scotsman was striding purposefully towards her, cutting off her planned path across the shore. The drunken look upon his face was warning enough that he did not have her well-being in mind. Trying to swallow down her mounting alarm, she hastily stuffed everything into the basket just as the stench of ale and stale sweat cloaked her. The moon was a silver halo behind him. Instinct made her pick up a fist-sized stone, praying to God she wouldn't have to use it.

"I see you're needin' me now, Mrs Mylchreest." he slurred dangerously, swaying above her. He reached down, yanking her roughly to her feet.

"I don't need you at all, sir, make no mistake!"

"My, but you're a spirited, bonny lassie! Just how I like 'em!" he said thickly into her ear.

She felt a clutch in her stomach as he breathed his foul breath into her hair. "Mr McKay!" she cried, as he pinned her to him, fragile as a butterfly he wished to crush.

He took her chin in a pinching grip between finger and thumb and brought his face close to hers. The rank odour of his unwashed skin mingled with the ale and baccy. She bit back the urge to retch.

In the moonlight he saw her whey-coloured face and fear in her eyes.Amused, he leaned forwards, enjoying his strength, his power. He smudged the blood that trickled on her swollen lip with his calloused thumb, and she flinched and cowered back at his touch. He roared with laughter and his warm spittle spotted her frozen cheek.

"Do not touch me!" she shrieked as loudly as she could, panic mounting as his free hand began to rummage, roughly, urgently at her bodice. She managed a scream as she struggled with him, against him, but the sound was ripped from her throat and carried away. His intentions plain, she was horrified to see that the shore was deserted in the persistent rain. She was without help.

"Stop! I'm with child, sir!" came her desperate, strangled sob as she voiced her news aloud for the first time since sharing it so happily with Roddy. It choked her, having to tell her precious secret to this brute. But he didn't flinch.

"Aye, but I have a need for you, *Katreeney*," he mumbled, shifting heavily. His hold on her loosened as he fumbled at her skirts. Katherine's fear morphed abruptly into a flair of murderous rage. He shifted again and her right arm fell loose. Her freed hand flew up, her weapon glinting sharp and deadly, to strike the back of his head.

But he spied a tell-tale flicker in her eyes and swung round just in time, the rock scratching his face, drawing his blood. He snatched at her wrist, twisting it agonisingly. She dropped the sparkling chunk of granite. Recovering quickly, he lunged at her, his fingers clamping so tight round her throat that she could feel tiny bubbles of saliva gurgling down her windpipe. Her eyes popped. Brilliant stars seemed to dazzle her. Surreal, suffocating clouds crowded in. She was about to black out. She kicked wildly before he cast her down savagely onto the sand.

"A paragon with a vicious streak," he mumbled, bending over her, pinning her down by her throat. He drew back his fist. She closed her eyes, numbed with terror, caring no more. His unfathomable hatefulness had already hit her. Then they heard a snap. The old leather cord of her necklace had broken. He tugged at it and held it up into the dim light, mesmerised by its luscious, rich colour as it sparkled above them, a beacon in the night.

"May it curse you!" she spat, wishing that the cherished purple glass was sharp. Sharp enough to pierce his flesh that he might bleed to death, here and now, before her very eyes.

"Little Manx witch!" he muttered, crossing his fingers quickly in the sign against witchcraft. Then as an extra safeguard he spat into the sand, saying "If it does no good then it does no harm."

His eyes swivelled back to her.

"Even I know your powers are useless if your blood's been spilled."

Katherine gasped. She was no witch, though he clearly believed she may be. His fist drew back again, his eyes just narrowed slits, brimming with menace. She curved away, waiting, helpless. But instead of striking her, he raised the necklace up again, very close to her face, turning it in the moonlight. She wondered at him. Was he bewitched? She dared not breathe.

"A worthless trinket," he slurred after some moments. "Much like yourself." Then, unexpectedly, he stood up, slipping the necklace into his pocket. He stepped over her, dusting his breeches, then strolled casually away across the sand.

She struggled to her feet, only to stumble back down onto her knees, shock washing over her. She wept, thanking God for her narrow escape, her deliverance from such evil.

After some time she lifted her basket. Roddy would kill McKay if he ever heard what the Scotsman had meant to do to her. He must never learn of it. She thought of her necklace, her charm.

'May this always keep you safe,' her father had said, and indeed it had this dreadful night.

"*Gura my' ed*, Dadda," she whispered up to the stars, wishing she kept it still.

★ ★ ★

Katherine stood up straight, her back aching. She gazed at the angry sea, more changeable than the weather itself. Their provider, yet also a cruel master. Had the sea not claimed her father for its own when she was a child? As a Peel girl she loved the sea, yet at times she hated it too. Its fruits, difficult and dangerous to harvest, were the Manxmen's staple diet, eked out with spuds and the *skilley*, the thin oatmeal porridge. Without the fishing they would be near starved.

Her mother Widow Qualtrough was also gathering the wrack, stooped, with her hair almost grey, yet she was not yet forty-five years old. Life was hard on her, with no husband to lean on. A lump rose in Katherine's throat and absentmindedly she felt for the little glass necklace. She had worn it ever since its making, even to bed. Her father had been drawn into her dreams because of it. But, of course, McKay kept it still. She ached for it, missing her father's presence in her dreams.

Roddy had asked her just once where it was, and she had lied that it was safe in the wooden box beneath their bed. Kitty had begged to wear it, and cried when Katherine told her to hush down about it. Katherine hated the lie, hated herself for telling it but above all else she hated the Scotsman. Though she had avoided him since that night he seemed, somehow, to be everywhere she went. If their paths crossed he would lick his lips, rake her with his wolf-grey eyes and murmur, "Ah, my sweet, sweet *Katreeney*," before bowing low.

He knew she had not uttered a word of his actions to her husband, but how could she? Roddy would kill him and be thrown into the dungeon of Peel Castle for a murderer, then be hanged like a rat in the rigging, before the whole of Peel. And then McKay's evil soul would haunt Katherine until her dying day.

"May my necklace curse you for as long as you have it," she whispered, just as she did each and every time he invaded her thoughts. Just as she did each and every time her eyes fell upon him or she heard his name. Just as she did after each and every nightmare he visited upon her.

"May it curse you, Galen McKay."

★ ★ ★

January 1744

The storm came from nowhere. The fleet had gone out as usual, only the stiffness of the breeze gave any hint of what was to come. Galen McKay was aboard the *Peel Lass*, cursing his bad luck at chancing upon some work on this day and in this weather.

The sea vented her fury and the fishing was forgotten as the skipper yelled "Batten down!"

A loose barrel or untidy net could send a man overboard so they fumbled with the thick ropes, trying to tie knots that would hold everything securely, ensuring everyone's safety. Only the Scotsman was idle.

A wave, higher than a house, crashed down. Galen careered across the deck. A barrel struck his leg and he yelped like a mad dog, only just grasping the iron rings holding the ropes tied at the deck edge. Roddy Mylchreest was coming to his aid. They had hated each other on sight, but Roddy's arm went round him all the same, dragging him sternwards.

"Good man, Roddy," called Juan, as he lashed ropes round anything else that might move.

The Scotsman wasn't hurt but offered no thanks, slumping down against the rail.

"Watch out, boys!"

They all heard the wave before it hit, roaring and hungry.

Galen McKay and Roddy stood no chance, being the only two, as yet, not tied to the boat. The smash lifted them both off their feet, slamming them back down onto the deck. Galen clung onto the rail and Roddy was caught in a rope hanging there, his right hand throbbing and broken. The lugger bucked and rolled.

"Seems you're needin' me now, Mr Mylchreest," Galen bawled into Roddy's ear, grasping his wrists.

The words had an edge to them. Roddy lifted his head, his brown curls plastered over his good-natured face. There was a look in Galen's eyes he'd rarely seen in a man, a look of pure unreasoned hatred. Roddy's blood, churning in his ears, ran icy cold.

The Scotsman glanced at the crew, watching now, fastened as they were at the opposite side of the deck, then called "Hold fast, man. Hold fast, Roddy Mylchreest!"

The words were deliberately meant for the crew and not to reassure Roddy. For Roddy was dangling dangerously over the deck's edge and it was the Scotsman who was holding him, not the other way round. Roddy's hand, a broken mangled mess, could not have held even a feather. He was at the Scotsman's mercy.

"Hold him! I'm comin'!" yelled Juan, beginning to unfasten himself.

Galen pulled Roddy in by his sleeves, their faces close

enough to touch. Their eyes locked.

"When you're goin' through Hell, keep going," bellowed the Scotsman.

Another wave hit. Roddy did not know his game, but it was clear he was playing one.

"What says you, McKay?"

"Ah, well, now you're asking. But do you want me as much as my little *Katreeney* does? Now there's a question ..." He left it dangling in the air.

"My Katherine?" said Roddy.

Galen smiled, licking his salty lips. "Forbidden fruit. Oh aye, always the sweetest. Aye, layin' with me these three months gone, and laughin' at the man she's married to. What d'you say to that, then?"

"Liar! She'd not lay with any other man!"

"How's she carryin' my bairn then?" Galen was enjoying the shock on Roddy' s grey face. "And she gave me this." He waggled his wrist.

Roddy gaped at the glinting purple glass necklace tied there. His head was spinning. Not a living soul knew of the baby yet, not even Katherine's own mother. Contempt contorted the face before him.

"Och ... best rid of ye," the Scotsman said.

He drew back smartly, unexpectedly, smashing Roddy' s forehead with his own. The sickening crunch went unheard. Only the wind screamed in protest.

Juan screamed "Man overboard!" as he slipped and slid across the deck as Roddy sank from view.

"I could nay hold 'im no more ... a dead weight he was," Galen said, turning slowly.

Juan, frantic at the loss of his boyhood friend, was already tying a loop in a rope to try to save him.

"But I was comin'! You had him fast! I was comin' – I saw

that you had him!"

"Aye, I did, didn't I?"

* * *

Who is ever really true? True to others and true to themselves?

As Roddy sinks, time seems to stand still. Water whooshes in his ears, the weight on him great, with his boots as heavy as two barrels of salt herring, dragging him to depths unknown.

His boots are all he can think of. As a small boy he had never owned any. Hand-me-downs when he got bigger, yes, but as a little 'un he'd gone barefoot like all his friends. He'd always longed for his own boots, some day, when he grew to be a man. Now he is that man, with boots of his own. Boots that will be the finish of him, dragging him deeper and deeper, to his early grave.

How can something once yearned for, something so longed for, be the death of a man?

Yet he has been lucky, very, very lucky. He had found his true love, his, gentle, cherished Katherine and been blessed with little Kitty, the very image of her mother. What more could a man want?

The pressure in his ears is terrible. His lungs want to burst. Time, he wants to scream. Time is what I want. Worth nothing, not a brass farthing, but now it is priceless, it is all he wants. But he is lost. Lost to the sea, unsure even if his wife really knows just how much he loves her.

Katherine, the only girl to have ever had his heart. All he had ever hoped and longed for. He'd believed she was happy. He was wrong.

Bitterness blurs his vision of her, laughing and smiling with Kitty on her knee. She *had* been more remote of late. Had the Scotsman spoken the truth? *Had* he wooed her? Had she really loved and lain with another? How did McKay know about the child she carried? Being slender, her petticoats wouldn't grow shorter until early spring most probably. She would have told him, if the child were his.

And what of the necklace? Was it a keepsake, a love token? Had he, Roddy Mylchreest, been duped by them both? How had he not seen their carrying on?

It was someone so longed and so yearned for who was going to kill him, he realised. Not with a dagger or a musket shot, but with a wicked deceit to pierce his heart, with the very vows, broken now, that she had pledged to him.

Tis too much to bear. Not my darling Katherine … my false of heart?

Final, tiny bubbles escape from his nose and mouth, bubbles of the purest Manx air, floating to the surface, where he longs to be.

My life is done.

He will never go home now – he has Galen McKay to thank for that.

Fumbling desperately, he cannot find his *crosh bollan*, the fisherman's charm, carried always for protection at sea. It is not in his pocket.

Aah … so there's the truth of it. My luck has run out, simple as that.

Closing his eyes, he yearns for his wife.

False to me? Oh, may it not be so. Katherine, my one true love. Be strong and be brave my sweet, sweet dearest …

* * *

As the storm raged over the Island and *Peel Lass* failed to return, the townsfolk began to fear the worst. Katherine prayed to the Almighty beside the fire. Hours later, something caught her eye on the mantelshelf, making the blood drain from her face. Roddy's *crosh bollan*! Her fingers tightened round it. It was as cold as death itself. A bad omen. Tears spilled silently, dampening her shawl.

"Please don't cry, Mammy."

Kitty, so noisy by day, was always silent as a cat by night. She climbed onto her lap.

"Let me loose your hair, Mammy, how Dadda likes it."

Kitty's fingers untangled her braid, as Katherine hummed a song Roddy liked to sing. Then her voice cracked and they clung to one another, terrified of the coming dawn.

"He'll come home safe to us, Mammy," Kitty told her later in bed, pressing small palms gently onto Katherine' s face, stroking it with a thumb still soggy from sucking. Then, nose to nose, she murmured "'Cos remember, he promises us, doesn't he? And he would *never* break a promise!" To Kitty, four years old and with a child's unblinking belief, it was as simple as that.

★ ★ ★

At daybreak, Annie Qualtrough came and Katherine sat pensively with her mother, and showed her Roddy's *crosh bollan.*

"Tsk, tsk, how's he forgotten that? Ah, 'tis terrible worrisome. When your father's boat was lost I never stopped prayin' all night long either." She looked at the blue circles under Katherine's eyes.

"You're a good girl, Katherine, and a fine wife and mother to little Kitty. God may smile on you yet."

"I've another on the way," Katherine sobbed, her hand on her belly.

Her mother held her close.

"Aye, I knew it, you've been so quiet lately." She took Katherine's hands. "Don't ever let your hope die, my love – not now, not ever! And you must teach your own children the same. Promise me, Katherine." Her eyes glinted with determination.

"Aye," Katherine whispered, "I promise."

★ ★ ★

Almost twenty-four hours later, Katherine lay wide awake and restless, a soul in turmoil, her mother still sleeping beside her for comfort and reassurance. First her father, now her husband, lost to the sea. Her fingers felt for her necklace. She had gifted it to Roddy when they were betrothed, but he had refused it, saying her father had made the charm to keep her safe for him and now it must keep her safe for her husband too. She had been glad to keep it. Now though, she was without her amulet and Roddy was without his. She rose from the bed.

In the kitchen, she swayed before the dying fire, listening to Kitty sleeping soundly on her pallet in the loft and the wind moaning down the chimney. Katherine glanced at the door. Outside, her spirit could soar, free and untroubled, into the wind.

Tucking Kitty up tight with a kiss, she padded barefoot across the room. Lifting the latch, her breath coming sharp and fast, she slipped outside. Away from her fireside, her mother and her sleeping child. Away to Roddy.

★ ★ ★

On the beach at first light, the Cashin brothers stopped dead. A woman, clearly not in her right mind, was waist-deep in the sea, struggling against the swell.

When they reached her she was coming up to the surface again, her face violet, her eyes sunken and haunted behind loose matted hair. They dragged her ashore. Rubbing her roughly on the sand, Peter breathed his own hot breath into her spidery hands.

"It's Katherine, Roddy's wife!" gasped Joseph, crossing himself as she babbled nonsense.

Moments later they were hammering on her cottage door.

"Dear lord!" cried Widow Qualtrough.

Peter pushed past to lay her on the bed.

She'll be all right, now she's home," Peter said to his brother.

Kitty, crouching behind the chair, clutched her dolly and her icy toes. "You look after your Mammy now, won't you?" Peter said kindly before she scurried away.

He rubbed a hand across his face. Katherine's bible lay on the table, with Roddy's *crosh bollan* on top. Peter could well imagine Katherine's torment. Kitty was singing a lullaby to her mammy.

"That child is the apple of Roddy's eye," Peter said to his brother. "She won't ever learn from me how close to being an orphan she came."

"Nor me," said Joseph grimly. "I swear it."

★ ★ ★

"There' s news! Mrs Mylchreest, Mrs Shimmin, Mrs Moore! News of the *Peel Lass*." Alf Clague battered on all the doors in Duke Street.

Women rushed out to hear that the lugger had run hard into the storm but had taken safe refuge in Castletown.

Katherine, weakened and weary, was dizzy with relief until Alf caught her eye.

The old man's face showed his anxiety with the transparency of a child's. Then he was gone.

Katherine felt he knew something that she too must soon learn. She shivered beneath the crisp moon as the wind whipped at her skirts. An east wind, an ill wind. Clutching

Kitty close, she hurried inside, slamming the door on the velvety night.

* * *

Snuffing out the last of the rush-lights, Katherine heard a soft, persistent tapping at the door. She lifted the latch. Alf Clague stood before her, twitchy and nervous.

"Mr Clague, whatever is it? You look all asunder. Alf, please!" She clutched his arm. "What's to tell? Let me know, but I must sit first!" She stumbled into a chair. He was reluctant to begin, trying to choose his words with care. He took a deep breath.

"Before the *Peel Lass* reached harbour they found there was a man overboard." He spoke slowly, softly, wringing his cap fiercely but his voice was kind.

"Happened fast. Storm was the worst our Juan's ever seen with waves the size of St Peter's church and a wind blasting straight from Hell itself. With the nets cast it was real dangerous. I'm sorry, Mrs Mylchreest, it was Roddy, he got washed over. Juan got a line to him and hauled him in, but he'd been under the water far too long."

"I see," murmured Katherine, but her eyes could see nothing behind her closed lids, only Roddy, smiling at her from the deck that last time. "My dearest, sweet Roddy is dead."

"Nay!" cried Alf, quite beside himself. "Oh, I'm terrible sorry for not saying it proper, Mrs Mylchreest. He's not dead, but not sensible neither. Jabbering away he is, no one knows what he's saying!"

"He's alive?" Katherine, chalk-faced, was already on her feet. "I thank the Lord for his mercy! I must go to him ... how will I go?" She groped blindly for her shawl.

"Hold on there, girl! You must wait. They'll bring him

home to you, soon as they can."

As Alf spoke the words she had feared she would never hear, they became strange and woolly as warm, peaty darkness smothered her.

* * *

The grey-faced, shrunken man wrapped in blankets and carried inside by the crew of the *Peel Lass* was barely recognisable as Katherine's strong, handsome Roddy. His body was alive, but his once lively, conker-brown eyes were dead. The storm had indeed stolen his sensibility. He was stricken with a pitiful dumbness, able only to mumble and moan like a sick animal. Katherine fussed over him "Thank you Juan, we are grateful he's home. I'll get him right, you see if I don't."

But the men looked doubtful and awkward, ashamed that even their shadows in the candlelight seemed stronger than their friend.

"That Galen McKay has much to answer for, Katherine," said Juan after the others had gone.

Katherine's blood chilled. She whispered her curse quickly.

"There were words of some sort. McKay's saying nothin', but he had a hold of Roddy one minute, the next ... well, he was gone."

"The Scotsman meant for him to drown?"

Juan couldn't meet her eye.

"He was under the water a long time, Katherine. 'Twas a miracle we fished 'im out at all. Don't know if we've not cursed you all by doin' it." His voice betrayed remorse and pity.

Katherine scrubbed away the angry tears coursing down her face. Her hatred for McKay licked like flames at her heart, stirring her soul. She reached out to gently touch Juan's clenched jaw.

"I *am* grateful to you, Juan. And Roddy will be too, one day … you'll see."

★ ★ ★

January 1745

Roddy's recovery was slow. Slow, but sure, Katherine reminded Kitty, and at last he was well enough to dandle his baby son, Alfie, upon his knee. And when he returned to the fishing he was more like his old self, though somewhat quieter and subdued.

The *Peel Lass* went out, regular as ever, but when a storm blew up the skipper turned her for home early, haunted still about Roddy going overboard. It had been a miracle he'd lived at all, let alone that within a year he was able to sit in church on Sundays, giving his thanks to his maker.

Peel folk had heard that Galen McKay had taken himself off, back to Scotland, most probably. No one knew for sure and nobody cared – they were glad to be rid of him.

★ ★ ★

Autumn 1745

September was wild, with seas high and stormy. Gales howled and cottages were damaged.

Only Kitty Mylchreest was happy with the weather because storms always brought the best treasure, unusual shells or strange things from shipwrecks, trapped after high tide.

Venturing into a cave late one afternoon, she came across a small, dimpled glass bottle. She held it to her eye like a spyglass. The cave was deep and dark, with a steady dripping to mark the passage of time like the ticking of a clock. As Kitty turned to leave a yellow slit of light illuminated the cave.

Blinking into the brightness, her eyes fell upon something else at the back of the cave. Propped there like a grotesque scarecrow was a body, the face veiled with a wide strip of seaweed which had dried out to become a tight death mask. The mouth gaped wide.

Dropping the bottle, Kitty scrabbled towards the daylight. Only when she reached the salty fresh air did her scream split the terrible silence at her back. Everyone on the shore ran to her. They fussed and soothed. Once she was calm, but still dumb with shock, her mammy and old Ted Teare went inside the cave to seek the cause of Kitty's distress.

"God bless us!" gasped Ted. "Who's this then?"

Reaching out a trembling hand, he peeled away the seaweed shroud, but the face was a bloated, rotting white ball. Not one single feature was recognisable.

"The poor man!" Katherine cried, turning her face away.

Ted hauled him out, bumping the body over the stones.

Fascinated by a peculiar wink of the light, Katherine looked on as a cord at the body's wrist became snagged on a rock. It snapped. Old Ted didn't notice her stoop down, nor did he see her blanch with shock and have to steady herself.

She slowly unfurled her hand, just as another hand had unfurled long ago. In her palm was her necklace, more battered than ever. It twinkled only slightly, being, by now, a very well-worn scrap indeed. She felt a small, secret smile curl into place as the body bobbed past her out of the cave.

"May the Devil take you, Galen McKay!" she called aloud, knowing full well that deaf old Ted would never hear her.

* * *

Roddy lay listening to his wife's gentle breathing as she slept, untroubled now that she knew Galen McKay was dead. Only she and Roddy knew the identity of the body in the cave. She had also told her husband about that November night on the shore, over a year ago, and how she had cursed the Scotsman ever since. Katherine's fear was that one day she would burn in the fires of Hell as punishment for her hexing.

Roddy had told her that even a nun would have cursed a man as evil as Galen McKay and that the Lord knew her to be a good, kind woman, without a bad bone in her body. She need have no fear. Roddy had experienced the bitter taste of hatred for the very first time in his life. His dislike of the Scotsman had indeed been well founded. He thanked the Lord for his wife's love.

There was a lesson to be heeded this day. A lesson about trusting to instinct, and that in the end, God willing, good would always prevail.

But they both knew that the most important lesson was about love. The kind of love that sees you through the very worst times and heals all wounds, however deep, like a magic salve. Yes, scars may remain, pulling and causing pain at times, but Roddy knew now, as he always had, that so long as his family's love prevailed, then nothing would ever harm them. Love was, after all, the only thing in life that really mattered.

Roddy sighed as he closed his eyes to sleep, thinking about the *Peel Lass*. Juan had come to him in the summertime to confess about a drunkard who had begged his passage to Scotland a few months before Roddy's return to the fishing. Practically penniless, he was, after losing at the gaming he was so fond of.

Checking that no one had seen the traveller, Juan had smiled grimly, thinking the early bird truly does always catch the worm. He had helped the man aboard and told him the trip would cost him nothing, it would be for old time's sake.

"Och, but that's good of you, Juan," came the reply, unaware of the winks between the men.

"Don't mention it. Us Peel crews always stick together," Juan said, placing a firm hand on Galen's shoulder.

"But I hear there's a storm brewin'," added the skipper softly, as he led him below. "Aye, and an ill wind blowin'…"

� june ✺

Race

Chris Ewan

We were way over the legal limit when we finally got on our motorbikes. I'd been drinking since lunchtime and Quinnin reckoned he'd had Stella on his cornflakes. It wasn't just us – everyone got legless on Mad Sunday. All along the prom half-cut Manxies were drinking with bearded German bikers, ogling tabloid 'stunners', whooping as big name riders pulled donuts and sent grey tyre smoke drifting into the night sky.

Quinnin had cornered me in one of the beer tents. He was with these two girls from across, poncing around in new leathers as if he was some kind of pro. He started giving me grief about my bike and I was drunk enough to talk back to him, telling the girls about his crash the previous year and how he'd screamed like a baby in the back of the ambulance. Quinnin didn't like it: he got all riled up. Drunken brink-manship ensued and he challenged me to a race.

"I'm over the limit," I told him, trying to escape and make my way back to the bar.

"Come on." He prodded me in the chest. "We'll do a Ritchie."

"A what?" asked one of the girls, giving Quinnin the opportunity to deliver his spiel.

Ritchie Shimmin, Quinnin explained, was a TT legend. Twelve times a race winner, twice in the wet. Ritchie was a great rider and a true Manxman but more than that, he was also a first-rate boozer. His party trick was riding the Mountain Course soused on Bushy's Bitter, at night, with no lights. So well did he know the roads, Ritchie would post times that were faster than most riders achieved during the day.

"No ta," I said, aiming to defuse the situation.

"Pussy," Quinnin said.

The girls sniggered into their alcopops, enjoying his posturing. One of them fixed me right in the eye, puckering her lips around her red plastic straw and sucking until her cheeks hollowed out. She was nice looking, had this elfin vibe what with her short hair and petite frame. The words *Biker Chick* were embossed on her T-shirt across her breasts.

"One lap," I said, holding her gaze. "With lights."

Quinnin chugged the last of his lager and crushed his plastic glass above my head, letting the foamy dregs drip onto my bonce. He belched in my face, then said, "Easy."

A crowd developed around our bikes. I could hear drunken cheering through my crash helmet, the noise distorted as though my ears were loaded with syrup. People were slapping me on the head and back, hitting me so hard that the blows made the cartilage in my spine crackle. I raised my tinted visor to stop my beer breath steaming the perspex and saw Quinnin pushing his rubber gloves into the webbing between his fingers. One of the girls was running her hand along his bicep. Biker Chick was standing beside me, chewing on her red straw, assessing my scrawny frame like a sceptical bidder at a bike auction.

I turned my focus to the track ahead, gripping my

handlebars tight and placing my booted feet onto my bike spurs. I revved hard and could hear Quinnin doing the same to my right. There was a countdown from 3 to 1. Then it was *Go.*

I dropped my clutch and screeched from the line, the front wheel of my bike rearing up as the horizon surged towards me. I traded gears, from first to sixth. I squeezed more gas into the tank and the speed-o needle quivered near the peak of its range. Bray Hill bottomed out. Quinnin was alongside me, edging in front. The first bend was looming. I cut my speed and leaned into the corner, then snaked right for the second. I felt the booze tilt inside my head as my padded kneecap grazed the ground. Aiming for the inside line, Quinnin's tyre crossed in front of me, his red light dazzling in the gloom. I jinked to the left, trying to ease past, but he weaved across the tarmac, forcing me to brake hard to avoid slamming into the wall. I lost ground and Quinnin's bike accelerated beyond the arc of my headlamp. Crowding over my handlebars, I cranked the throttle, concentrating on the flickering white line of the road and nothing else.

Thirty-seven-and-a-half miles – after eight pints of ale it can pass in no time at all. Whole passages of the race were lost to me, like periodic bouts of amnesia. I had no recollection of passing Greeba Castle, or of skimming through the big right-hander at Ballacraine, or of leaping the hump bridge at Ballaugh. All that mattered to me was the shifting band of asphalt that sped beneath my tyres, the keening of my engine as it neared the top of its range and the occasional red blips of Quinnin's brakelight up ahead.

By the time I reached the Mountain Road it felt like my groin had merged with the petrol tank, as if I'd become a part of my machine. I imagined I could feel where the grip was surest and that I could push harder because of it. Shedding my last residues of caution, I gave it everything I had. Slowly, Quinnin's bike began to ease into range.

At Onchan, we swung right, then right again onto the finishing straight. I carried momentum out of the corner and found myself parallel with Quinnin. He looked across at me, eyes wary now, but he still had the nerve to mouth, "Loser" at me.

Angling my bike towards his, I thought about reaching out and squeezing his brake lever, sending him spinning into the straw-bales lining the side of the road, his bike throwing up sparks from the tarmac and then exploding violently in the darkness. Quinnin had a similar idea. He raised his biker boot in the air and slammed it into the faring near my front suspension. My bike lurched sideways. I lost my grip on my handlebars and began to fall. The world pirouetted above me and my helmet struck the ground hard, followed by my splayed arms and legs. I tumbled once and came to rest, grazing my elbow badly.

There were raucous cheers and shouts. I lifted my dazed head from the floor and found Biker Chick peering down at me, a shocked expression on her face. Quinnin was standing on his bike, punching the air triumphantly, a group of drunken lads jumping around him, spilling beer and toasting his victory with their plastic glasses held aloft. The arcade screen in front of him screamed the word *FIRST* and dance music pulsed from the *SEGA* speakers to my side. I slapped my palm against my spring-mounted bike, cursing his underhand tactics. Then I fumbled for another pound coin, yelling, "Best of three," at the top of my voice.

july

Aidan Alemson achieved a BA from the University of Queensland, Brisbane and then studied art history and painting in Florence, Italy. He has contributed to various short films and documentaries. Aidan has written a novel entitled *The Point However Is To Change It*, a double-novella *Wolfhound The Troubleshooter* and a stage play *The Mesopotamian Legacy*; all published by Artisan Productions, Brisbane, Australia.

His most recent poetry was included in the anthologies *Whispers on the Breeze*, *A Sense of Place* and *The Funny Thing!*, all published by United Press of London. He won second prize in the Short Story section of the Olive Lamming Memorial Literary Competition 2009. In addition, his short stories 'Hommy-Beg' and 'The Third Eye' were included in *A Tail for All Seasons* Volumes 1 and 2 respectively.

The Niarbyl Tail

Aidan Alemson

"There's Niarbyl Bay down there. Beautiful place. Unique. But its rocks are powerful strange. Every once in a while something happens to trigger them off and if you're around at the wrong time it could drive you spare … At least that's what I've come to believe."

Dollin Cashen continued to regale his two remaining passengers with colourful local tales as he turned his Number 7 bus into a lane bearing the Manx Gaelic name *Bayr-yn-arbyl* (Road of the Tail of the Rocks).

"For example, we're now driving down towards the Niarbyl fault line. This road divides two neighbouring farms, Creglea and Ballacooil. During the first decade of the twentieth century there was bad blood, a real *jeel*, between the two respective farmers, leading to acts of violence."

"What was it all about, buddy?" asked Brent Avery in his resonant American accent.

"Sheep-bothering for starters."

Brent glanced askance through his glasses at his beige-coiffured wife Mimi, sitting beside him in her chino jumpsuit.

She shrugged in all innocence.

"Sheep jumping over fences. They crossed the line and got slaughtered. Cattle were driven over the cliff. One farmer near killed the other. The local community were gripped by fear and split in two over who or what was to blame."

"You think the rocks sorta triggered it?" asked Mimi.

Dollin laughed. "More a case of the rocks being triggered off by something happening, then reverberating in a way that causes human emotions to fly over the top ... It's only a feeling I have. No doubt you'll think I've rocks in my head."

"Not at all," chorused the amused bemused tourists as the small bus turned into the Niarbyl Café and Visitor Centre car park. As the Averys alighted, the bald-headed Dollin laughed heartily and called after them, "I'm just a bus driver who fancies himself a tour guide. Have a good time and I'll be back to collect you at 2.30."

* * *

Well-satisfied with their lunch of Queenie scallops and fries washed down with Diet Coke, the Averys exited the comfortable Niarbyl Café, all set to walk it off while exploring the rocky cove below.

As they wended their way down the road to the pebbly beach, the pungent smell of seaweed spiced the air. It was as stimulating as the salty ozone-laden breeze. Squawking herring gulls flew sorties overhead or stood like sentries on rocky outcrops alongside their rivals the oystercatchers. Their breast feathers were puffed out by a strong gust which blustered across the Irish Sea onto the westerly Manx coastline. With its picturesque arrangement of sea, cliffs, tumbling hills and cottages, Niarbyl Bay offered an outstanding scenic composition.

"Gee Mimi, this sure is different to what we've got in the

States. It's a piece of old-world charm. There's even an ancient cannon cemented in there."

At that moment there was a break in the clouds. Shafts of light illuminated the landscape. The tide had ebbed. Mimi nodded in excitement. She pointed towards a group of rocks that extended into the sea.

"Oh look, Brent! That must be the 'Tail'. They say you can walk over its 'vertebrae'."

"Tail of what?"

"Well, I'm not too sure now, but the Celtic folktale section of the book I bought at the House of *Man-oh-man* at Peel mentions Teeval, Princess of the Ocean. She takes on different shapes such as a mermaid siren who could lure mortal men to their doom on the rocks."

"Quite a gal. Reminds me of my ex."

"Uh-huh ... Oh wow! I can see it – that could be Teeval's tail and there's her head way to the south. She's curved around the sapphire bay in her mantle of emeralds."

"Yeah. Right." Although knowing his second wife to be fanciful, Brent thought that the southward curve of high green hills sloping dramatically to the shoreline did tend to overexcite the imagination. To him, they suggested the humps of a giant prehistoric sea monster with its fossilized tail extending into the waves. Then his gaze focused on the highest hill, Cronk-ny-Irree Laa.

"Holy smoke! Take a look at that, will ya Mimi. Looks like a bushfire but I can't see any flames."

"No, honey. The guidebook says what looks like smoke is really trapped wisps of rising mist."

Brent nodded his Seattle Mariners baseball cap in mechanical agreement, somewhat irritated by how his wife always managed to one-up him with her regurgitated pearls of wisdom. She smiled at him ingenuously, her hazel eyes sparkling with delight.

"Isn't *Near Bill* lovely! A real gem of a place."

They took digital photos of one another in front of a traditional Manx twin cottage with a tethered thatched roof, whitewashed stone walls and triple chimneys. Nearby were some red kayaks stored beside an illustrated information board, but nobody else was around. The couple made their way northward around the promontory, champing over large smooth pebbles strewn with tagliatelle-like strands of yellowish-brown kelp and washed-up trash. Mimi's attention was drawn to the rock formations of compacted sediments which towered above them. The geological pressures had been so immense that the stratification was almost perpendicular.

"This is what I wanted to show you here, honey."

She opened her sharkskin tote bag, took out a booklet and read to her husband:

"The Manx Group mudstone slates originate from Gondwana, of which southern England, Africa and Australia are parts. They're around 480 million years old. The Dalby Group sandstones north of Niarbyl come from Laurentia, of which Scotland and North America are parts. The contact between these two rock groups is a major geological fault. It's the only known remnant of the Lapetus Ocean which once separated these primeval super-continents".

Her husband was agog, for once actually astonished by the depth of his wife's research.

"You mean, out of the whole Atlantic Ocean, the surgical stitches of Europe and America are exposed in this little boondocks beach?"

"Seems so. That fissure must be the fault line. See the different colored stone on either side."

"Outstanding! On the Discovery Channel they showed how, unlike volcanoes, fault lines like these can leak energy real slow; causing a build-up of electro-magnetic forces in the surrounding area."

The Averys took yet more photos of each other straddling the continental divide as effortlessly as mythological colossi could have done. Well pleased, they made their way back around the cliff until they reached its fractured Tail. It too had been formed by the frightening forces of combined destruction and creation aeons ago.

"How about a shot of us standing together on that outcrop? I'll set the auto-timer."

Brent carefully positioned his camera, then assisted his wife in climbing up onto the rock as the cold surf splashed around it.

"Okay honey, hold up your right arm and pretend to be the Statue of Liberty standing on Liberty Island."

"Yeah. It's like a little piece of North America in the middle of the British Isles."

"From what you've read, I think this bit's probably part of the Gondwana chunk ... but what the heck! The Limeys are in need of some self-liberation anyhow."

Laughing together, the Averys broke out of their studio-style pose to embrace in the bracing salty air. Their smiles met in a lingering kiss – just as the auto-timer on their camera finally clicked in.

They could hear someone wolf-whistling at their spontaneous display of love American-style. Disengaging, they looked across the cove to notice a family all dressed in hiking boots and knapsacks, marching in single file along a coastal path which stretched past the other two houses on the shore. The gang of four cheekily waved at the pair. The Averys waved back, amused, as the family trekked on out of view towards the ruined eighth-century chapel at Lag-ny-Keeilley.

"Let's check out where those guys are going," suggested

Mimi.

The American couple descended carefully from the jagged rock, with the gentlemanly Brent assisting his wife down in the manner of overweight ballet dancers executing a *pas de deux*.

"Hang on a moment, chicken. I just wanna get a little old souvenir before we go," said Brent. He used a piece of slate as a crude chisel to chip off a fragment. "Gonna get this little fella mounted when we get back home. It'll make a great conversation piece," he added, slipping the rock fragment into the outside pocket of his summer jacket.

They hopscotched awkwardly across the moss-covered rockpools towards a centrally located bungalow with a well-maintained flower garden and a tractor with an empty boat trailer parked out front. Not wanting to appear nosy, the tourists followed the hikers' path along a sea wall towards a small whitewashed Manx cottage with a mouldy earthen-tiled roof. As it was partially built into the side of the cliff, the path practically snaked its way overhead. The cottage had a sash window and a red front door with a circular plaque above it. No smoke belched from its chimneys.

"Looks like a doll's house that fell off a cargo ship and got washed up here in a storm," Brent laughed. He moseyed around to the Lilliputian front porch to peer through the red-framed window.

"It's dark inside. Looks like no one's been here since the last Ice Age. Tell you what, I'll use the flash to lighten it up."

Brent positioned his camera right up close to the window and pushed the 'shoot' button. The flash exposed more than he'd bargained for: an anxious face, hovering towards him like the head of a mummy that had been needlessly unwrapped. Brent sprang back in shock, letting go of his expensive camera which fortunately was strapped around his neck.

"Oh my God! Je-sus, what was that?"

His greatest critic couldn't resist: "Your own reflection, perhaps?"

Before Brent could respond, they heard the door of the cottage being unbolted and creaking open. A diminutive figure emerged to confront the two tourists. It was a little old lady with thin white hair and a wrinkled face which was as naturally scarred as the nearby cliff face. Her rheumy dark eyes radiated rage. If she had possessed more teeth she would have bitten the intruders.

"Who do you think you are, taking photographs of me in my own home! I'm no heritage exhibit! Bugger off!"

Brent Avery was upset too, but more out of shame than anger.

"I'm awful sorry, ma'am. I didn't think anyone lived here."

Mimi stood by her husband. "That's true. We thought maybe your cottage was some kinda storage facility. You know – fishermen's nets and stuff."

Neither tourist believed their lame explanations would assuage the local woman's rage. She stood supporting herself with her left hand leaning against the outer stone wall, wearing an ill-fitting faded silk dress. To their surprise, the old woman's angry expression softened as she turned to address Mimi.

"You're ... you're a Canuck!"

Before Mimi could reply, Brent stepped forward. "She sure is. This is my wife Mimi. My name's Brent; Brent Avery. We're from Seattle, Washington State."

"Hi. Sorry to disturb you," said Mimi, unsure whether to shake hands. "We're real impressed by your Island – especially with *Near Bill* here."

Brent kept the momentum going. "We sure are. It looks even better in real life than on the internet."

"In the net?"

"No, the internet. We bought our July vacation package online."

"On a line? Oh, you want to fish. Sorry, can't help."

"Ah, no ma'am. I'm no fisherman. I was a computer systems analyst for the Forward Slash Corporation in Seattle. Then one day I realized I was working more than living. So I cashed in my silicon chips to spend more time with my lovely wife and our family. But first there's a European grand tour to take care of; every little nook and cranny."

The local lady smiled. "Including my own humble abode."

Brent was unable to answer back. His wife jumped in. "Ah … We've got two kids: Randy is married with two kids of his own, while Candy is divorced with joint custody of a little girl. It's kinda strange being a grandma in your fifties."

The elderly woman looked wistful. "I wouldn't know … Never had little ones … Never got married."

Mimi glanced at Brent who was a tad irked that she'd unwittingly pushed it too far and undone his effective diplomacy. Nevertheless, the homeowner stared curiously at the female intruder.

"So you're definitely a Canuck?"

"I am originally Canadian; from just outside Vancouver. It's not far from the US border, in the Pacific Northwest. How do you know the difference?"

"She thought she'd corrected her accent. It's *aboot* time she did," teased her Yankee spouse.

The Manxwoman smiled sadly at Mimi. "I used to know a Canadian fella. He was stationed here on the Island during Number Two."

"Number Two?"

"Yessir. The Second Big One. He was a navigator on those

Halifax bombers before he came over here – flew all the way to Germany and back. Said his aeroplane looked like a moth-eaten blanket by the time they landed."

"Was there an Allied airbase around here?" asked Brent.

"An RAF base, yessir. Up in the north at Jurby and also at Andreas. But they were proper training bases. Oh, there was also *HMS Urley* at Ronaldsway with all those Fairey Barracudas and Fairey Swordfish whizzing past. *Themselves* could never abide the use of the 'F-word'."

"Fairies," mouthed Mimi for Brent's benefit.

"My fella Tod was helping train new flyboys to get up and down safe and kick the Jerries in the pants in between, like what he'd done."

Mr Avery chuckled. "Ha. You summed the whole darn thing up pretty good."

"The Canucks and the Anzacs came over quicker than the Yanks' Eagle Squadrons – as soon as it started, being part of the Empire. They were brave boys. Really nicely natured too."

"See honey," joked Mimi, "I've got a pro-Canadian ally of my own, in the face of US domination."

Mr Avery glanced at his quartz-movement wristwatch, thinking to himself, 'By the sound of the introduction, this lonesome senior citizen's reminiscences are gonna be about as long as that particular conflict.'

"During the war I was a coastwatcher in the Observer Corps," related the Manxwoman. "I volunteered to sit in a pillbox cabin farther up the hill there just past Dalby village. The leftover oldsters couldn't see so good. My job was to peep through the slot window half the day with a pair of field glasses, looking for enemy ships, subs and aeroplanes. If I saw any suspicious activity, I'd liaise with the nearby radar station. Guess I came in handy if they blew a fuse. Those sirens sounded awfully scary. The only time our church bells could be rung was at the threat of a German invasion."

"Was there a German raid here?" asked Brent.

"Just a jettison night bombing, but not on my watch. Dalby put the Island on alert. A Luftwaffe stray dropped four bombs nearby that caused large craters. My Nan was rattled out of bed. I wondered if the big radar masts were the target, but it could've been they were trying to climb over yon hill. Luckily only a frog was killed."

"Yep. Those Frenchies do tend to get in the way."

"During my day watch, apart from our Allied craft, I mostly saw baskers, seals, seabirds, butterflies, the Mountains of Mourne across ... and Tod." Her croaky voice faltered as she remembered. "He was on leave of duty from Jurby for the day. It was late August 1944. The tide of war was turning by then. Most of the fellas spent their leave at the pub. Tod spent it 'whale watching' as he called it: wandering along the coastal paths with field glasses looking for departing basking sharks ... until he noticed me. He poked his pointy nose right in through the pillbox slot and declared: 'I surrender, cupcake'."

Mimi laughed. "See, we Canucks have got the gift of the gab too. Why didn't you ever use that line on me, honey?"

"Didn't need to. I'd already won the encounter."

The old woman wasn't listening to the tourists' raillery. She was immersed in her own stream of consciousness.

"Earlier, in 1942, I saw a young German flyboy who'd been washed up on the Tail. I tried to save him, but sadly he was already dead."

Brent was surprised. "But he was the enemy."

Mimi was touched by the old lady's attitude. Her own maiden name was Seeberg. Finding out about the Island's internment camps for enemy aliens during both world wars reminded her of how her own forebears had been interned in British Columbia during the First World War.

"At that moment all I could see was a young life lost. Perhaps he was the sweetheart of a girl like me, even though I'd never really loved before, not until I met Tod. We'd meet up in the pillbox. He called me his 'jet-eyed gal'. That summer stretched all the way to mid-December; an Indian summer of our own."

Mimi recalled the delight of young love. Brent, stung long before by a nasty divorce from his first wife Barb, wasn't quite as moved.

"When my coastwatching duties were done, we'd walk hand-in-hand along the fields below Dalby to my Nan's home here in Niarbyl. She'd been looking after me since my parents died in a fire when I was six. Nan was a widow, so we kept one another company in this very cottage. Yessir, it was two's a crowd in here! Nan did odd jobs to make ends meet. Earlier on, she'd done housework for the Australian music hall star Florrie Forde on her regular holidays next door."

"I take it your Nan didn't mind Tod being a foreign guy?"

The old woman's eyes glinted in annoyance.

Brent Avery gulped, thinking, 'I only want her to get over the mushy stuff.'

"Nan didn't approve of anyone who'd take me away from her. So we sat on the Tail of the rocks over there, Tod and I. We hugged and kissed, knowing full well that Nan was watching our every move through this very window."

Mimi pointed at where they'd been standing. "Yeah, we were just taking photos there. I could feel the Tail was a ... like ... special spot."

"It's special to me too. It's the last place on this earth where I held the love of my life ... Now Nan's gone and I'm the one who's cursed to stare at it for the rest of my lonely days."

Mimi clutched her mouth, suddenly realizing.

"Oh my God! Tod was killed!"

A few tears trickled down the old woman's furrowed face. "Tod had to fly off to the Battle of the Bulge. Our side needed as many flyboys as possible to knock Jerry for six all the way back to Berlin. He was transferred to a US airbase in the South of England. He promised to write to me, but there was nothing for three months."

"Sadly that battle was damn brutal, ma'am. The Krauts were hell-bent on splitting the Allied line in half."

"I was going out of my mind. Didn't know if Tod were alive or dead ... I learnt later he was 'somewhere over Europe'. That made it worse – only a fraction of the bomber boys made it back intact. I knew he was such a good navigator that he'd take his Flying Fortress bang on target ..."

Her voice trailed off, shot down by emotional flak. It took her a moment to regain her composure. Mimi wanted to pat the old lady's bony shoulder in comfort but she looked too frail to touch. She kept leaning against her cottage wall, like a feeble human buttress.

"That's when Nan and I fell out. She tried to break us up. I told her I wanted to marry Tod and emigrate to Canada. He lived in a town called Moose Jaw."

"I know of it. Never been there myself," remarked Mimi. "It's in Saskatchewan Province, south of Saskatoon. Quite a rowdy place from what I've heard. Great name though."

"Well the moment my Nan heard of it she had a fit! Said she'd sworn on my parents' graves that she'd take care of me. She wouldn't allow me to waste my life in some Wild West backwater."

"Uh-huh," grunted Brent, with an atypical sense of irony.

"Then came the letter ... I met our village postman on my way to the pillbox. He handed me a formal-looking letter

158

stamped from across. I tore it open. It said that Tod had been killed in action. I near collapsed. I ran down the lane and didn't stop till I was halfway along the Tail. Couldn't see a thing; my eyes were so teary. There could've been an entire fleet of Nazi battleships at anchor off Niarbyl, but I wouldn't have seen them. All I could think of was Tod and how I wanted to join him as quick as possible. Then I slipped on some slimy moss and knocked my head. Hours passed without me knowing."

"Oh, you poor dear!"

"When I came to, I heard my Nan shouting. I turned round. Part of the Tail behind me had submerged. What had been shallow rockpools between two humps of rock was a gulf of swirling water. Nan was on the other side, hollering at me. At her age, she'd already risked her life getting that far up the Tail. Then I saw she'd brought a rope and wanted me to catch it off her throw. I was in shock, frozen to the spot. It was then that I saw her about to enter the sea, desperate to save me. That brought me to my senses. I answered her call. After several attempts, I caught the rope. I took to the waves; gripping and paddling forward while Nan was pulling me in. Before too long we were both safe and blubbering like babies."

Mimi gasped. "I can imagine!"

"Then you'll never believe it: just a month before war's end, the postman brought me a letter from Tod. I recognised his handwriting immediately. He'd made it safely back from the devastated Continent, back to the Ridgewell American airbase in Essex. Said he'd soon be on his way back here and that he loved me ... We'd be married."

"Hey, that's great. So the official letter was a goof-up."

"Worse sir – it near killed me. Nan was wonderful. Said she wanted to make up for how she'd behaved earlier. She gave me her blessing for a new life as Tod's wife in Canada."

By now Mr Avery was as enthused as when loading up a

new software package.

"I'm real happy for you, lady. After what you'd experienced ..."

"Wait on a moment, honey," interrupted Mrs Avery, her brow knitted in concern, "I'm pretty sure she mentioned she never – never saw Tod again. Don't tell us he didn't make it back to the Isle of Man? That would be too cruel."

The Manxwoman didn't reply immediately. She needed to take stock of the reality of a vanished past.

"Tod did return to the Island – in a way. The war was coming to a close. After receiving his letter, I knew he'd be here with me by the end of it. In my head I could even hear the church bell ringing joyfully for us. Nan altered a wedding dress for me. It'd been used by successive cousins around the Island, with each one storing it for the next marital relay runner. She even made this special going-away outfit from a silk drogue used for anti-aircraft target practice. She dyed it puce red with *scriss-ny-greg*; a sea moss. The drogue had floated onto the Tail, adrift from Knock-y-Vriew. See how lovely the dress still is. I thought I'd be heading across the pond with the man of my dreams ... but it wasn't to be."

Mimi interrupted again, tactfully, "If it's too painful, we understand."

The old woman shook her head. She appeared quite wan.

"You've come all the way from Tod's country. Our meeting was meant to be. Tod wrote to say he'd fly in on the 23rd of April 1945; St George's Day. I didn't know exactly what time he'd be coming in. I assumed it would be on an RAF aeroplane. He never turned up."

"No details at all?"

"No sir. I waited in the cold outside the Jurby Airfield perimeter fence from early that morning. At around 10.30, I heard a loud noise up near North Barrule – that's a huge hill

... Oh, it's strange. Early in the war, I'd given my savings in a public appeal for a Spitfire for the RAF – a fighter plane named *North Barrule*. It took me a while to realise that the leftover mist on the summit was mixed with a cloud of smoke belching out from a big fire on the eastern slope ... Word soon came through that an aeroplane had crashed into North Barrule: a bomber – not a German one, an Allied one ... an American B-17."

"Oh my God!" Mimi clutched her face, tinkling her wind-chime earrings. Her husband was equally upset.

"Tragic. B-17 Flying Fortresses had a crew of about seven."

"More than that. On that day there were 31 souls lost in the crash. The bomber was packed not with bombs but passengers: airmen from their Essex base en route to Belfast for some R&R. They'd slogged for two years without a break. Then Fate dealt the death card. Playing cards and debris littered the hillside. I could never go up there though. Too painful."

"I'm so sorry, ma'am. Back home we call them the 'Glorious Generation'."

"Yessir – glorious they were indeed ... and my Tod was one of them. I'll wager my soul he was on board that Yankee bomber, coming back to me. He gave his word he would. The air crash investigators used the boys' dog tags to identify them. They claimed that all 31 passengers and crew on the B-17 were accounted for; that all of them were US personnel. There was no record of a Flight Sergeant Tod Timmins on secondment from the Royal Canadian Air Force. But why else would they be flying so low in the middle of the Irish Sea? They were experienced pilots with flight charts. They wouldn't be trying to avoid their own side's ground radar. No, there's only one possible explanation: Tod had hitched a ride on that bomber.

They were dropping him off at Jurby Airfield on their way to Northern Ireland. Must have been. What other explanation could there be? Tod was being flown in to marry me."

Brent and Mimi stared worriedly at one another. There were other possible explanations, but neither could see the point in stating them. Brent, as was his wont, came the closest.

"Ma'am, I'm no aviation expert, although my brother does work for Boeing which is based in our hometown. What I do know is that fog and wind shear are particularly perilous – even for modern aircraft with sophisticated onboard radar and GPS satellite navigation. Imagine what it was like in those old propeller planes of the 1940s; those brave boys were flying by the seat of their pants in comparison. A hell of a lot of them lost their lives in crashes."

The Manxwoman's tears were drying up. All the while she took stock of the male stranger's words. She blew her nose on a handkerchief kept in her dress pocket. Mimi noticed the initials 'DS' embroidered on it. Brent looked at his watch again: they were running out of time.

"I'm pretty sure, in fact I'm certain, that if your boyfriend were truly on that bomber which crashed then the US author-ities would have notified the Canadians."

"I wrote to the Timmins family care of Moose Jaw, but there was no reply. The Air Force wouldn't tell me anything. I had to glean what I could … I know it was a cover-up. The Americans lied their heads off rather than admit the truth. If Tod had been navigating then I know they would have landed safely at Jurby on St George's Day 1945."

Brent Avery had had enough. Nobody was gonna sully Uncle Sam's coat-tails. "Maybe he *was* the navigator. That could be the *real* reason why they covered it up."

"Brent. No."

Ignoring his wife's plea, he continued, "Or maybe he wasn't on the plane at all. Did you ever consider that, lady?"

There was a rasping intake of breath as the words struck. Sixty-five years of pain flared from the woman's eyes as she trained them like a double-barrelled ack-ack gun at the American man's large nose.

"How dare you say that about my Tod! You've betrayed my trust."

Brent gave the woman a withering glare back, before solemnly addressing his wife.

"We gotta go now, Mimi. It's nearly a quarter past two already. The bus won't wait for us. Period."

Wordlessly, Mimi met the old Manxwoman's wounded gaze, imploring her to see that she truly cared but could say nothing without making it worse. Mr Avery put his arm around his wife's waist and firmly ushered her away from the cottage. He stopped suddenly. Withdrawing the Gondwana rock memento from his jacket pocket, he flung it angrily back towards the Tail, muttering, "I just remembered an old Injun jinx that it's bad luck to take stones from their natural site."

The old woman staggered back against the whitewashed wall.

"Arrgh! Typical know-all Yank. If it hadn't been for you lot, my Tod would still be alive. You took him away from me, you Yankee bastards! Why won't you admit it? You killed him!"

The Manxwoman's previously enervated voice had developed a second wind. Her bitter words followed the tourists as they stumbled back across the shore and retraced their steps up the road to the café car park. Her anguished cries echoed off the jagged rocks and looming cliffs.

Niarbyl Bay had ceased to be a tranquil place.

★ ★ ★

163

"Je-sus, what a nerve!" Brent complained to his wife, once they'd reached the comparative safety of the Peel-bound bus.

"You gotta be understanding, honey. Those were terrible times she lived thru."

"Gimme a break. She's a goddamn fruitcake! Imagine dishonoring the memory of our boys who sacrificed their lives over here to keep her free. Je-sus! No wonder that Canuck didn't wanna return to marry her. He's probably back home in Moose Jaw even as we speak; surrounded by his great-grandkids and an agreeable squaw. Way to go, buddy, way to go!"

Mimi felt miserable but let it drop. She knew it was better to let him get it out of his system. They had to catch a flight to Belfast themselves the next day. It would be their last stopover before returning to the USA.

"I'm so looking forward to seeing our own grandkids again," she thought as she gazed out the bus window at the western horizon beyond the Niarbyl cliffs. In the firmament above, jet planes were spinning vapour contrails like skyspider webs as they crisscrossed the Atlantic.

"It may be the place where North America and Europe meet," reflected the Canadian woman, "but I feel so far from home."

The single-decker bus rolled on through Dalby's narrow high street, passing an impressive neo-Gothic church. Earlier in the day it had appeared to Brent as being quaint – now it looked ominous. The pointed capstones of its flèche buttresses resembled a battery of surface-to-air missiles, seemingly ready to be launched at winged demonic invaders.

Farther along, nestled in a farmer's paddock sloping down to the shoreline, stood a large gorse-covered bulge which seemed unnatural.

"I wonder if that's an ancient Celtic burial barrow?" Mimi remarked, hoping to distract her husband from his brooding.

Brent merely grunted, unable to either confirm or deny. However, another voice answered her question, raised above the rumble of the diesel engine. It was that of Dollin Cashen, their amiable bus driver, who fancied himself as a tour guide.

"Aw no. That's what's left of an old World War Two radar station. The farmer stores his animal feed in it now. The big transmitter masts were demolished a while back."

The only other passengers on the small bus, a blonde teenage mother with a toddler parked beside her in a pushchair, looked up. The mother wondered whether the history lecture was for her benefit, but soon smiled when the comeovers seated up front responded.

"Thank you, Driver."

"Yep."

"Enjoyed your trip to Niarbyl?"

Mimi piped up before Brent had a chance to think of a smart-ass response.

"Sure did. Took a whole bunch of photos to show the folks back home."

Her husband took the cue to switch on his digital SLR camera. He checked the day's take to keep himself distracted. The little boy squawked to gain his mother's attention. She tickled his chin, making him instantly gurgle with delight. Undeterred by the cacophony, Dollin kept the conversation going. His was usually the quietist route on the Island.

"I suppose you took a picture of the old cottage. It often features in the postcards and films."

The young mother spoke up: "*Waking Ned*." Her child assumed she was praising him and eagerly responded: "King Ned! King Ned!"

"No, that were the other one," Dollin laughingly corrected the local pair. "I'm referring to the small one at the far end of the cove. You know."

"Do we ever."

Mimi hastily answered over Brent: "A Manx doll's house. Real pretty."

"Well now, there's a strange tale linked to that little cottage. My late grandfather was the local postman round these parts during the war. Granddad cycled around Dalby and down to Niarbyl to deliver the post to the RAF Officers' Mess where the café now stands, and to the bay dwellers; including Sarah Skillicorn who lived in that cottage with her granddaughter Daisy. She was a kind-hearted, vivacious girl. All in the Patrick parish were fond of her. She had a wartime romance with a Canadian airman based at Jurby. Anyway, he flew off to finish off the Third Reich. Poor Daisy nearly went spare, worrying if he'd survive. She was in tears awaiting his letters. Granddad felt like a one-way go-between."

Brent Avery had heard it all before and didn't particularly want to hear it again. His bespectacled brown eyes stayed glued to his handheld slideshow. The young mother did though – it was one piece of local *skeet* she wasn't yet aware of. Her uncomprehending child didn't appreciate the lack of attention; his giggles soon reverted to disgruntled wails.

"Aye tot, that's a fairly accurate impression of the state Crazy Daisy, as they branded her, was in right enough … Oh, I shouldn't call her so. The poor girl suffered a terrible trauma just before war's end."

"Yeah, she told us all about it," remarked Mimi.

Dollin's flow of words ceased. It was a full moment before he spoke again. Mimi noticed that his tone had lost its lightheartedness.

"Did you just say *she* told you?"

"Uh-huh. Chatting outside her cottage."

The driver took a while to mull over it; never taking his alert eyes off the road.

"Must have been someone else."

"Naw. It was Crazy Daisy all right," grumbled Brent. "She damn near spoilt the outing."

"Couldn't be. That little cottage has been empty since her Nan Sarah died."

"Oh. She could've just been visiting her childhood home. I noticed the monogrammed initials 'DS' on her kerchief. A very old lady with thin white hair and dark eyes. About five foot two. She told us all about her Nan helping prepare for her wedding with Tod and how the Flying Fortress had crashed into some big hill here. She figured he'd hitched a ride on it."

"That's what Daisy claimed, but then shortly afterwards she was taken away to Ballamona."

"Balla-whata?"

"Ballamona. That's a mental asylum," the young mother answered Mimi.

"She was locked up there for most of her life. She was convinced her sweetheart was on that bomber, but no one can be sure. Her Nan was a *jowsha*, that's an old grouch, but she loved Daisy. Just nine days before that crash, there was a similar one. Another American Flying Fortress, on its way to Belfast as well. It hit a hill not far away, killing all on board. Daisy had come down with a stomach bug and knew nowt of it. Sarah hid the news from her ... but she wondered later, after Daisy lost her mind, whether Tod could have taken the earlier flight to surprise her. His disappearance still remains a mystery. Officially he went AWOL."

Brent tuned in as Dollin continued.

"During the hostilities, what with all the training and the comings and goings of planes on both sides, there'd been nowt but noise. A couple of the older folk started whispering that as Themselves simply cannot abide noise they'd called on their magic host Manannan to put a stop to it all with his mantle of mist."

"*Themselves?* You mean fairies? Tell me you're not serious, buddy," retorted Brent.

"Oh it's just old talk, but many did think the second B-17 crash was mighty strange. It's still the worst aviation disaster in Manx history. The weather was mainly clear, apart from some lingering mist on North Barrule, named after the Norse 'Watch and Ward'. The air crash investigators couldn't understand why, on nearing the Isle of Man, the experienced pilot descended to such a dangerous altitude, only 500 feet above sea level. As I said, it was only days since the earlier B-17 crash and all Allied air crews had been put on alert to watch out for our high ground. Anyway, for poor Daisy the absence of Tod was devastating. A fortnight after the crash, when the Dalby church bell started ringing to celebrate VE Day, she cracked up and lost her mind."

Brent's anger rapidly evaporated. 'Why didn't I keep my big mouth shut? Maybe this Manx driver guy's right: it *was* those damn rocks that screwed me up and got me all riled,' he thought.

Mimi and Brent stared deeply at one another. They experienced a rare moment of marital telepathy. She firmly squeezed his hand.

"Ah, Driver, do you happen to know where Miss Daisy actually lives now? You see, I'd like to send her roses and a MoneyGram."

"That's kind of you. Yessir. Daisy's presently at Ballatessan Nursing Home in Peel. She's bedridden from a severe stroke. Can hardly move a muscle, poor girl. Like being both dead and alive."

The Averys both jolted up in their seats as if the bus had hit a pothole.

Brent hurriedly fast-forwarded the digital photos to the shot he'd taken through the cottage window. He showed it to Mimi. What he'd seen with his own eyes didn't show up in the image. The old woman's face hadn't been captured at all: only an orb-like light that could've been the flash reflecting off the windowpane.

"Oh my God! She's a living ghost!"

The teenage mother smirked at Mimi's outburst. She pressed the bell for the Glen Maye stop next up. Mr Avery then assisted her by lifting the child's pushchair off the bus and she wished them a safe trip home.

As he was five minutes early and no one was waiting to board, Dollin Cashen closed the bus doors and cut the engine. He turned in his driver's seat to address the two tourists more informally.

"I wouldn't be saying this, but from what you've told me I believe that Daisy's somehow come through to you … Now, here's a secret that not even Daisy's aware of. After her breakdown, her Nan Sarah Skillicorn was consumed by guilt. She confided to Granddad that she'd used her cousin's typewriter to type up a copy of the letter she herself had received when her own husband was killed in the Great War. She changed just the names and dates. This she sealed in an envelope addressed to Daisy and forwarded it with a note to a friend across, simply asking her to post it back. She figured rightly that her granddaughter wouldn't have had a clue of such official notification procedures; after all, Daisy was only Tod's girlfriend, not his wife or relative."

"That's an awful thing to do," declared Mimi.

"At the time, she thought she was doing the right thing. Tod hadn't written in several months. Sarah always believed that he was a womaniser having a fling at Daisy's expense and that he'd no intention of returning. She wanted the naive girl to get her life back on track."

"Sheesh! The plot thickens."

"No one really knows the truth, mister. Later, when Daisy got Tod's real letter she told her Nan he was coming to marry her. Sarah feared she'd misjudged the man. But after Daisy's breakdown, Sarah read Tod's letter herself. He'd merely written that he was coming back and that he loved his jet-eyed Manx beauty. Being an innocent country girl, Daisy had assumed he meant they'd marry. Poor Sarah was beside herself, thinking it was the double whammy caused by her own foolish letter that had driven her granddaughter insane."

"It's all so sad and strange. Poor Daisy instantly recognized my Canadian accent and seemed kinda hopeful. Perhaps she tuned in somehow and thought I'd brought news of Tod – but how could it happen? I noticed her left hand was leaning on the cottage wall all the time."

"You're not suggesting she was plugged into it, honey; like some sorta power transformer?"

Dollin's blue eyes were pensive. "None of us can know how Daisy came through. My sixth sense tells me it's the Niarbyl rocks that helped make it possible. My thinking is that after the plane crash the fierceness of her obsession was reinforced by the power of the rocks around her – including those of her own cottage. They originated millions of years ago in Gondwanaland. I've read about natives who locate and communicate while separated by hundreds of miles. They believe in the special power of their sacred Gondwana stones. It's all part of it back there; like a natural radar installation."

"That's weird. Her breakdown – was it delusional or something?" asked Brent, sounding concerned.

Dollin was quiet for a moment, thinking how to put it into words.

"Whatever it be called, it was as though the intensity of

170

her emotions caused a split: a human fault line rupturing her soul and severing her psyche in two."

The normally garrulous Averys were rendered speechless by the extraordinary pathos of it all. United in mind, they reacted with understanding to Dollin's words. They both felt that their visit to Niarbyl had somehow melded them closer together. Whether triggered by the power of its transmitting rocks or by the signals sent by Daisy remained mystifying. It was an encryption that not even the Bletchley Park computer *Colossus* could ever have deciphered.

❦ August ❧

Alan Lawton was born in the village of Micklehurst in the midst of the Pennines and moved to the Isle of Man in 1962. Alan worked for many years in the farming and construction industries and also served for a time in the armed forces. He has a degree with the Open University and has undertaken research work for the University of Liverpool on the structure of the Manx construction industry.

Alan is a keen historian and writer and achieved first place in the Olive Lamming short story competition in 1979. His short stories 'A Walk Along the North Quay of Douglas' and 'Death Tram' were included in previous volumes of *A Tail for All Seasons* and his first novel *The Wanderers of the Water Realm* is shortly to be published by MP Publishing.

Now retired, Alan lives quietly in Onchan with his longtime partner and concentrates on writing, light gardening and culinary challenges.

catch The foxdale Ripper!

Alan Lawton

The rattle and clank of the antiquated lift warned Corporal Caley that his tiny detective agency was about to receive its first prospective client for almost three days. He was certainly pleased to hear the metallic clatter, for the bills from his irate creditors had recently begun outnumbering the cheques from satisfied customers by a ratio of three to one. Even the solitary sandwich peddler, who still visited the rundown office block in downtown Douglas, had begun fobbing him off with stale baps that tasted worse than his ex-wife's cooking. Most of his work now came from matrimonial matters and debt collecting.

He turned to Shirley Kinrade, his personal assistant and close friend, "I wonder if our new client's first words are going to be, 'I'm sure that my husband is having an affair with that tart with the wooden leg living next door', or 'The vicar owes me for two used tyres. I want you to break his right leg.'"

"I don't care what they start with," Shirley replied with a shake of her head, "as long as they end up by giving us a nice fat retainer. I haven't been paid for two weeks and it's the beginning of August and little Charlie needs a new pair of sandals. Children grow out of them so quickly at his age."

The door of the outer office swung open before Corporal could frame his reply and he was mildly surprised when Finlow Corkish crossed the threshold. The two men knew each other very well having been educated together at Ballakermeen High School, but their paths had divided upon graduation, Corporal having joined the London Metropolitan Constabulary as soon as possible, whilst Finlow had begun a career in accountancy, eventually leading to his present position as Senior Manager of a large and influential offshore investment company.

Finlow normally possessed a waspish sense of humour and might well have begun the meeting by reminding the detective of the strange first name that he had received from his father, a Corporal in the Grenadier Guards. But not today, for Finlow was white as a sheet and clearly upset. The investigator led him into his private office and seated him on the old sofa that occupied the far corner of the room. He then retrieved a bottle of rum and two glasses from a filing cabinet and poured out two stiff measures of the fiery liquid.

"I reckon that you haven't come to invite me to one of your garden parties," Corporal began. "Best tell me what's bothering you so much."

"That confounded Foxdale Ripper – what else?" Finlow replied. "I've just come from a meeting with several of the largest financiers who do business with my company. They're all thinking of selling their mansion houses, quitting the Island and taking their assets with them if someone doesn't get their finger out and catch the villain within the next two months. I've also heard that some of the estate agencies are complaining about the falling value of luxury properties and some hoteliers are panicking over the mass cancellations of bookings."

"I can see your problem," the detective mused. "Two brutal unsolved murders are causing near panic amongst your investors ... Now if there was to be a third ..."

"Then the economic damage would be catastrophic," Finlow broke in. "And we would find ourselves living in a fear-ridden society with everyone mistrusting their neighbours. It would be terrible."

He paused and took a sip of rum.

"The Isle of Man Constabulary has released very little information, save that two extremely brutal murders have been committed and the investigation is being given the highest priority ... But a strong rumour is spreading amongst the Island's business community, suggesting the police are hampered by a lack of information and are nowhere near making an arrest.

"All we know for certain is that the first victim was a retired banker named Carl Braur who dwelt in St John's and his body was found lying naked on a piece of waste ground near the 'Snuff the Wind' mine above Foxdale, and that's how the killer got his name. The victim's throat had been cut from ear to ear, he'd been disembowelled as cleanly as a pig in an abattoir and all of his intestines were missing. There's not much doubt about the gruesome details, because the corpse was discovered by a party of twenty local hikers and some of them were disturbed enough to go blabbing the news all over the Island. Rumours also suggest that the second murder was an exact copy of the first except the corpse was found floating in the stream below Glen Maye. The victim was a speculative builder called John Baron who lived with his family in the village of Foxdale."

"I can understand your problems," Corporal said. "But what do you expect me to do about it?"

"We need your help in catching the killer," Finlow replied.

"You were quite a high flyer in your days with the Metropolitan Police and you were destined for great things if that crashed police car hadn't put an end to your career."

The accountant continued quickly before the detective was able to recover from his surprise and regain his powers of speech. "Plenty of folk have deluded themselves into believing that the killer is someone who visits the Island in order to commit his crimes, but others are convinced that our villain is a local man who holds a deep grudge against Manx society. Perhaps he belongs to one of the groups who failed to benefit from the Island's current prosperity, possibly a fisherman or a small farmer, even a disgruntled hotelier who has become unhinged through watching his livelihood dwindling away."

Finlow continued without a pause. "You were born in St John's and you know just about everybody in the west of the Island. All we ask is that you nose about and see if you can discover anything that may be of use to the enquiry; you were renowned for having an intuitive way of getting results whilst you were with the Met. Perhaps you still have your old touch?"

"You must be mad … Totally barking mad!" Corporal replied as soon as he was able to get a word in edgeways, "The police wouldn't stand for someone interfering with their investigation. I would risk losing my private investigator's licence and probably worse. I wouldn't have stood for it when I was in the Met – not for a single damned second."

Finlow shook his head. "The word is that the police would be glad of new information from any source, besides, my billionaire patrons carry plenty of influence in the right quarters. My clients are prepared to reward you with top rates of pay and a very generous bonus if you dig up information that leads to an arrest. Come on, what do you say?"

"I still say that you're all mad!" the detective replied and then he pulled a handful of unpaid bills from a drawer in his desk. "But these pieces of paper say that I'm your man and I'll start tomorrow."

★ ★ ★

Finlow Corkish had hardly reached the lift before Shirley burst into the inner office.

"That old intercom works just fine," she said with an irate shake of her red locks. "I heard every single word and I can't believe that you were so stupid as to accept that man's commission. You risk having an angry Chief Constable in front of you and a mad killer stalking you from behind."

She paused and slipped her arms around him.

"Look, we've been more than boss and secretary for quite a while now and I worry about you, I really do. Ring that damned accountant up and tell him that you've changed your mind. We can manage somehow!"

Corporal gently kissed her on the cheek. "Where's the risk in asking a few questions?" he replied. "I can plod around the west of the Island for a couple of weeks and earn enough cash to pay off our debts. If I catch a single thread of useful information then I'll ring up the Constabulary and let them take the risks."

"You can't kid me," Shirley replied. "Finlow's stirred up your old hunter's Instinct and you can't wait to get on yonder villains trail ... But if you're dead set on pursuing this enquiry then I'll be with you every step of the ...."

The door of the outer office swung open and the secretary's four-year-old son ran inside, followed by Shirley's twin sister Helen.

"I wanna puppy!" Charlie yelled. "The other kids at school have dogs. I want one."

Helen sighed. "He's been like this ever since one of his

179

friends brought a pet dog to school. Take no notice of him and he'll get tired of demanding what he can't have."

But Charlie was still shouting for a puppy when his mother locked up the office and took him home.

★ ★ ★

The morning was dry and sunny when Corporal climbed into his battered old Ford and collected Shirley and her son from the small terraced house which they occupied in upper Douglas.

"Wanna puppy ... Wanna dog," Charlie repeated all the way to school and his mother was heartily glad to see him running into the playground.

"He's driving me nuts," Shirley said with a groan. "But that's him gone until the afternoon. Now where do we begin with our enquiries'?" she asked as she refastened her seat belt.

"We're heading for St John's," Corporal replied, "and having a cup of tea with an old friend of mine who owns a smallholding in the lee of Slieu Whallian Mountain. I've known Olaf Bell for as long as I can remember and you can rely on Olaf to know everything that's going on in the district. I wouldn't call him a 'Skeet' but he's something of an expert on other folk's affairs!"

The old Ford's engine spluttered and banged noisily as the vehicle passed through the village of St John's and crossed the intersection into the Patrick Road. Corporal briefly glanced at his companion as the car began picking up speed.

"Olaf is a fairly easygoing sort of fella," he said. "But he's a bit queer around women ever since his wife took off with his twin brother about ten years ago, so you'd best let me do most of the talking."

The detective steered his car along a rough track and into a farmyard that fronted a small two-storyed house and a run of rather dilapidated farm buildings. He was relieved to see that a dirty bicycle, festooned with gardening tools, was leaning against the farmhouse wall.

"Thank goodness for that," he remarked to Shirley, "Olaf's at home and not away at his work. He earns his living by doing gardens to supplement the few quid that he makes by offering donkey rides at most of the fairs held on the Island. He was once a prosperous market gardener until the supermarkets put an end to his livelihood."

A small stocky man of about fifty years of age answered the door, ushered the pair into a small sitting-room at the front of his house and quickly produced the almost ritual offering of bonnag and strong tea.

"How are you getting along?" the private detective enquired. "It must be almost twelve months since I last drove up your lane."

"Oh fair to middling," the gardener answered. "Better since I demolished my commercial greenhouses and stuck to weedin' folks' flowerbeds to pay the bills, but I've kept hold of one small greenhouse just to give me a supply of tomatoes for my own table – remind me to give you a few before you go."

The investigator took a sip of tea. "The times have been hard for folks who are still working in the traditional industries," he said. "And not everyone has adjusted as well as yourself. I wouldn't be surprised if some people around here are holding grudges against those who flaunt their wealth by building fine houses and driving around the countryside in expensive cars."

Olaf gave the investigator a shrewd look. "You'll be refer-ring to yonder fella that folks call the 'Foxdale Ripper' – and you'll be wondering if I know anyone who fits the bill?"

"That had crossed my mind," Corporal answered. "Can

you name any possible suspects or do you wish to keep your thoughts to yourself?"

"Now I don't like makin' trouble for my neighbours," the gardener said. "But butchering folks like cattle is beyond all reason and a couple of candidates do immediately spring to mind. Philip Christian of Ballahoward Farm would be the obvious choice," he continued. "Christian used to milk a hundred pedigree Holsteins, until the poor returns from the sale of liquid milk and rising costs drove him out of business. He cursed the financial sector from Heaven to Hell and back and he's noted for standing outside the Keys and blackguarding the MHKs as they pass in and out of the place. He earns a few quid as a bouncer around the Douglas nightclubs and I don't doubt that he's angry enough to do the odd murder."

He paused to swallow a mouthful of tea. "There's also Widow Corrin who lives in Glen Maye. She and her late husband used to own a boarding house in Douglas, until the collapse of the tourist trade forced them to sell their property. Aye, she's been a very bitter woman since her husband hung himself from a tree in the garden and she's not slow to speak her mind. She's used to hard work and as strong as any man and she'd certainly be physically capable of doing the killings."

"Did you know any of the victims?" Shirley asked.

And much to Corporal's surprise, the gardener answered with a smile. "Bless you lass, I knew both of them. Carl Braur was a German by birth and he settled on the Island some time after the Second World War. He was an accountant by profession and he made a stack of money by playing the stock market. He lived alone in a small cottage on the edge of St John's and was liked and respected by everyone in the district. Can't think why anyone would wish to murder him!"

"What about Baron?" the private investigator asked.

182

"Aye, well, he was a different kettle of fish!" The gardener replied. "He was a young man who was 'on the make', as the old folks would remark. He specialised in getting hold of disused barns and farmhouses for a song and converting them into desirable residences, as the estate agents would say. He seemed to enjoy robbing cash-strapped country folk of their property, on one hand, and failing to pay his subcontractors on the other. Save for his wife and three kids, you would have a job finding anyone who wouldn't like to murder him!"

At that moment a loud braying erupted from the nearby stables and Olaf rose to his feet. "My donkeys are calling for their breakfast," he said. "And then I must take a bush-saw to a stand of overgrown leylandii at the other side of the village. But first I'll get those tomatoes that I promised you."

★ ★ ★

Corporal parked his car in front of the Tynwald Inn and the two colleagues were soon enjoying refreshing glasses of ice-cold shandy in a secluded corner of the bar.

"You certainly made a hit with the gardener," Corporal said after quenching his thirst. "I thought that he would ignore you, but he took to you straight away and that's unusual. Even so, he was probably wrong in suggesting that Phillip Christian could be our killer. I knew him from my schooldays and he was always ready to use his fists in good times or in bad. I once visited his farm and tried to collect a bad debt for a client, but I never got the cash out of him and finished up being pushed into a pile of manure for my trouble. Philip Christian could easily kill someone in a fit of rage, but to logically plan a murder and carry it out in cold blood would be quite beyond him."

"What about that widow, the one who lives in Glen Maye?" Shirley suggested. "Could she have been responsible?"

Corporal gave a reluctant nod. "I knew Margaret Corrin well in the days when she ran a boarding house with her late husband. She was a strapping lass and physically capable of doing the deed, but they say that she went to pieces after her husband hung himself. I owe her a call so we'll give her 'a coat of lookin' at' before we head back to Douglas."

* * *

The old Ford made its way along the Patrick road, turned left at the junction with the Peel to Dalby highway and about ten minutes later the vehicle reached the outskirts of Glen Maye. Corporal braked hard and swung the car up a rough country lane and drew to a halt outside an old stone-built Manx cottage.

It was Margaret Corrin herself who answered the detective's knock and he was instantly shocked by her appearance. She had aged long beyond her years and the dress that had once fitted her statuesque frame now hung loosely upon her emaciated body like a grotesque cloak, and her eyes betrayed the loneliness and pain that was racking her apart. But she recognised her visitor immediately.

"Corporal Caley," she said with obvious pleasure. "Come into my sitting-room and bring your young lady with you. I'm fair glad to see you both for I don't get many visitors since my husband died."

Corporal looked around the sitting-room and found seating space for himself and Shirley amidst the clutter of old newspapers and empty food cartons. He had exchanged only a few words with the woman before he realised that she was incapable of being a murderer and no possible danger to anyone but herself.

At first Margaret was able to conduct a lucid conversation with her guests, but she quickly began losing her concentration and the detective realised that he must ask his questions as quickly as possible.

"Nasty business that murder in the village," he said. "I expect that all your neighbours are talking about it?"

The woman thought for a moment. "No, only the young policeman who called not long ago. He wanted to know if I'd noticed anything unusual and so he spent some time viewing the tyres on my husband's old car that's been lying in the garage ..."

She broke off for a while. "But I told him that I've only seen the Devil prowling past my window and he left soon afterwards."

Corporal shook his head and steered the conversation back to their shared memories of the good times spent in the woman's lodging house in Douglas. After about an hour he made his excuses and the pair left the cottage.

The return drive to Douglas was uneventful, until the mobile phone in Corporal's pocket began ringing incessantly and he pulled off the road to take the call. He was visibly shaken when he put the instrument away and turned to Shirley.

"That was Finlow Corkish. He said that a usually reliable source of information, within the government service, had quietly confirmed to him that the Ripper's victims had been deliberately drained of blood before being transported to the locations where their bodies had been discovered."

"I've changed my mind about this investigation," Shirley whispered in quiet anger. The man must be caught before he kills again!"

* * *

The pair did not return to their office by the shortest route but made a detour in order to collect Charlie from school.

"It's not fair ... I wanna dog like the other kids," he yelled as he ran out of the school gates, but his tirade suddenly ended when he accidently collided with Corporal's crash-injured leg. The detective grimaced with pain and Shirley turned to him after strapping her child into his car seat.

"Your leg is giving you trouble again," she said, stating the obvious.

"Navy rum and half-mouldy baps isn't the best diet to keep a man fit and active. You'd best come to my house in Douglas and have a good feed of my homemade meat and potato pie. Then you can sleep on a proper bed in my spare room, not on that broken-down sofa back at your office. Come along now, let's get a move on!"

Later that evening, Shirley made her colleague lie prone upon his bed in the spare room and she carefully laid a poultice upon his injured leg to reduce the inflammation.

"I would love to sleep with you tonight," she said as she smoothed down the poultice. "For there's little comfort in a lonely bed, but when my husband left me for another woman, I swore that I would never let Charlie watch me bedding a long succession of 'uncles'. My son deserves better ... I hope you understand."

"Aye, the lad deserves much better," Corporal agreed as the nagging pain began receding. "Now I'd best get some sleep or I won't be much use in the morning."

★ ★ ★

The following seven days were particularly hectic for the two colleagues. They visited many of the farms from St John's through to Kirk Michael in the hope of obtaining the odd scrap of information that might help their enquiry.

They listened to the gossip in all the pubs along their route, and then at Shirley's suggestion she visited numerous church halls and other places that were commonly frequented by women and young children in the faint hope of obtaining a new lead. But all they heard was the latest crop of wild rumours and discovered absolutely nothing of substance.

On the fourth day Corporal returned to the house carrying a little brown puppy with a white spot on its back.

"Farmer Corlett's bitch had a litter of puppies and this is the only one without a new home. I brought it here to save its life, but I'll take it to the MSPCA if you can't manage it."

Shirley saw the look of unparalleled joy upon her son's face and she uttered a sigh of resignation.

"Another shitty little baby to housetrain," she said. "At least it should put an end to Charlie's endless whining, though unfortunately he's going to stay with his Aunt Helen for a few days and he won't enjoy leaving his new friend behind."

On the seventh evening, Corporal enjoyed a particularly good cottage pie in Shirley's kitchen and retired early to bed in the hope of gaining a good night's sleep. However, the many intricacies of the Ripper case afforded him no rest.

How did the Foxdale Ripper select his victims?

Where did the murderer kill and disembowel them?

And how were the remains transported to their various places of disposal in absolute secrecy?

There seemed to be no answer to these questions and he was forced to admit that he was no further forward with his investigation than on that day in early August when Finlow Corkish had entered his office. Even so, he felt intuitively that some small clue lay hidden within the meagre amount of information that had been teased out in the course of the past week; some little fact that would burst the case wide open. He lay in the darkness and forced himself to consider every aspect of the investigation, from the very first day of the enquiry until the moment that he retired to his bedroom, and he repeated the process time after time.

The light of dawn was beginning to illuminate the bedroom window when his questing mind seized upon the elusive clue.

"The donkeys," he repeated aloud. "It's the bloody donkeys!"

Without pausing for a moment's thought, he quickly dressed and made his way down to his car that was parked outside the house. The old vehicle coughed and spluttered into life and soon Corporal was driving through Douglas in the direction of the Peel road. Despite its age and condition, the old Ford covered the distance to St John's in less than half an hour and the detective parked his car on the Patrick road only a short distance from the smallholding of Olaf Bell.

It was now full daylight and Corporal had no difficulty in reaching the group of outbuildings lying near the gardener's house. He quietly crept towards the dilapidated stable block where Olaf kept his donkeys. He unlatched the half-door of the first box and was greeted by a mare with a foal. The second box contained the gardener's three working donkeys. However, the detective let out a gasp when he peered into the third and final box, for a large male donkey, almost the size of a full grown mule, was looking back at him whilst contentedly munching upon its generous ration of hay.

"So that's how it was done!" he said to himself. "Now I'd best get back to the car and contact the police."

Corporal had begun retracing his steps when he noticed that the sliding door to Olaf's last remaining greenhouse was partly open and that a single naked light bulb was illuminating the rows of tomato vines inside. The detective's curiosity was aroused and he slipped inside, where he was immediately greeted by the stench of corruption emanating from a bucket of black clotted blood that was standing upon one of the stagings. At almost the same moment his eyes fell upon one of the ropes supporting the rows of flourishing vines and to his horror he realised that it was manufactured from crudely cured human intestines. He remembered the sandwiches that Shirley had made from Olaf's delicious tomatoes and he began retching violently. He was so sick that he hardly felt the gardener's pruning knife slicing into his unprotected neck.

★ ★ ★

"How are you feeling?" Finlow Corkish enquired, as he entered Corporal's private room in Noble's Hospital. "The last time that I visited this room you were unconscious and had more tubes inside you than Pulrose power station."

"I'm not doing too badly," the detective replied in a weak and rather hoarse voice. "The surgeon says that I can leave the hospital in a couple of weeks. The medical staff are looking after me really well, but I'll be fair glad to enjoy a bit of sunshine before the winter sets in."

"The hospital did a mighty job of work on him," Shirley added from her seat beside the detective's bed. "Corporal had about as much blood left in him as a vegetarian sausage when the paramedics arrived and got a line into him."

Finlow pulled up a spare chair and joined Shirley alongside the bed.

"There are a few details about this case that I don't fully understand," he said, turning to the red-haired secretary.

"Tell us, Mrs Kinrade, how were you in a position to save Corporal's life when he was attacked by that damned gardener?"

She smiled. "I knew from experience that Corporal often erred on the side of impetuosity and I decided to watch his back as far as I was able. Even so, it was purely good luck that I was awake and heard him creeping out of my house on the final night of our enquiry; I tailed him in my own car to the gardener's smallholding at St John's and I was only just in time to save him when Olaf assaulted him with his pruning knife. I didn't use any fancy tactics; I simply struck the gardener over the head with a ten-inch clay plant pot that happened to be full of wet soil at the time. The paramedics had to patch him up as well," she said grimly. "The rest you know."

Finlow then turned his attention to the wounded private detective.

"When did you suspect that Olaf was the killer? Was it when he regaled you with worthless information when you visited him at his farmhouse?"

Corporal would have shaken his head, but the dressings around his neck prevented all movement.

"No, not until that final sleepless night," he replied. "Although it did seem extremely strange that Olaf was over-polite to Shirley when we interviewed him at his farmhouse, for he didn't normally have much time for women. But I never believed that Olaf could possibly have been our killer, for he appeared to have no means of moving the corpses after butchering them. He lost his driving licence years ago and he always used a haulage contractor whenever any of his livestock needed shifting. But on that final night, I recalled that Olaf's late father had been a muleteer in the murderous Italian campaign of the Second World War and I remembered the old man's tales of bringing the dead down from the mountains upon the backs of army mules. Then everything became clear to me.

"The gardener had probably killed and butchered his victims in the disused vegetable packing shed that lay behind his house, for the premises would have been ideal for washing and preparing the corpses for transportation. The moment that I discovered that large beast of burden in Olaf's stable I knew for certain that he was the killer and I also knew how he moved the bodies to their various places of disposal.

"Olaf was born and raised in the lee of the mountains and he knew the old miners' paths and sheep tracks like the back of his hand. He could easily traverse them in sunshine or black darkness, in winter or summer. He probably led that surefooted beast across the open moor in the dead of night, with the wrapped corpses carried upon its back and with only the mountain sheep and the black hill cows to bear witness.

"If the gardener needed to pass human habitation, then he would simply have muffled the animal's hoofs like the cavalry raiders did in the old days. Meanwhile, the police were casting about like blind-worms looking for incriminating car tracks. A few animal footprints would have attracted little attention and they would have been swept away by the first shower of rain. I also remembered Widow Corrin saying that she saw the Devil prowling past her window. She probably caught a glimpse of Olaf taking his second victim for disposal in the Glen Maye stream, for the lane running past her cottage leads directly onto the open mountain ..."

Corporal began gasping for breath, for the long period of speech was beginning to take its toll and Shirley helped him to sip a little water so that he could complete his testimony.

"But what I could never understand was how Olaf was able to lure his victims to his smallholding in the first place."

Finlow wiped a few drops of spilled water from the detective's chin. "I can go some way in answering that question," he said. "It's rumoured that the police were able to get a few words out of the gardener before he went completely catatonic and was shipped off the Island to an institution for the criminally insane near Liverpool. It seems that he met his first victim whilst the man was out for a walk along the Patrick road and he invited him home for a game of cards. The old German must have drawn the ace of spades because he was probably dead within the hour."

He paused. "The final movements of John Baron, the second victim, are likely to remain a mystery from this time hence. But it's said that the Manx constabulary intends to keep the case open indefinitely, for they feel certain that the answer to some of their 'missing persons' cases will be found lying buried beneath the heather of the Manx uplands."

Finlay reached for his coat. "I suppose you'll be reopening your detective agency as soon as you get on your feet. Now I've a fraud case that's ..."

"Not damned likely," Shirley interrupted. "Because I'm going to marry Corporal before he gets himself killed ... Or I'll have nobody to walk the dog."

◖ september ◗

Elaine Aulton lives in Ramsey and splits her time between writing and teaching. Elaine started 2010 on a high by winning the Olive Lamming short story competition and has since won an online Womag competition and been shortlisted for the International Fish Publishing short story competition. Prior to this year Elaine has been a finalist and winner of the *Mail on Sunday* novel-writing competition and regularly has articles and stories published in various national magazines either under her own name or under the pen name of Ellan Moore.

Her short stories 'The Carrasdhoo', 'The Monks' Treasure' and 'The Bridge' have all been included in previous volumes of *A Tail for All Seasons*.

The curse of finn mac cuill

Elaine Aulton

"Nearly there," Sheelley said. With one hand she clutched the bible tightly to her chest, inside her waterproof, protecting it from the persistent September drizzle. Her other hand sheltered her eyes as she squinted at the astonishing phenomenon ahead of them. "Watch out! Rocks!"

Drew turned his head slightly. The waves were indeed sucking and splashing against jagged rocks that were rising from the sea, the last of the sun reflecting off them, causing them to glow orange against the midnight-blue of the waves. He thrust the oars against the water, whitening his knuckles, making the rowing boat slew a little. But too late. They scraped and tipped against one of the rocks. The ozone smell of disturbed seaweed swirled round them.

"Hold on," he said as a wave slapped hard and splashed them both. Drew coughed and wiped wet hair from his face that through exertion was as red as his cagoule, pulled the hood off, and looked over his shoulder. "We're so close, Sheelley ... How long have we got?"

She stood suddenly, crying out, "I see someone. I can't

believe it." The boat rocked the other way, making her stumble. "I can't believe it, Drew. Two. Two people on the beach. *Hey! Hey!*" She waved, lost her balance and fell into the bottom of the boat. "It's a man and a woman," she gasped.

"For heaven's sake, stop pratting about." Drew leaned over the side and pushed an oar hard against one of the rocks. There was an ominous, deep, scraping sound and the boat merely tipped where it was. "I don't think we can go any further. How long have we got? How long?"

Sheelley looked at her watch, worried. "We didn't know it would be this far out. Must be nearly time by now. The books all said half an hour." She struggled to a sitting position, looking at the rocks between them and the shore of the risen island. "Drew? How will we get to that beach?"

He gave a low whistle. "No time. These rocks have caught her fast." He shipped the oars and held onto the gunwale. "I'll go across them. Stay here." Drew slipped and slithered to keep his footing across the weedy rocks, using hands and feet to make his way. He splashed deep into the pools between them but struggled on. The setting sun shone underneath the umbrella clouds and brushed the surreal scene with orange hues, casting long, black, undulating shadows. Sheelley squinted after him, her heart thumping: fear for his safety; disbelief that the island was actually here; panic from racing against the clock.

She stood up again in the grounded rowing boat, making it shift and scrape. The drizzle grew heavier. The man and woman were hurrying away from the stony beach and towards the low, rocky cliff, oblivious to Drew, and to her. She called again, "Hey! Look. We're coming." As Sheelley waved her arms she realised she still clutched the bible. "Drew, wait. Wait!"

Drew was hunched over, clambering almost crab-like over

the last remaining rocks between him and the beach. He stood, and launched himself into the surf, running and stumbling onto the shingle, a bright red figure with a long black shadow against the greyness of the island.

Sheelley saw the woman shade her eyes and point at Drew. Sheelley yelled, *"Drew. Here!"* He turned to face her and she waved the bible at him.

Drew staggered a few feet back into the surf, then retreated and went back up the beach. He beckoned with his whole arm for her to follow. Sheelley clambered over the side of the boat and stood ankle-deep in water on a submerged rock. She saw Drew still beckoning. The couple were crossing the beach towards him. Sheelley took a step and fell forward, pain lancing her knees. She stood again, and saw that his arm movement had changed. Of course. He wanted her to throw the bible to him.

Sheelley balanced herself, then threw the bible as hard as she could. It sailed over the rocks in an arc, its cover spreading like wings, and the pages riffling in midair. Its arc truncated; the weight of the exposed pages making it fall short, into the waves.

Drew took a couple of steps into the sea, and from where Sheelley stood she watched the two figures approaching him. Drew retraced his steps to go to them, pointing back towards her but without looking.

Sheelley screamed, *"No time. Pick it up!"*

Drew took a further step up the beach, still pointing at her but obviously talking to the couple. A knot of frustration balled up under Sheelley's ribcage. "Stupid, stupid, stupid," she muttered. She leaped forwards onto a weed-covered rock, her foot shot sideways as she landed on slick weed and she pitched onto her face. The sudden shock of it took her breath and made her ears ring. She scrambled up, vaguely aware that her face hurt. Her nostrils stung and her eyes clenched shut involuntarily. She scrubbed the heel of her hand across her eyes, and in a blur saw Drew waving animatedly. Then he froze, arm outstretched.

Drew's cagoule seemed to be getting darker. Sheelley wiped her eyes again. Drew's red cagoule darkened to umber; then, as she stared, the colour leached from it. The woman's long green skirt was changing. Becoming grey. The man was obscured by Drew, but he, too, was unmoving.

Sheelley heard a scream. It was her own voice.

Three figures stood on the shingle beach: one of them still pointing at her, although his head was turned towards his companions. All three were rigid. Grey.

Statues.

The rock she stood on shuddered, making her lose her footing and she sprawled forward again. She landed on another rock that lay just beneath the surface of the sea. Sheelley felt this rock shudder too. She raised herself up on her arms, and watched in horror as the sea moved up her forearms, to her elbows, and up towards her shoulders. 'No time', she thought. She splashed towards the rowing boat that now bobbed loose of rocks. As she caught hold of the gunwale she looked for Drew. He and the two others were a motionless tableau as the sea swirled around their knees. By the time she'd painfully hauled herself into the boat, the sea was churning around their chests, and the rowing boat was floating free.

Sheelley grasped the oars. She turned the boat back towards Port Soderick and sat facing the stricken island that was silently sliding from view. The drizzle had stopped. The last of the sunset reflected dapples of orange that moved and merged on the choppy water, gliding closer together as the island sank. Seagulls squawked loudly overhead. The expanse of sea became unbroken. Drew had gone. She retched, and vomited over the side.

* * *

"We have cleaned up your face and hands, and we are admitting you for observation, Sheelley. Once you are on the ward, the police will be wanting to talk to you." The duty doctor was smiling at her. Sheelley stared at him without speaking. She sucked in a shuddering breath. "Do you understand?" the doctor said.

Sheelley's lips moved. "He's gone," she whispered.

The doctor nodded to someone behind Sheelley; firm hands grasped her arms and half-lifted, half-guided her to a wheelchair.

A young policewoman appeared round the pastel curtains of the hospital bed, twenty minutes later. The lights were subdued, and everything seemed hushed and distant.

The policewoman spoke in a muted voice, matching the hospital quiet. "Sheelley Cain? I'm WPC Laura Walker. Call me Laura. I need to talk to you, find out what's going on." Sheelley shivered although the ward was warm.

The curtains moved again, and Sheelley's mother lunged at the bed and hugged her daughter. "Oh, love. What's happened?" She held her at arm's length and a puzzled expression crossed her features. "What's happened to your face?" She glanced down at Sheelley's limp arms and saw the bandages. "And your hands?" She noticed Laura. "What are the police doing here?"

"We need to speak to Sheelley."

"Well, I'm her mother. Brenda."

"Good. Glad you're here."

Sheelley allowed herself to be hugged again, but as soon as her mother let go, she slumped back against the pillows like an empty glove puppet. "You won't find him."

"What?" the other two said together.

"He's under the sea," Sheelley whispered.

WPC Laura Walker leaned closer, and Sheelley's mother jumped back saying, "Drew? Are you talking about Drew? Where is he?"

Sheelley's eyes gazed blankly at the space between her mother and Laura. "We saw it. He was on the island. It took him down, too."

Brenda's mouth sagged open. Laura said, "Who is Drew?" After a long silence Brenda said, "Drew McBride. Sheelley's fiancé. They've been engaged for three months now. Getting married next summer. What's happened?"

WPC Laura Walker indicated for Brenda to sit down. Then she said, "Your daughter was brought here by a motorist who found her walking along the Old Castletown Road. She was staggering and hysterical. She'd suffered some facial injuries. He brought her straight to Noble's A and E, and they called us."

"Someone from here called me too. They told me she was fine, but I was so worried. Where's Drew? What's happened?"

Laura pursed her lips. "That's what we need to find out."

Brenda sat on the bed with her arms around her daughter, and finally Sheelley's incoherent and stumbling story was written in Laura Walker's notebook.

The WPC closed her book and frowned. "For what it's worth, I think the doc should have another look at her. She's rambling."

Brenda nodded, reluctantly.

"I'll go and have a word. Magic islands and statues. We're wasting time. We need to find Drew McBride." Her radio crackled. She hurried into the corridor, listening to it, then came back to Sheelley's bed. "His car's parked at Port

Soderick."

Sheelley looked up, suddenly. "I couldn't drive it. He's got the keys in his pocket. Oh, Drew." Her voice broke.

Laura said, slowly, "Where. Is. Drew?"

"Under the sea. I told you."

Laura swept the curtains aside, speaking urgently into her radio. Brenda caught the words, 'coastguard' and 'emergency'.

★ ★ ★

Brenda dozed in the chair next to her daughter's bed. Sheelley remained wide awake, staring ahead. Occasionally tears would seep down and wet the butterfly stitches on her cheek. As the hospital started waking up: humming and clattering and squeaking, the windows brightening as the sky announced dawn, a sudden bang made her focus. A man's voice, "Where is she?" and heavy footsteps. Sheelley sat forward, expectant.

"Drew," she said. Brenda woke.

"Where, love?"

The man's voice again, "Where is she?"

Sheelley yanked her cover off, "He's here. He's all right."

The curtain that shrouded her from the corridor was ripped back and Mr McBride, followed by a nurse, came right up to the bed.

"Sheelley, where's our Drew? I've had the police. What were you kids doing?" His eyes were red, and stale alcohol fumes wafted from him.

Sheelley said, "I thought you were Drew."

The nurse was firm. "I'm sorry, you shouldn't be here. I must ask you to leave."

Mr McBride ignored her and looked at Sheelley's legs. "You poor lamb. What happened to you?" His big hands tenderly replaced the sheet. "You're all cuts and ..." He reached out a finger and touched one of her bandaged hands.

"Please, sir," the nurse said.

Brenda touched the nurse's elbow. "It's all right. He's fine."

Mr McBride sat on the bed; no one noticed the nurse's tight, exasperated sigh.

Sheelley spoke in a low monotone. "He climbed over the rocks, to get to the island. When I followed I slipped. I panicked. I didn't know I'd hurt myself. I had to get back into the boat."

"Boat?"

"Juan's old rowing boat. We towed it down last year, and tied it up by the funicular. Ready for if – when – we needed it."

Mr McBride shook his head slowly, with a slight smile. "You kids. Always harping on about bloody myths and legends. I'd've thought in your twenties you'd both grow out of it. So, where's our Drew? Did he bring the boat back? Is he hurt?"

Sheelley stared into his red-rimmed eyes. She tried to speak but nothing came out. Finally she managed a strangled, "He turned to stone. He went down with the island."

★ ★ ★

Laura shifted on her uncomfortable hard chair. The room felt claustrophobic but she waited to hear what they'd been called for.

"This is a potential murder enquiry." The Chief Constable peered at his notes. "We have no body, but we know that Mr Drew McBride has disappeared." He looked up at those assembled in the stuffy room. The radiator was on and the window shut, filmed with condensation. "Mr Drew McBride was last seen in the company of his fiancée, Miss Sheelley Cain, on the afternoon of 28th September. We have ascertained that he did not leave the Isle of Man, either from the Sea Terminal or the airport.

"There has been zero activity of his bank accounts. Those same accounts show no unusual deposits or withdrawals in the months preceding his disappearance."

One of the officers raised a hand. "Sir, how about the fiancée? What about her accounts?"

"Nothing suspicious. However, Drew McBride has disappeared taking nothing. Just the clothes he was wearing, and from Miss Cain's statement he also had his wallet and car keys. His black Saxo was unlocked in the car park at Port Soderick. She is sticking to her story that he turned into a lump of stone and sank into the sea, on an island that only appears every seven years."

There was a snigger from some of them in the room.

The Chief Constable raised his eyebrows. "Divers have found nothing. Something is very off. We're upping manpower to locate Drew McBride." He wagged a finger towards WPC Walker. "I want you in the team to investigate Sheelley Cain. She talks to you."

Someone in the room murmured, "Cain girl's a nutter."

"Is that your professional opinion?" snapped the Chief Constable. Taut silence, then, after a pause, "Right, as I said: even though we don't have a body yet, we're treating this as a potential murder enquiry."

★ ★ ★

WPC Laura Walker already had basic information: Sheelley Elizabeth Cain, aged twenty-two. Met Drew McBride at the Museum Library two years ago, when she was twenty and he was twenty-four.

Sheelley now sat opposite Laura, looking thinner, with

dark circles beneath her eyes. Her bruises had faded and the cuts had healed. She held her mug of coffee with both hands and seemed eager to talk. "He'd been there the day before," she said, "and we'd just smiled at each other. Next day I went in and he was there again so I said hello. He asked me what I was doing. I showed him this ..." She handed Laura a well-thumbed copy of *More Manx Myths*, with a bookmark at page 28.

"'The Submerged Island,'" Laura read aloud. She looked at the cover. "Dennis W. Turner. Researches Manx history, doesn't he?"

"Yes. And you see there? He mentions Nora Cain. I'm a Cain, so I wanted to find out more. Find out where he discovered names and dates. Drew read it. He was intrigued."

Laura started reading. When she looked up she said in a gentle voice, "You believe this, don't you?"

There was a long silence between them. Sheelley put her mug down, untouched. "He helped me look. There was an 1891 book by A.W. Moore, and in there it referred to one by Train, written in 1845. Drew found it. He asked me to go out for lunch to keep him company, as his reward for finding the right book. We've been together ever since." She caught her breath and her eyes filled.

Laura asked again. "Did you believe this legend?"

Sheelley blinked the tears away. "*Did* I? Not really. Not then. We sort of tried to persuade each other that it might be true, and that there could be a connection because of my name. And because *my* granddad also told me a version of the sunken isle."

Laura read aloud, "*Her grandsire told her of the land beneath the sea.*" She looked up. "But it says that Nora and her lover died because of a spell. Sheelley, it's just a legend."

Sheelley looked up sharply. "It's not a legend, though, is

it? It's a curse."

Laura tapped the open book. "So, the people of the island are supposed to have insulted this mighty wizard –"

"Finn Mac Cuill."

"Right, Finn Mac Cuill, and his revenge was to sink it?"

"Yes." She stared intently into Laura's eyes. "And Finn Mac Cuill's curse has taken Drew. I have to save him."

"I'm saying this as a friend. Your ... version of events of the night Drew disappeared is peculiar. You're asking us to believe that this –" she waved the book, "is fact. That once every seven years this island surfaces, but only for half an hour. But surely you can tell the difference between fact and fiction? Please, Sheelley, reconsider. Your mental health will be questioned."

"Drew and I were messing around."

Laura leaned forward, eagerly.

"We'd been down Port Soderick every night in September. Sad place. Nothing stays. Water sports, paddling pool, pub, kiddies' playground – they all go, don't they? I think it's the curse."

Laura made an impatient sound, but Sheelley didn't seem to notice. "We'd prepared, with the bible and the boat. We were going to stay until it was dark. It's really spooky there when it's dark, you know. It started to rain so we tried to shelter under the arch. But when it happened ..." Her eyes unfocused and her voice softened. "The swell was rattling the stones, and I was leaning back on Drew and he had his arms round me. I felt his arms go really tight and he whispered, "Look!" Even in the rain I saw the sea churning, out beyond the bay. And then something lifted out of the sea, and we ran to the wall. The sea surged in and walloped the wall, coming right up the slipway. You should have seen it. And we could see it. It got higher, rising up and up. Even though it was raining it was shining orange from the sun, and we could see it. The island. We stared because we couldn't believe our eyes. The sound the sea made ... the sight of that land ... we lifted our boat easily – excitement and adrenaline, I think – and we started badly, both with an oar. Drew took over and he rowed like a madman. I don't know how long it took. At first it was like a mirage, and we didn't seem to gain on the island. And then we were nearly there." She stopped, looking into the distance as if she could see the island again.

Laura waited for her to continue. Finally she said, "Then what?"

Sheelley started, and looked at her mug of coffee. She spoke as if to the coffee, her voice now flat. "You already know. I told you. I described it to you."

"You said there were two others. Where did they come from, Sheelley?"

"They were already there. They were hurrying away from the shore." She laughed, suddenly. "Perhaps, seven years ago, it was glorious weather. And when they surfaced this time the rain surprised them." She looked at Laura. "Their clothes were like those drawings of peasants of long ago. Dull colours. The man had a brown sleeveless tunic and trousers tucked into boots, and a green hat. She had a long swamp-green dress, tied round the waist, and a green scarf round her head. No one wears stuff like that any more. Drew was talking to them."

Laura made an odd noise.

"What?" Sheelley demanded.

"If what you say is true, how *could* he talk to them? They wouldn't speak English, now would they?"

Sheelley gazed into the distance again. She murmured, "Speaking Manx? That's why he was gesticulating so much. It must be."

There was an awkward pause. Laura stood up and shrugged

into her jacket. "I have to go. You'll be seeing someone later. A psychiatrist."

"Then I'll be able to go home?"

Laura pursed her lips and shook her head slightly. "I don't know, Sheelley. I honestly don't know."

* * *

When Sheelley was discharged from Grianagh Court she was unprepared for what met her. In Shoprite she was blatantly snubbed by one of Drew's cousins. Mr McBride hung up on her when she phoned. Against her mother's advice she went to Drew's house, and stood at the door, knocking and ringing. She felt sure Mr McBride was in. She leaned her ear against the peeling paint of the front door. She heard the sound of a door closing, muffled through the wood. A minute later she heard the unmistakeable sound of an engine starting, and then she watched as Mr McBride drove his van out of the back lane and straight past her, staring resolutely ahead.

When she walked into the pub with the few friends who stood by her, she was unprepared for the venomous, "You've got a nerve. You know what you did to Drew McBride." She turned just in time to see Mr McBride's ex-girlfriend's arm racing towards her. Next second she was soaking, lager streaming down her face. Without a word she left the pub; the only sound breaking the silence was the hum of the slot-machine.

Brenda, too, got the cold shoulder from some of her acquaintances.

"No smoke without fire," became a common, overheard phrase. Sheelley withdrew, becoming a shadow, fading away.

Laura visited. She tried, unsuccessfully, to hide her shock at the deterioration in Sheelley. "I wanted to tell you in person, there won't be an inquest."

Brenda put a protective arm around her daughter and

spluttered, "What are you talking about? Inquest? Have you found Drew?"

"No. But the Attorney General can ask the Coroner to hold an inquest without a body, if it's believed that a death has occurred. We have no evidence that this is so."

Brenda nodded thoughtfully and sighed. Then she forced a cheerful smile and said over-brightly, "Would you like a cup of tea? We were going to have one."

"Yes. Please." Laura waited until Brenda left the room, then leaned forward and whispered urgently, "Sheelley. What are you doing to yourself?"

Sheelley looked up at her, dull-eyed.

"Are you trying to live out the rest of that ridiculous curse? Eh? Be like Nora Cain and pine your life away? Are you?"

Sheelley looked puzzled.

"You should see yourself," Laura continued. "Fight it. Don't let Finn Mac-bloody-Cuill win."

A spark of understanding ignited in Sheelley's eyes. She placed her thin hand over Laura's and whispered, "Thank you."

When Brenda bustled in with a tray of tea and biscuits, Sheelley said, "Mum, I've decided. I'm going to America. Visit dad and his new family. Go travelling. Something. Anything."

Brenda threw a shocked glance at Laura. She stood quite still, holding the tray and scrunched her eyes closed. She pressed her lips together, then forced a smile. "That's a very good idea, love," she said in a stifled voice. "A very good idea."

★ ★ ★

Seven years later

A slim woman with her hair in a long, thick plait walked out of the gloom of the Sea Terminal in Douglas, into the bright September sunshine. She weaved through the waiting taxis and cars dropping off and collecting passengers. She wore a battered rucksack over a vivid orange and purple shirt. She crossed the road and headed towards Victoria Street. As she rounded the corner she almost collided with a pushchair.

"Laura Walker," she cried, incredulously.

The woman with the pushchair stopped dead and looked puzzled. "Actually, it's Laura Richmond now."

Sheelley took her sunglasses off. As she did so, Laura exclaimed, "Sheelley Cain. I didn't recognise you. You've grown your hair."

There was an embarrassed pause, then Sheelley bent to face level to the toddler in the pushchair. She grinned at the chubby little chap, busily sucking a dummy. When she stood up she said, "You're a mother?"

"Two boys. The older one started school this term." Sheelley straightened and Laura looked her up and down and laughed. "Your travels have done you proud. You look fabulous. When did you –"

"I just got off the boat. I ... um..."

Laura said, "Judging by the small amount of luggage, you're visiting. Come to see your mum?"

Sheelley smiled. "She finally married Michael and lives in Dublin now."

Laura did a quick calculation. "Unfinished business, then?" she asked.

Sheelley bit her lip and hoisted her rucksack. "Unfinished business," she agreed.

"Good luck."

The women nodded at each other, and Sheelley strode up the hill, watched by a thoughtful Laura.

Sheelley rented a car for the week and bought an inflatable dinghy. Since leaving the Isle of Man, this was all she'd planned for. She had a soft leather-bound bible that used to belong to her dad's grandmother, small and well-worn. Prickling with anticipation she drove to Port Soderick. She parked in the dilapidated car park and strolled through the glen. The wooden climbing frames and swings that once nestled in a hollow in the glen were gone now, she saw. She allowed her path to finally bring her to the shore; the remaining buildings on the sea-front were boarded-up, but showed depressing signs of vandalism. Where the brightly-hued playground had been was just an empty area of thigh-high weeds, with a blackened area from an old bonfire. She turned her back on the neglect and stared out at a calm, deep-blue sea, waves stroking the striated cliffs on both sides of the narrow bay as it ebbed. The tide-table had shown that the tide would be going out. That would help. Sunset would be a little after seven. She could feel her heart beating faster already. The taste of the air was tangy with salt, and the scent of earth and stone.

She went back to the car, drove it round to the sea wall and hid the keys behind the sun visor. She readied the dinghy, and dragged it into the sea. The sky was changing hue, from baby blue to a steely grey-blue on the eastern horizon. Her eyes ached from watching. Imperceptibly, the sky and sea darkened, then little sparkles of yellow-orange on the waves heralded the sunset. Sheelley could barely swallow. Seagulls called from above, wheeling over the cliffs. She stared and stared at the horizon, willing the island to rise.

What if it was the wrong day? What if she'd missed it already? What if …? She whimpered and started rowing out of the bay. Almost as soon as she'd gained deep water, the sea surged and pushed her back towards the rocky cove. Panicking, she rowed harder, and tried to look over her shoulder. Another wave surged, and she saw sunlight glinting from something that hadn't been there before. Sheelley gripped the oars with slippery palms and rowed as though in a race. "I *will* do it!" she shouted to the sky.

Sweat trickled down her neck and back, and she puffed and gasped as she rowed. A rowing machine was placid, nothing like this alternating wrenching, stuttering, palm-searing effort. She turned her head again and saw a flash of red.

"Oh," sobbed from her throat as she realised it was Drew. Drew was still with the two people. She could see them clearly. Tears sprang unbidden and fractured her view. To wipe her eyes she let go of an oar, then scrabbled frantically to catch hold of it again so that she didn't lose any time.

Over the noise of her heavy breathing, her heartbeat hammering in her ears, the sea – she thought she heard a shout. She turned her head once more. She saw rocks, sliding up from the waves. Some of them were fierce, although black seaweed appeared plentiful. Sheelley slowed her rowing, not wanting to rupture the inflatable edging of her boat. She guided herself past the first row of rocks, then saw that more were rising. Something moved beneath the soft base of her boat, and she saw a lump rising in the stern as if a long bony finger were being pushed upwards. She shoved at it with her foot, and realised it was solid rock. The stern of the dinghy began to lift.

Sheelley looked to the island. Drew was running along the shore towards her. It dawned on her that she'd rowed much farther along the beach than where they'd grounded seven years before, *and* that she was further out than when they'd been in the rowing boat.

The dinghy started to fold and she knew she couldn't

release it. Holding the little bible tightly Sheelley leaped into the sea, aiming for the next barrier of rocks. She thrashed about, gaining purchase and scrambling over the rocky eruptions, then splashing back into the sea. She kept going. She heard her name called and lifted her head. Drew was wading into the sea, coming to rescue her.

There was another rocky outcrop, filled with pools and covered with black weed. She dived towards it, and hauled herself through the slippery and sharp obstacles. Time mattered so much, and having to fight through the sea and weed-covered rocks was stealing too many precious minutes.

"Sheelley?" Drew's voice sounded high and panic-stricken. She stretched out and his hand clasped hers.

"Drew. I got here."

He pulled her up and she staggered into his arms. "Drew, we have to put the bible on the shore."

He leaned away from her, shock and confusion on his face. "Sheelley?" he said again. "I turned round and you'd vanished … I was frantic … couldn't see you. Sheelley, is it you?"

"Yes. It's me. Come on."

"But … you've changed."

"Yes."

They lurched hand in hand over the uneven rocks towards the shore. The couple dressed in peasant clothes were much nearer, the woman holding her skirts up as she hurried along the shingle. The woman was calling something, but Sheelley didn't understand a word.

Drew pulled her forward, out of the sea onto the beach. As it scrunched under her feet, Sheelley breathed, "This will break Finn Mac Cuill's curse." She gently laid the bible on the shingle, then stood and looked at Drew.

"Sheelley?" he said once more. They looked into one another's eyes.

"It's been seven years, Drew. Seven years." Her voice broke. Drew hesitantly embraced her, and then suddenly held her tight as she wept into his neck.

The peasant couple reached them, both speaking together. The man bent down and picked up the bible, turning it over and over in his hands, curiously.

Sheelley sniffed to compose herself and turned to face them. Drew said, keeping one arm firmly around her shoulders, "I think they're speaking Manx."

Sheelley smiled cautiously at the woman, aware of the wide-eyed speculation she was receiving. The man spoke, thrusting his chin to indicate the low cliffs behind that caught the last of the sunset. Sheelley looked briefly, then turned and looked back at the Isle of Man, silhouetted against a beautiful dying ember sky. She put an arm around Drew's waist. The island would stay here, the curse broken. She had done it. She had laid the bible on the land while it was fully raised from the sea.

She looked down, moved her feet in disbelief and cried out, "Where is it?"

Drew seemed confused. "Where's what?"

"The bible. It's gone."

"What? It can't –"

"It was right there." Sheelley's voice sounded shrill. "Right there." They both frantically scanned the shingle.

The man spoke unintelligibly again, and held up the small, leather-bound bible. Sheelley was unable to speak. She broke from Drew's arms and snatched the bible back, gasping, "No, no, no, no, no." She bent and pressed the bible against the pebbles as if trying to force it below the surface, tears of complete frustration welling up. She raised her face to Drew, crouched with her hand pushing on the bible on the shore.

★ ★ ★

Laura watched from her vantage point on the hill above Marine Drive, binoculars to her eyes. She held her breath as she saw the red cagoule darken, the orange and purple turn to sepia, the two in green and brown become greyish. Laura exhaled in horror. Her heart was pounding painfully and she felt faint, but she was unable to take her eyes from the implausible scene. Sheelley was crouched, Drew bending towards her, the other two standing upright.

Dismayed, she watched the colour leave them completely; they remained immobile; the sea sucked the island and its statues down, caressing the still figures. Then they were gone.

As she lowered the binoculars something caught her eye and she swiftly peered through them again. It was Sheelley's grey and yellow dinghy, rising and falling with the swell, being pulled towards the centre of the island as the last of it sank from sight.

Poor Sheelley, poor Drew. Laura had investigated Sheelley's claims, and she too had read how to break Finn Mac Cuill's curse. Like Sheelley, she'd become obsessed. When they'd met earlier she assumed that Sheelley knew exactly what to do. A bible had to be placed when the island was in its original position, when it had reached the right height. Laura had seen it rising for fifteen minutes, then sinking for fifteen minutes. That meant that the island was only at the correct altitude for a few seconds. So, if a bible was placed too soon or too late, the critical time would be missed. Or, perhaps, because that man picked the bible up again ...

Laura lowered her binoculars. She watched as if in a dream while the highest point of the island shimmered, blood-red, as it submerged. Gone.

Gone. Lost among the waves and legend.

october

Colin Fleetney was born in Kent and lived there until the 1980s when he moved to the Island to become the vicar of Lezayre. Before being ordained Colin worked as a seagoing engineer and then as a hospital engineer in a large psychiatric hospital. After ordination he worked as a hospital chaplain and then became Team Vicar for five parishes outside Canterbury.

Now retired and living in Port Erin with his Manx wife Joan he contributes factual articles to magazines in the UK as well as writing short stories and building working steam engines in his garden shed.

His stories 'The Bracelet', 'You are Standing into Danger' and 'When Children Play' have been published in the previous two volumes of *A Tail for All Seasons*.

The steeplejack's Tale

Colin Fleetney

My name is Bob Wilkes and I'm a steeplejack, but I'm no Fred Dibnah. I've never dropped a mill chimney and hopefully you'll never see me on TV. I'm a loner. I was born and bred in Carlisle and I'm proud of the fact that I still live in the house in which I was born. Lady friends? Oh yes, they come along from time to time, but as soon as I sense that they're becoming, shall I say 'serious', I end the relationship. To put it simply, I'm not going to give half my grub away in order to get the other half cooked. No, I'm a free agent. I answer to no one. The only, shall I say regular, fixture in my life is my Saturday evening session in the Dog and Gun on the Gretna road in Carlisle. And the only time I miss that appointment is when work calls me over to the Isle of Man. I have clients all over the north-west, mainly, of course, the Church, but also country houses and town halls. Very little of my work is done on spec, so to speak, as I generally have a five-year contract with clients. This system makes for easy money. I visit the site, examine the job by using binoculars, and of course always see that there is work to be done. I pitch up my ladders, erect a bit of scaffolding around the supposed job, scrape off a bit of moss, slap a bit of mortar here and there, sit up there for an hour or two, then dismantle my gear and charge a hefty fee. If the client looks like the adventurous type, and a few are, believe me, I take a bit more care. They just might want to climb up and see what I've done. Most, however, would not go near my ladders and are content to look at the job through my binoculars, not that they know what they're looking at. This work provides a reasonable income but my real income comes from a sideline.

A year or two ago I got talking, in a Welcome Break, to a couple of elderly American tourists. They were searching for records of their ancestors who emigrated to the States early in the nineteenth century. When I met them they had just visited a church out in the back of beyond and been shown the entry in the Baptismal Register of the woman's great-something-or-other grandmother and then, in the Marriage Register, the same woman's marriage. They were now on their way to the Keswick area somewhere, to trace the man's ancestors.

What interested me was the fact that they said that they would have willingly paid money – real money – to own the actual pages from those old, mouldering registers. They would frame and display them proudly, they said. I made discreet enquiries on the web and found that there were people, hundreds of people, and not only in the States, who would pay for the genuine thing as opposed to photocopies.

Now, I have occasionally done people 'favours' over the years . In one case I was asked to leave my ladders rigged up the front of a certain country house for one night longer than I needed. This I did, and someone climbed my ladders, entered through a skylight and helped themselves to silverware and jewellery. A day or two later word was got to me that if ever I needed help of any kind just mention it to a certain man in a certain pub in Carlisle.

So I 'said the word' and, after a few days, a set of skeleton-keys, keys that would unlock virtually any ordinary door or safe, was dropped through my letter box.

I got an opportunity to try out the keys when I had a request from a man in Kansas who wanted the page of a register recording the baptism of his great-whatever grandfather, in, he believed 1805. He gave me the details and the name of the village; it is in the Lake District, and indicated that money was no object – just get the page.

The church in question was on my books so I contacted the vicar and the church secretary suggesting that I take a look at the bell turret and weathervane after the recent gales. They, of course, agreed, ever mindful of their insurance. The small church is remote and the vicar lives in a village several miles away. Ideal! I made a quick inspection of the turret, weathervane and the bell housing. All was in order.

Then I turned to the real work of the morning. The church door was easy to unlock, a simple massive and crude lock made to look several hundred years old but actually made in the 1920s. After a bit of probing and fiddling, it turned to my key with a satisfying 'clunk'.

The vestry was simply a curtained-off corner at the back of the church. I pushed through the heavy, dusty, red curtains letting them close behind me with a rattling of brass rings. I've been in countless vestries and this one was typical; a massive Victorian table acting as a desk, a matching chair with a sagging seat. A big wardrobe in which, I had no doubt, would hang a collection of motheaten, damp and iron-mould stained choirboys' cassocks and surplices, not used these past twenty years. I didn't bother to look because I was only interested in the safe. Well 'safe' is perhaps too strong a word for the big cast-iron box standing next to the table. Apart from the wind sighing over the roof and the distant cawing of rooks, all was silent as I knelt and peered at the massive box. The top of the box was the hinged lid and the keyhole was in the front. I tried several keys and got one jammed, causing me several minutes of near-panic. Yes, I learned from that old iron box; I learned to respect the skill of the locksmiths of two hundred years ago. Anyway, I finally freed my key, changed it for another and, after a bit more fiddling, felt the tumblers move and heard the lock open.

Inside, neatly stacked, were the registers and, wrapped in green velvet cloth, the church plate used in the Holy Communion service. The oldest registers went back to the early 1700s. The silver plate did not interest me. A page or two from a seventeenth-century register would not be missed for possibly years, but church plate, no way. If that disappeared, all hell would break loose within days.

I found the name in question easily, incredibly easily, such is the care the Church of England takes, not only in recording everything, but also in keeping those records on site. Acting on impulse I also searched the Marriage Register for the 1830s and found the man's marriage. I neatly removed both pages with my Jiffy knife and quite simply that was that. I had earned myself £1,000.

I received enquiries from people with Manx connections. This was not, of course, surprising, for the Manx, like the Irish, had, due to appalling economic hardship, emigrated all over the world. I was therefore pleased that my five-year maintenance contract on several Manx church towers was due, and within a month of the above incident, equipped with certain details, I was aboard the Isle of Man boat, *King Orry*, bound for Douglas.

I had booked in, once again, at my regular boarding house in Ramsey. A grey plaster and stucco, tall and narrow Victorian building, it was typical of the hundreds that once did business on the Island, but were now (October 1995) fast vanishing. Anyway, I always enjoyed staying with Mr and Mrs Callister. They took great pride in their house and cooked good food, and plenty of it, which was important when you had been working in the open-air all day. And they had off-road parking big enough to take my lorry. All in all an ideal situation.

I arrived at the Callisters' around 7.30 in the evening after one of those flat, calm crossings that you occasionally experience on the Irish Sea. I then had a leisurely drive north on the coast road to Ramsey, followed by a splendid meal and a pleasant evening with the Callisters, being their only guest.

The next morning I drove west, through Sulby and Kirk Michael, on through Cronk-y-Voddy and down through breathtakingly beautiful Glen Helen to St John's. The inspection of the spire of the Chapel Royal was the job I liked least. That spire is, without a doubt, the most looked at and photographed spire on the Island and therefore demanded that I cut no corners and put my best work into it. It is also a 'needle' spire. Tall, yes, of course, but also narrow and very slender. Have a look at it – a real look at it, some time. Would you like to climb it? No. And neither do I. It's like climbing a pole, and it tends to tremble slightly when heavy traffic passes by on the main road. No, St John's spire is not the best of jobs.

The following day, a grey, still and warmish day, saw me in Peel, on the roof of the Cathedral tower. This tower once supported the tallest spire on the Island – and also the heaviest. It was carefully dismantled late in the nineteenth century as it was causing structural damage to the tower and then, with all the pieces lettered and numbered, it was stored under the trees behind the Cathedral and there it remains, a moss-covered stack of shaped stone and ironwork.

They like me to inspect the spire-base on the tower roof

and the lead sheeting – it's a simple enough job. Perhaps one day I'll get the job of re-erecting the spire, you never know.

On the next day, a Friday, I intended to keep the first of two private 'business appointments' that would, if successful, be worth a great deal of money to me. Rushen Parish Church was a long way from Ramsey, but a very pleasant drive. Mr Callister had suggested that, south of Upper Foxdale, I should turn right and take the lonely road up past the Rushen mines and, with the great bulk of South Barrule on my left, go straight across the crossroads he called 'Round Table' and on, towards a high, rounded hill with a cairn on its summit that had been in sight since I drove by the old mines, Cronk-ny-Irree Laa. Then, with aircraft below me and the south of the Island laid out like a relief map, I descended in a series of switch-back dips and bends, to, I almost said 'ground level'. What a stunning ride! Yet the Manx take this beauty in their stride. So many places are incredibly lovely here.

I called at the vicarage, and soon had my ladders up to the domed top of the bell-turret. An hour's work showed me that the stonework required no work. I wire-brushed the bell, checked and greased its bearings. I put a coat of wood preservative on the yoke and checked the condition of the rope – in all, another hour or so.

Early afternoon found me in the Allendale, an upstairs cafe of the old sort, just opposite Port Erin railway station. I've used the Allendale several times, no airs and graces, just plentiful, straightforward food. There was something nagging at me – something I needed to get in Port Erin, but what?

Back at the church I ignored the outside door to the vestry. A visitor would use the main door. I tried the door – unlocked! I walked in as a visitor might, respectful but confident. The building seemed empty but, as I walked up the aisle I turned to check up in the organ gallery. Empty. In the chancel I tried the vestry door. Unlocked! This was incredible luck. Luck that vanished at that moment when I heard the chatter of voices and footsteps approaching the main door.

A group of women walked in, and fell silent when they saw me studying the big east window. I slowly turned, nodded casually and remarked on the window's beauty and told them who I was. Ice broken, they said that they had an afternoon's work facing them, decorating the church for a wedding the next day. I listened to their various problems for a minute or two then said I had work to do.

As I climbed my ladders I said, under my breath, "Damn, damn, damn" to the rhythm of my feet on the rungs of the ladder. I then spent a long, boring afternoon partly up on the turret or, as the afternoon wore on and the wind grew chill, down in the cab of the lorry after I had dismantled my ladders. All the while the women came and went in cars, and the church swallowed countless bunches and armfuls of flowers and what looked like a couple of moving bushes of greenery.

Finally the last woman drove away and I prepared to have another go at the vestry. I climbed out of the cab – and the vicar walked around the corner. We had a chat and I made some remark about the long drive back to Ramsey and started the engine.

I was after two pages in the Rushen registers, two pages that, to me, were worth probably £2,000 and I was not leaving the south without them. I drove back to Port Erin, parked by the station and waited. I went to the Allendale again for a cup of tea and a bun and I remembered what it was that I had wanted – a Manx stamp to post the register sheets back to the Dog and Gun. Unless I was going away the next day and I could carry them in my bag, I always got rid of them. I'd drop them in the first postbox on my way from Rushen Church to Ramsey.

The main door was still unlocked, and after a quick glance round, I made for the chancel and the vestry door, which stood open. Fingering my skeleton keys in my pocket I stepped down, into the vestry. No safe! A table, with inkwell and blotter, chair and cupboard. The cupboard was locked and took me all of two minutes fiddling with my keys and – there they were – the registers!

I was searching for two entries but found three for the family in question and then, acting on a hunch, found another in the 1920s. Brilliant! Within a minute I had the pages in question neatly cut from the three registers and blessedly safe in a big envelope. Mine!

As I relocked the cupboard I heard voices. This I could not believe. I had pulled the vestry door closed, but not latched it. I peered through the crack. Seven middle-aged women and three men, all holding sheets of paper, were coming down the aisle. Two other men were talking just inside the door, then one disappeared and I heard footsteps on the stairs. The other man hurried down the aisle after the group. Music – they were holding music. My God, it's the choir. Choir practice! Of course, for the wedding tomorrow. As if to confirm my fears I heard the organ gently hiss and sigh as its bellows filled.

The women and the three men filed into the choir stalls and the other man stood with his back to the empty church. He checked that they were ready, glanced over his shoulder to the distant organ gallery and nodded to the young man up there on the organ bench. He then turned to the choir, and asked, "Ready?" They all nodded or murmured. "Now *watch* me, watch me all the time, right?" He raised his arms, paused, and then added, "And *listen* to each other." He indicated to the organist and they were off.

I spent the following forty minutes trapped in the vestry, happy when they were singing, but fearful someone would need to come into the vestry when they were not singing. Under other circumstances I might have enjoyed them. I know a little about music, and they sounded pretty good. I was, however, relieved when the conductor called it a day. I drove back to Ramsey with snatches of a catchy melody tantalizing me.

The next day, Saturday, saw me at Kirk Christ, Lezayre. It was not a good day. The Lezayre Tops, that steep, high escarpment that runs from Sky Hill west to the mouth of Sulby Glen, had mist spilling like water over their crests, driven by a steady wind. The mist was dissolving long before it reached the base of the tops and it was calm down at the church, but that could change. As they say, 'You get a lot of weather for your money on the Isle of Man'.

I pitched my ladders up the south side of the tower, the side facing the Churchtown road. Once at the top of the tower, some sixty feet from the ground, I climbed into the foot-wide stone gutter and walked, or rather, leaning against the base of the spire, edged my way right round the tower and spire to inspect the masonry and the four lead drainage spouts and the decorative gargoyles, one positioned at each corner of the tower.

Each gargoyle represented a profession. One held a square and compass representing, I suppose, the architect who built the church. Another was, of course, a priest. Another was holding a pen and book in its claws – a clerk, I suppose. The fourth was playing some kind of small, stringed instrument. Like all gargoyles, their heads were a mixture of reptile and human – I hope the four men commemorated by those gargoyles didn't look like them! Just below each gargoyle there was a long, lead pipe that carried the stormwater that runs down the spire well out, clear of the walls of the tower. Even at that height there was an accumulation of leaves in the gutter and all four pipes needed rodding out. I finished the job by scrubbing the gargoyles with washing-up liquid. If decorative stonework like gargoyles are white and clean-looking when seen from the ground, and the crosses on the pinnacles of spires have been attended to, people think a lot of work has been done.

Sixty feet further up found me lashing my scaffold boards in a square, round the capstone and weather vane at the top of the spire. The spire was in a reasonable condition but the vane, having experienced almost one hundred and fifty years of Manx weather, was in a pretty poor state, so I slapped a coat of silver Hammerite on it.

Then I sat there leaning against the vane while my scaffold boards creaked in the breeze. I puffed at a cigarette, my legs swinging in space, as I gazed around and waited. At that height, the trees bordering the main road from Sky Hill right through to Kerrowmoar looked magnificent, every shade of brown, gold and red. To the north, across the Plain of Ayre, I could see the white and red lighthouse at the Point of Ayre. All very fine, but soon now the autumn gales and driving rain would strip those leaves away to expose black, thrashing branches, and the Plain of Ayre would look drab and sullen. With the weather soon to close in, the sextons were working Saturday as well.

My wait suddenly came to an end and I tossed my cigarette down and watched as it was caught by the breeze to be wafted away – a white speck vanishing far below. I had been, all this time, watching the two sextons in the cemetery across the Churchtown road. I had seen the vicar drive away while I gave the gargoyles a wash and brush up. I wanted the sextons out of the way because I had vital business in the vestry. They were stripping ivy off the headstones that surrounded the clear area in the Eastern Ground, the area where the first Kirk Christ had stood. You could see the shape of the old church clearly from where I sat. All that's left of that church is, so they say, the Holy Communion silver and the church bell hanging in the tower under where I was sitting. Anyway, the sextons suddenly stopped work. They then stacked their tools against the wall of the ruined schoolhouse down by the Churchtown road and made for their hut. Afternoon teabreak! No, better than that. As I watched, they loaded a lawnmower into their van and drove away.

Within five minutes I was down on the ground. After grabbing the cardboard file lying on the passenger seat of my lorry I made for the church door. The door, set in the base of the tower was, I knew, unlocked. I paused for a few moments just inside the church, looking carefully and listening. It was mid-afternoon, just the time most people do church work, so I had to be careful. I could not be certain that someone had not slipped into the church through a side door to arrange flowers or to do cleaning. So I stood by the font, with all my senses keyed up. Apart from the sound of the breeze in the trees around the church, there was silence. Kirk Christ is a big church; long, wide and with a gallery at the west end. As I walked up the aisle and out from under the gallery, I could not resist turning and looking up into the twilight gloom, but no face gazed down at me.

There are two vestries, one situated to the north and one to the south of the chancel. I chose wrongly, I chose the one on the south side and found myself surrounded by all kinds of vases and equipment for flower arranging. I retreated to the chancel, then I cautiously tried the door of the north vestry. It was unlocked. I stepped down into the clergy vestry. Cupboards, a chest of drawers, a roll-top desk and matching chair, all new with the church, I estimated. On the walls, photographs of several self-important looking bishops and a painting of the old church which, to me, looked identical with Malew Church. Modern, fitted carpet throughout. The safe, a robust-looking dark green Milner 'Bulwark' of, I reckoned, 1900, stood in the corner.

I squatted down, flipped open my leather keypouch, swung the polished brass keyhole cover to one side and selected what appeared to me to be a likely key. That old Milner was no pushover. In all I tried four keys during which time I heard all kinds of noises – vehicles down on the main road and vehicles on the Churchtown road. One sounded as if it was pulling into the church driveway. I can tell you I was sweating when, finally, the old Milner conceded defeat and its tumblers clicked over, releasing the door lever.

As I lifted the lever it gave a satisfying 'clunk' and as I pulled, the great, thick door swung open smoothly. The upper part consisted of shelves on which were the registers and the church plate – silver pattens, chalices and jugs. I examined it – I couldn't resist it. It was heavy, solid silver, some engraved with a dedication to 'Our Gracious Sovereign Lady, Queen Anne', would you believe? Other pieces were from the time of William the Fourth. Placed in the right hands it would be worth a fortune. But, no matter, I carefully put it back. So far as I was concerned it was dynamite.

The oldest registers were bound in cream calfskin and blocked in gold. I had all the details written in my notebook and spent the next half hour searching from William and Mary's reign up to mid-Victorian times for births, marriages and deaths. It was hard work in that I had half an ear, more than half an ear, attuned to any sounds and believe me, I was jumpy! Incredibly, I found all that I was asked to search for. I got to work with my Jiffy knife and soon had all the relevant pages neatly removed and inside the folder. Of course, with my entry on each page there were nine others, but, there you are. What did President Truman say; 'You can't make an ome-lette without breaking eggs'? Anyway, those pages would be worth almost £5,000 to me. A good afternoon's work, indeed!

It was then that I heard the sound of the main door opening, followed instantly by footsteps coming, and coming fast, up the aisle. Jiffy knife in one hand, folder on the desk and safe door open wide, my God! I pocketed the knife, virtually threw the folder between the safe and the wall and gently closed the safe door carefully because I dared not let it thump. Then, as the footsteps mounted the chancel steps, I turned the locking lever which, so far as my nerves were concerned, emitted a tremendous 'Clunk'. I had just straightened up when the vicar walked in.

I was prepared for the confrontation. The vicar, of course, was not, and he visibly jumped when he saw me standing in the middle of his vestry.

I 'took the high ground' as they say. "I'm Bob Wilkes, the steeplejack," I said. "I am very interested in the old church and was told there was a picture of it in here."

Most vicars are incredibly enthusiastic when you ask them anything about their churches. This man was no exception. After explaining that the picture was painted in 1840 by someone who actually knew the old church, he insisted that we walk across to the cemetery and look at the site in some detail. My heart sank!

Once up in the cemetery he paused and gazed up at the church tower and spire. "My word, you've done well up there," he said. "The weathervane looks magnificent and the gargoyles look new."

I made some kind of modest-sounding noise. Then I was treated to a tour of the site of the old church – its crypt is, apparently, still there, under the turf. He then showed me where the stone for the present church came from – a small quarry now engulfed in trees, behind the sexton's house. He finally insisted that I went across the road to the vicarage for a cup of tea. I needed it, I can tell you! I could have done with a large slice or two of cake, as well.

After the cup of tea and a tour of his garden the vicar walked back with me to the church to do some paperwork in the vestry. I therefore conceded defeat, climbed into the lorry and headed back to Ramsey. On the way back to the Callisters', all I could think about was retrieving my folder from behind that safe. There was only one thing for it; I would have to go back to the church during the night. Risky, yes, but well worth it, and, anyway, I was booked on the boat the next morning so I had no choice.

* * *

After supper Bob Wilkes told the Callisters that he intended to drive around for a bit, possibly out to Andreas, Jurby or even the Point of Ayre. The novelty of driving at night on the peaceful Manx roads appealed to him, he said. They gave him a key and said, "See you at breakfast."

It would have been sheer stupidity to take the lorry into Churchtown late at that time of night so, a little past midnight, he pulled in under the Ballakillingan chestnut trees, about one hundred yards from the Lezayre War Memorial. He waited for some ten minutes to see if he had aroused any interest. The weather had deteriorated. The wind had increased and a fine but persistent rain had set in. The mist that had spilled and curled over the edge of the Lezayre Tops during the afternoon had thickened to fog, which, saturated by the rain, was now thick at road level.

He sat listening to the tick-tick of the engine as it cooled, and the sighing of the wind around the cab. Finally he climbed out of the cab and shivered in the chill of the rain and fog. He checked once again in his pocket for the skeleton keys and his pencil torch. Both okay. Zipping his anorak up under his chin, he hunched his shoulders and set out for the church.

By God, but it was dark! From the moving leaves invisible above his head, the wind sent miniature cascades of cold water that seemed to know exactly where his anorak ended and his neck started. The night was, he realised, full of noise, of sounds that could not instantly be given a comforting name. Strange sounds, unsettling sounds. Once or twice he stopped and listened intently and, smiling at his anxiety, he realised that the sounds were branches moving in the wind and rubbing together.

Walking as he was on the Ballakillingan side of the road, facing towards Sulby, he nearly missed the Churchtown turn-off. He suddenly saw, as the wind caused the fog to part for a few seconds, the tall cross of the War Memorial, black against the fog, just across the road.

Now he needed to be careful, for on his left behind the garden wall was a house. Keeping close to the wall, he carefully picked his way up the short hill, more a slope really, towards the gates of the church garden. It was further from the main road than he had realised.

In the swirling water-filled darkness, he was suddenly aware of an indistinct blackness looming above him on his right. The east end of the church, of course! A very fit man, he was surprised that he was glad to stop for breath. Somewhere just ahead, to his left, was the sexton's house and beyond it, on both sides of the road, Lezayre Cemetery – huge, containing, so the vicar had said this afternoon, far more people than were alive in Ramsey. Wilkes shuddered as he listened to the wind whispering and sighing through the trees that clothed the Lezayre Tops. It crossed his mind that he was earning his anticipated £5,000.

He walked off the road through the open gate and his shoes crunched loudly on to the loose gravelled surface of the church drive. He stopped. He had intended to go to the main west door in the tower, but that was closer to the sexton's house. No, better use the south side vestry door; it was just along a few feet from where he was standing. The church wall, shiny black with water, reared up on his right, the roof lost in the fog. Suddenly there they were, the steps up to the vestry door.

It was a simple Yale-type lock and he heard it click open within a couple of minutes of probing and fiddling. He cautiously pushed open the door, and, carefully placing his feet, he stepped inside and gently closed the door behind him. He waited, every sense keyed up. Noise. It was just the wind hissing and sighing round the building and over the roof. Okay. He switched on the pencil-torch and took a quick look around. Sink, draining board, vases, boxes, junk. He walked over to the door into the church and, switching off the torch, he carefully turned the knob.

He stepped out into the chancel and felt a good quality carpet under his feet. In the near-absolute darkness he sensed space; vast, empty space, space through which the wind, strong outside, breathed and played weakly. There were little sounds, too. He listened intently, sifting and examining them. Somewhere a page of an open book was fluttering. Somewhere a curtain was shifting, rippling, moving very slightly and its brass rings were fidgeting. Once again it crossed his mind that he was earning his £5,000.

He switched the torch on for a few seconds. Risky, but he simply could not resist the temptation. There was something, well, comforting in a silly way, in the tiny beam sweeping round the church. The puny, concentrated narrow beam was lost, swallowed up in the blackness of the vast building, stretching out beyond the choir stalls and the pulpit. Across the chancel the organ loomed, its pipes flashing a series of reflections as his torch beam passed across them. To his right the communion rails, then the altar, and then the great, towering east window. Window! He instantly switched off the torch.

After a few seconds, with arms outstretched before him, he slowly made his way across the chancel to the north vestry door. After several steps he flicked the torch on and off and found the door just in front of him. It opened and he stepped down into the vestry.

With a sense of physical as well as mental relief he reached behind him and pulled the door closed and switched on the torch and there, standing by the safe, was a tall figure. In the second or two that it took for him to play the torch beam over the figure he took in a white gown, reaching to the floor. Round the waist was a white girdle with tassled ends. In its hands it held a scroll of paper. But the face! Snake eyes, a flat nose with flared nostrils, lips drawn back in a rictus grin displaying tiny, sharply pointed teeth.

Wilkes turned, stumbled on the step, wrenched open the door that flew back, with a crash. He stumbled, dropped his torch, wildly grabbed at it, recovered it and, with shaking hands directed it back, into the vestry. The figure was stirring. It was moving, yes, moving very slowly towards him! For a moment he could not breathe, even. He backed away, gasped, turned, aimed the torch beam across the chancel, seeking the other vestry door, then leapt, stumbled, dropped the torch which clattered somewhere and went out. Just the thick dark – it enclosed him, choked him. He stumbled across the chancel, arms outstretched before him, seeking the door to freedom and all the while he was surrounded by a terrible, high-pitched shrieking, a blubbering howl that rose and fell, rose and fell. He missed the vestry door and fell headlong across the end of the choir stalls. For only seconds he lay there terrified, engulfed in pain and sucking in breath. It flashed across his mind that the sound, that awful sound, was him screaming. He grabbed at the woodwork, and slightly dazed and with his shins hurting like hell, he heaved himself to his feet and started to run. He ran through the treacly blackness, towards the centre of the church to the main aisle that led to the main west door. He had forgotten the chancel steps and, after only eight feet, shouting in fear, he once again fell heavily and cut his face on the edge of the front pew. Moaning, he heaved himself up and started off again, but he had forgotten that Kirk Christ has two side aisles and no central aisle. Once again he slammed into the woodwork of the front pew, winding himself and bruising his ribs.

Completely disorientated, he ran blindly. A heavy curtain seemed to wrap itself round him and, with a clattering of brass rails and rings, it brought him to the floor. He leapt from pew to pew, over the backs, skidding on seat runners, falling, struggling to his feet, falling again. He winded himself against the massive stone font and, partially recovering, cannoned into a glass-topped table and bookcases. Finally he fell through swing doors into the porch, the base of the tower, and found a stone step and followed it, up, up. "Help me, God, help me, help me. Oh God, help me!"

The sexton always unlocked the church at 7.45a.m. He crunched through the wet gravel to the west door . Beyond the weathervane, fretted against the sky, the clouds were breaking and as he watched, the patches of blue were expanding. The wind had blown itself out during the night and the fog had cleared. All things considered it could be a good day, he thought as his key turned in the lock and he pushed open the door.

Whistling, he walked through the tower, pushed open the swing doors – and stopped whistling. Vandals, he thought. Bloody vandals. Oh, the Vicar's going to have a fit when he sees this little lot.

The two bookcases holding hymn books and prayer books were overturned. Several hundred books were scattered over a wide area. Many had broken spines where they had been trampled on. The book table was overturned, its glass top smashed. The children's corner looked as if a herd of cows had stampeded across it, little chairs smashed and tumbled everywhere. The sexton walked slowly up the north aisle. Someone had been jumping from pew to pew, leaping over the backs and swinging on the heavy curtains that separated off the rear part of the church. Curtains and rails hung, sagging and broken, brass rings scattered around. He looked no further and shaking his head, he turned, went back, and locking the door behind him, hurried to the vicarage. There would be no services today.

They found Bob Wilkes on the first floor of the tower. He was curled up in the foetal position, eyes tightly closed. He refused to acknowledge anyone, say anything or open his eyes. He had, obviously, spent several hours wantonly desecrating the church. It must have been carried out while he was in an ungovernable rage because he had hurt himself badly during the process. He was a mass of minor cuts and bruises. An examination would later find that he had broken fingers and cracked ribs. He was taken to Ramsey Cottage Hospital and then on to Noble's. At first he refused to speak – to talk at all. After a few days he said, "The clerk knew what I'd done and he came for me." When questioned by the police he simply repeated that sentence over and over again.

Within a few days Wilkes was transferred to England and, after a month or two at a general hospital, they found it necessary to transfer him to a secure wing. He tended to rush about at night and harm himself. That was fifteen years ago. He is still there. Still in the same secure unit. Still on the same ward. And during all those long years he has said nothing but, "The clerk knew what I'd done and he came for me." He has repeated that phrase in answer to any question thousands upon thousands of times.

★ ★ ★

At the time of what the police called 'the incident' they, and the vicar, went to great lengths to discover why Wilkes had acted as he did. The fact of the matter was that Wilkes had broken into a locked church – a set of skeleton keys had been found on him. The vicar had checked the safe. He found it locked and its contents, the church plate and £23, untouched. The vicar said that he had talked with Wilkes during the previous afternoon. They had discussed the picture of old Kirk Christ, hanging in the vestry. He had then admired Wilkes's work on the spire and had shown him the site of the old church. They had ended up at the vicarage for a cup of tea – all very ordinary, really. Wilkes appeared to be under no stress and certainly exhibited no anger towards the vicar.

"We walked back to the church together," the vicar said. "Mr Wilkes dismantled his ladders and stowed them on his lorry. He drove off and I had work to do in the vestry. The next day, Sunday, being the Festival of All Souls, the Sunday School were doing a presentation during the morning service and I wanted to make a space for them to stand their Archangel Michael. You see, they and their teachers had made, by using a borrowed dressmaker's dummy, a splendid life-size angel. It looked totally lifelike, quite magnificent. They had made a head for it – a really lovely head with a beautiful face. They had dressed it in one of my albs and made a scroll of heavy paper for it to hold. It looked, as I say, so very lifelike. The Sunday School ladies were going to stand it in the vestry during the evening so that it could easily be carried out into the church during the children's presentation. Of course, poor Mr Wilkes wrecked it. He had dragged it halfway through the vestry door. Tragic, so tragic, that he should vent his spite on the children's work."

november

Allison Fletcher was educated at Ramsey Grammar School and then trained as a nurse at the Old Nobles Hospital.

She has since retired from nursing and now lives quietly in a bluebell wood on the west coast where she spends her time between her two loves of writing and gardening.

Allison came third in the Olive Lamming award for fiction in 2010 and this is her first published short story.

вoу meets girl

Allison Fletcher

Alex could feel himself falling.

He had been falling for so long that there seemed little point in worrying about it, in fact very little worried him any more.

Detached and almost abnormally relaxed, he allowed himself to freefall into the darkness. Registering one brief moment of panic he became conscious of his heart beating wildly in his chest and looking up he watched the diluted memory of all that he had ever been drifting into the distance.

Alice grabbed at the upholstery as the taxi slid round yet another corner in the thick fog, the rain lashing so hard against the windows the wipers could hardly cope. Since leaving Ramsey she had lost all idea of where they actually were; Mannanan had cast his cloak like a woollen shroud and visibility on the mountain was reduced to inches.

Despite reassurances from the driver she had convinced herself the baby would be born in the cab and only the prospect of careering to their deaths in some rain-soaked gully was likely to prevent this happening.

She was wrong. Alex George Richardson was born half an hour after they reached the maternity hospital on one of the stormiest November nights on record and although she hadn't wanted him she took the screaming bundle from the midwife and held him to her breast.

As mothers went she was more efficient than affectionate. Love, like money, was a commodity in short supply in the Richardson household, where two generations eked out an existence on a few acres of rabbit-bitten Ayres.

Alex recognized early on that his father would be the main provider of what little affection he was likely to receive and once he could walk they were seldom found apart. Alex loved his father and, without ever having to be told, he knew his father loved him.

Within a few years a sister arrived and Alex had loved her too. Leaning against the old pram, in a sunny corner of the yard, he stood over her as she slept, his grandmother's chickens scratching about at his feet. Moving in her sleep, Linda would reach out and grasp at the air until he placed one of his little fingers in her own and so he would stand waiting patiently for the day when she would take her first faltering steps and sit on the ground beside him.

With big blue eyes and great mops of blond hair it was often difficult to tell them apart, although their grandfather regularly took Alex into the back yard and clipped away the curls. The old man wasn't having a grandson who looked like a girl. Large tears rolled silently down the boy's face as he watched the breeze catch the fallen tresses and blow them into little drifts below the step.

As they grew, the two blond heads were always together, while they made daisy chains in the orchard or ran over the Ayres to the water's edge. Socks and shoes left on the beach, they played at being chased by the tide, arriving home tired and wet to pick through their beachcombing finds.

When it was too cold to go out they retreated to the front hall, draughty and damp and bathed in a strange red glow as the daylight filtered through the stained glass windows. This space became the centre of their imaginary world, the home of their secrets and the stage of their fantasies; here they rummaged through their mother's paste jewellery and paraded about for hours in her old clothes. In his memory the scents of early childhood were always the sharp tang of the sea mingled with damp and mothballs.

By the time she was five he had already fallen into the role of responsible other and would walk her the half mile up to the main road to wait for the school bus. Alex carrying their lunch in brown paper bags, jam oozing from the sandwiches, they'd make the slow climb hand in hand, naming the birds and flowers as they went, gently moving with the seasons.

Soon, without him even noticing, they had grown.

Linda no longer needed him to walk her to the bus or occupy her free time; she made friends of her own. Giggling friends, who arrived on their bicycles or came skipping down the road in pairs, taking her away to hide in quiet corners and whisper secrets. A private, all-female club to which he was no longer invited.

Alex moved up to the Grammar School and went out before her in the mornings, trudging alone to the top of the road and returning later with a bag of homework that had to be set aside while he helped around the farm.

And so he filled his time with chores, doing whatever was asked of him, although his heart and his head were always somewhere else. On the days when there was no work to do he'd sit alone, reading, waiting for his father to come in – and then one day he didn't.

He never came home again.

For the first time in his life Alex became aware of a deep sadness, a sense of hopelessness that lived inside him like a worm, waiting its opportunity to plunge him into a dark world full of despair.

On the day of the funeral he had climbed out of the bathroom window and run all the way to Bride churchyard only to be caught and returned home by an over-protective neighbour.

Aunts and uncles crowded in around the naughty boy, an exclusion zone appeared and the already distant mother became forever out of reach.

His grandfather very shortly followed his father into the ground and Alex found himself alone in a house full of women. The stock and the fields were quickly sold and absorbed into the farm next door, and only the orchard with its few elderly hens and the decaying house remained.

Alex spent as little time as possible there and escaped to wander the Ayres whenever he could. Sitting alone in the shelter of a dune, the sea grass rustling above his head, or walking for hours with the wind tugging at his hair and the spray camouflaging the tears that streaked his face.

When he was at home he would find himself standing alone in the hall listening for the echoes of a happier time. No one else noticed; self-absorbed, the three grieving females almost stopped noticing Alex as he moved like a shadow about the house. None of them commented on the scratches and abrasions his pretty boy good looks attracted from the tougher elements at school and he very quickly learnt to keep his problems to himself, gradually falling more deeply into the world of the worm.

Still, life of a sort went on, the process of growing and becoming less of a financial burden falling more heavily on

Alex than his sister. And so they drifted apart.

His exams came and went. 'A bright, although introverted boy,' said his report, 'he could go far if encouraged.'

"No extended education for Alex," said his mother. "Out of school and into work as soon as possible."

He joined the army, deciding it would be easier to send money home than to continue his lonely existence in the house full of women. His mother and grandmother encouraged him; in their hearts they were glad to see the morose young man leave.

They all went to see him off, a month before his seventeenth birthday, taking the boat bus to the ferry terminal. He found a place at the stern where he could see the landing stage and picked them out huddled together, his mother and grandmother in their dowdy, out of fashion clothes and Linda, a bright spark in coloured tights, waving madly as the boat pulled out of the harbour. The familiar sting of the spray hit his face as the vessel turned into the wind and with one final movement of his hand he left his childhood behind and set out hoping to find his place in the world, a place that would accommodate him and allow him to be happy.

And he was for a while, although the male closeness seemed alien and uncouth after the restrained female household. He worked hard at fitting in and tried to ignore the sense of being while not belonging but when he fell exhausted into his bed at night the worm was always there, reminding him that he was different. By sheer strength of will he rose above it, staying to be bullied and teased, tortured and trained and ultimately befriended in a haphazard sort of way.

Gradually the introverted boy became a man, reluctantly joining in on riotous nights out in strange towns, anxious to feel part of the norm. On one drunken weekend leave he met Maddie. She reminded him of his sister, with her blue eyes and blonde hair, so in a way she reminded him of himself. She hung back from her tipsy and precocious friends, her shyness making it easier for him to approach her.

They both seemed out of place in the noisy bar, and escaping, they walked the streets for hours, eating chips and sharing histories.

Eventually they ended up in her bed.

Alex was never quite certain he had fallen in love with Maddie, or she with him, but those nights he spent with her were less likely to be invaded by the worm than many others and it was possible that he loved her for this reason alone.

Returning home briefly to attend his grandmother's funeral he told his mother he was married and three months later, after the birth of his son, the three of them paid a flying visit.

Linda, grown and with a boyfriend of her own, cooed over the baby and then flew out for a night on the town. His mother, never close, seemed more distant than ever and not particularly overjoyed at the arrival of her grandson.

After the landlocked army bases he was glad to be back on the Island and spent what time he could walking his old haunts, disturbing the terns and watching the gannets diving far out from the shoreline, happy to feel the spray on his face and the wind against his body. Maddie hated the visit and was glad to escape back to their married quarters.

Alex didn't return home again until after his divorce and discharge from the army, by which time Linda was married and living in Italy and his mother bedridden and in the final grip of the cancer that had been consuming her for years, her medication so strong that she slipped fitfully in and out of sleep with only a rare lucid moment.

He quickly realised she either wasn't interested or wasn't capable of absorbing what he said and so he never told her about the breakdown of his marriage. She never found out about his descent into the world of the worm and how this had brought about his eventual discharge from the army and she died peacefully one afternoon, as he sat with her, without ever knowing that only his regular visits to a psychiatrist were stopping him taking the rest of her medication and lying down on the bed beside her.

Linda came home briefly for the funeral and spent a few hours rummaging through the house. She didn't want to stay, she didn't want any of it, it was too dark and depressing, too gloomy; a house full of sad memories. She told him to sell it and move on, then she did, back to Italy and the sun.

For a few weeks he wandered about the place, emptying cupboards and missing appointments. Without any sense of purpose he sorted out the accumulation of a lifetime that wasn't his until one day he caught sight of himself in a mirror. Over his clothes he'd thrown his mother's old silk dressing gown, bright and embroidered with an oriental pattern, whilst around his neck hung a couple of strings of his grandmother's beads.

In one brief moment he turned on the worm.

The 'For Sale' sign went up.

★ ★ ★

The lift slowed in its descent and eventually hiccoughed to a stop; with a shush the doors parted and its occupants moved forward in a rush to be out. All except one. A tall, slim woman hung back, catching sight of her reflection in the now empty mirrored interior. As no one else entered the compartment she took a moment to smile at her grainy image. Although nearly forty her hair was still thick and blond and fell in heavy curls around the collar of her silky blouse, her eyes were bright and blue and seemed to sparkle in her suntanned face. Beneath her blouse the implants nestled comfortably into her skimpy bra as she ran her hand carefully over her figure.

She liked what she saw and taking a deep breath, she shouldered her bag and walked out of the lift, her kitten heels click clacking on the tiled floor. Alexa smiled to herself as she walked through the foyer and out onto the sunlit promenade; far out in the bay she could see gannets diving for fish.

Falling was easy, you just had to be confident about where you wanted to land.

✳ December ✳

Dollin Kelly was born in Port St. Mary in 1931 and was educated at Rushen Central School, the Royal Masonic schools and St. Johns College, York. For many years he taught in Manchester and then the Isle of Man and is now retired and living back in Port St. Mary.

Dollin was the winner of the Olive Lamming 2010 prize for a non-fiction story.

A funny thing happened on the way home from school

Dollin Kelly

It has been a long-standing joke in our family that after 3rd September 1939 and the declaration of war by Britain on Nazi Germany any parents of young children in the UK having connections, however tenuous, with the Isle of Man, despatched their offspring with great rapidity to brothers, sisters, aunts, grandparents, cousins – even mere friends – who lived in the presumed peace and tranquility of an island the Germans would not bother to bomb.

That, actually, is not the joke.

The joke is that *our* mother sent my brother, Juan, and me in the opposite direction: perhaps she had a hidden message for us which our juvenile subtlety was too immature to recognise. Anyway on 18th September we found ourselves being escorted by our mother to, and deposited in, the Royal Masonic Institution for Boys (Junior) School, Bushey, Hertfordshire – about thirteen miles north of Piccadilly Circus and, on a clear day with the wind behind it, almost within the sound of Bow Bells. When the wind was in the other direction we had a very clear stink from Benskin's Brewery at Watford, a mile to the north.

For the sake of this tale, I'll 'fast-forward' to our journey home for the Christmas holidays in December 1940. By this time we were hardened war veterans, having experienced the introduction of our school to high explosive and incendiary bombs, dropped by the aforementioned Germans, plus the various sentiments that go with sleeping on the floor – three bodies to two mattresses – in one of two reinforced ground floor rooms ('play box' and 'boot') while the orchestra of falling bombs, answering ack-ack fire and the continuo of droning aeroplanes, played its lullaby above our otherwise peaceful rooftops. Also Juan and I had been part of the contingent of about one-eighth of the school whose mothers (we were all fatherless) had opted to have us stay at school for the entire summer holiday because it might be 'too unsafe in our own homes'. We, therefore, also had seen the most northerly skirmishes of the Battle of Britain fought over our heads during the memorably hot days of August and early September 1940.

In those days most children were shown a new journey once. After that they were expected to be savvy enough to undertake the same trip on their own or with their peers without expecting an adult to accompany them, particularly if they were only travelling between their school and home. If a nine or ten-year-old wanted to buy a bus, train or boat ticket, no one questioned it and the term 'unaccompanied child' had not yet been invented. That December, five Manx boys left Bushey in one party for the longed-for sanctuary of the Island and for Christmas at home. We were Jimmy Taggart, aged 12 from Ramsey and his brother John, aged 11, both of whom also had spent the summer holidays at school; Saul Cregeen, aged 10 from Onchan; my brother Juan, celebrating his eleventh birthday, and I, just 9 years old at the time.

All went well until we arrived at the Prince's Landing Stage at Liverpool where the *Victoria* was lying alongside with no signs of having steam up ready for departure. The term 'customer relations' had also not been invented in those days but a typical Steam Packet crewman was at the bottom of the gangplank (and here my 78 years of memory might now be subject to a little colourful exaggeration), shouting to anyone who dared approach the 'boat' (as Steam Packet vessels were always referred to until the coming of the first ro-ro) "Clear-off! The boat isn't sailing today! German aircraft mined the Mersey this morning and the navy's now sweeping it. Phone tomorrow at noon and we'll give you further orders." Steam Packet crewmen never left anyone in doubt as to who was in charge.

The Ramsey boys said, "Oh, we've got an auntie in Liverpool. Goodbye," and immediately disappeared, leaving no forwarding address. I asked Cregeen if, perchance, *he* might have an auntie in Liverpool but answer came there none. Even for those days, I suppose, it was a bit tough for a boy celebrating his eleventh birthday, a ten-year-old and a nine-year-old to be abandoned on the landing stage in this way and I *don't* consider today's children are mollycoddled when carriers give them special protection.

Fortunately, Juan and I, before the war, had stayed in Liverpool with Mr and Mrs Will Scott, acquaintances of our parents who had particularly befriended us after our father died. We had stayed with them at their house in Derby Lane, Old Swan. Both of us knew the way and that the number of the tram which would get us there was 19. We suggested to Cregeen that he come with us. I hope his mother was forever grateful afterwards that he accepted our offer of the Scotts' hospitality.

It is, perhaps, worth considering what we might have done had Juan and I not known the Scotts. We definitely would not have made a drama out of the event and the one certain point is that we wouldn't have died. We would have revealed our plight to the nearest passing stranger or nearest policeman – neither of which solutions would, I'm afraid, appeal to many of today's children taught by their parents to be terrified of the former and mistrustful of the latter.

Mind you, it would have taken huge bravery on our part to have approached the seaman at the bottom of the gangplank.

Children's perceptions, of course, are different from adults': it was only quite a bit later in life that it occurred to me that the Scotts were pretty prosperous members of the merchant class. They owned several sweet shops throughout Liverpool and one at the Four Roads, Port St Mary. Part of each was a post office where Will was the designated sub-post-master though, obviously, others did the work. (Manx post offices were still a part of the British GPO in those days.) The Scotts did not own a motor car (as we did) but they did have a holiday cottage attached to the Port St Mary shop and a weekend retreat in North Wales. Their house in West Derby never struck me as being anything special as there were, and still are, hundreds of houses like it in the Isle of Man. We called them boarding houses or, even, private hotels but the Scotts' four-storey-plus-basement double-fronted Edwardian end of terrace edifice with large front and back gardens was a private house. They mightn't have owned a car but they did have a coach house and stable (disused) and were the only family I have ever stayed with which had a butler, *and* an intercom phone system in every room in the house.

Accompanied by oohs and ahhs and lovely, warm hugs they welcomed we three orphans of the storm of war. We were fed and watered, our mothers were contacted and we were shown where we would be sleeping – on mattresses on the floor of their cellar to which the family had been reintroduced just the night before after months free from any bombing at all around Liverpool! Bombs fell heavily that night, sending their familiar shudders up through the floor, and the accompanying ack-ack provided a comforting feeling of *déjà vu* to help us settle. We yarned and played board games till around midnight when Mr Scott took us up to the billiard room which was under the eaves and had a fairly large skylight. He told us that we would remember the sight he was showing us for the rest of our lives: Saul Cregeen and my brother Juan are dead long years ago but Mr Scott was right; I remember that sight in detail even now.

At least half of the horizon visible from that window was a distant mass of flame with the sky to a great height reflecting a violent orange. Mr Scott explained that the targets which had been successfully hit were the Liverpool Docks. When we did eventually take the tram to the boat for home we saw that a goodly number of downtown properties had also been hit. Despite Liverpool's having been designated City of Culture just recently, many of those buildings are still derelict.

I think we probably arrived in Liverpool on a Tuesday. During the war only one boat operated the Douglas–Liverpool route so there was only a boat in either direction every other day and, of course, no boat on Sundays. (Just like the IOM railways, Sunday boat services were unknown until about the 1960s.) Around 11.00a.m. the next day the sirens mournfully groaned into action as the Luftwaffe was once again over the Mersey. Distant explosions were heard but, as instructed, we duly phoned the Steam Packet agent, Thomas Orford Ltd, at midday. "The Mersey's been mined again: the navy is out again trying to clear the channel. Phone again, same time tomorrow."

That night and 'the same time tomorrow' the story was the same, and again during the following twenty-four hours: bombing raids by night and mining raids by day. The Scotts were wonderful but what about the people on the Island? The Mersey was paralysed: no passenger or cargo boat from Liverpool since the previous Saturday; things must have been becoming desperate. So too at the Liverpool end: the Steam Packet must have been really keen to get the mails, newspapers and perishable goods normally carried by the *Victoria* over to the Island, not to mention all the extra people converging on the port *en route* for their Christmas holidays, so on the Friday Orfords said, "Try again later", which the Scotts duly did and eventually tentative directions were given to make for the Pier Head ready for a provisional 7.00p.m. sailing.

I think that that was actually about the time when the boat did finally sail. It was absolutely crammed with people. Soldiers, sailors, airmen, men on their own, women on their own, families with babes in arms and every one of us looking worn out as we crammed together wherever we could find somewhere to stand. I don't even remember where Juan was for most of the journey. The crowd's momentum had propelled me down into the aft well-deck where I recollect being ring-fenced by three or four chaps in khaki when, suddenly, not ten minutes after departing the pier, there was a tremendous crash, the boat shook, then shivered and all the already 'blacked out' lights of wartime went out, then on, then out again – exactly like film-makers were later to portray such scenes in the multitude of war films which are still shown on our TVs today. The women hadn't stopped screaming before two more enormous explosions in very quick succession rocked the boat but, mercifully, the lights came on within a matter of seconds and, slowly, following a good few relieved exhalations of stifled breath, conversation was resumed and shortly after, normal behaviour as the realisation dawned that we didn't seem to be sinking and, in fact, the *Victoria* was steaming on without so much as a pause.

That's it, really: the rest of the journey was uneventful. We arrived at the Edward Pier somewhere around midnight. The water was at full ebb but we soon picked out our grandfather and our mother amongst the faces peering dangerously over the precipitous edge of the pier which was high above deck level. Juan and I both delved into our strong carrier bags obtained in Liverpool to hold aloft the bargain of bargains we had jointly acquired on a shopping expedition into town. In the middle of a war where bombs were regularly dropped on railways, docks, homes, shops, factories and anything else Jerry thought it worth having a go at; where millions of tons of shipping were being destroyed in half the oceans of the world simply to starve Britain into submission, what had we been able to buy for sixpence each that we were so keen to show our nearest and dearest? It defies belief but it's true. What we had bought were three (the third for our sister, Esther) newly imported, live tortoises!

A little something extra ...

Alison Ogden is 15 and a student at St. Ninians's High School, Douglas. Alison is an avid reader and loves to write, and apart from winning the IOM Young Crime Writer's Award has also won the Spirit of Normandy Trust Young Historian Senior Award 2010. This award was open to all schools across the UK for the best essay on any aspect of the D-Day landings.

About the CWA

The Crime Writers' Association, of which I am a member, is a professional body that represents the interests of writers of crime fiction and non-fiction throughout the British Isles and beyond. This year, the CWA organised its first National Crime Fiction Week, which proved to be a real success. The Young Crime Writers' Competition was at the very heart of the preparations for National Crime Fiction Week, and I was delighted by the high standard of stories submitted by young writers in the Isle of Man. Congratulations again to Alison Ogden, our very talented local winner, and sincere thanks and appreciation to Priory Press for re-printing Alison's pacey and exhilarating story here. Enjoy!

Chris Ewan

Dead End

Alison Ogden

"Kez! What we gonna do? What we gonna do?" Danny frantically paces the room, rubbing his shaking hands through his dark, greasy hair.

"Shut up and le' me think for a minute!"

"But Kez – you jus' killed her!"

"You think I don't already know that! Now shut up!"

I glance at the body, blood slowly staining the carpet a dark crimson. From the en-suite, a tap drips monotonously, sending hollow echoes through the blackness of the room. I shake my head. It wasn't meant to go down like this.

"Kez," he hisses.

"What?"

"We gotta get outta here. The cops'll be here any minute." He hurriedly checks the empty street below through the slats in the venetian blinds. Only the pale glimmer from a street light pierces the stillness of night.

"It's not the cops we have to worry about," I murmur.

It was meant to be routine; it was so simple. Everything would have gone smoothly if it wasn't for the stupid bitch pulling Danny's balaclava off. She saw him. That was her mistake. My reaction was automatic. And now she lies at my feet, another problem.

A thousand others churn through my head till I become almost sick with the thought of our predicament; my predicament. Danny won't squeal, but I promised the boss I'd look after him. But it got out of hand.

"Jesus Christ, Kez. What are we doin'? Come on man. Think o' somethin'. Before the cops get 'ere!"

I grab him, shoving him hard against a wall, clamping my hand over his mouth.

"Shut the hell up, Danny! I'm thinking what to do. Just keep yer trap shut."

He yanks my hand from over his face, pushing me away.

"Okay man. Okay. Jesus. Yer don't 'ave to grab me."

I tear my eyes from him, to the body, then to the knife in my hand. Her blood, beginning to congeal on the blade, is turning to thick, black ink.

My eyes flicker towards her. She could've done something with her life. Shame. But you never mess with the boss. And once you're working for him, there's only one way out. Some people just don't get that. She was one of them. Not any more.

"We need to get rid of her."

"What? Hell, I'm not goin' anywhere near her."

"Don't worry Danny, she's dead. If only you'd paid more attention. I knew this was a mistake." I mutter the last words harshly under my breath.

"Kez, she came out o' nowhere. It isn't my fault. I just didn't see her."

"Then you should've opened your bloody eyes," I snarl back.

I'm in enough trouble already without having a stroppy

teenager giving me lip. What's the boss going to say when he finds out one of his best girls got whacked because his nephew got in the way. It was a scare. A reminder to let her know she has to pay up sooner or later. But I screwed it up. I lost my temper. And now I've got to find a way out of this.

My blood runs cold as the squeal of a siren hurtles by and flashing blue lights blur past the window. Instinctively, I drop to the floor. Danny's eyes are as wide as saucers as he copies. The scream of tyres on wet tarmac. I hold my breath. My heart pummels my ribcage as footsteps sound from below the window.

The woman's blonde hair is so close I could almost touch its bleached, combed silkiness. Sickly sweet perfume and the metallic stench of blood assault my nostrils, making me gag. But I can't move. I mustn't move. Danny lays quivering across the room from me. Poor kid, only nineteen. Deep voices drift upwards from the street, filling the room with eerie, distant murmurs.

"All quiet on the western front," laughs one of them.

"Yup. Means I can go home and have a good night's sleep," the other cheerfully remarks.

Moments later, the engine starts and the car rolls away. I exhale.

"That was close," Danny stutters, getting shakily to his feet.

"Too close," I agree.

We take a few seconds to come out of the shock.

"What are we gonna do with her?" he asks. "Kez. Sooner or later my uncle's gonna notice she ain't been workin' an' we're gonna be …"

"I know."

My head hurts from thinking. There's no easy way out of this, but I've got to think of something.

"We tell the boss."

"What? Are you mad? You tell him what happened an' he's gonna go crazy."

"An' if we don't?" I reply.

"We're screwed," he whispers helplessly, knowingly.

"No. I am. You're his nephew. I'm dispensible," I reassure him.

A clock on the bedside table ticks away mindlessly; dogs a few blocks away growl to the skies and the tap continues to drip. The radiator gurgles, making Danny leap half a metre in the air.

"It's the heating."

He spins around nervously, fretfully scanning the room, half expecting someone to jump him.

"Find a sheet, or something to wrap her up in and tie her hands."

"Where the hell am I …?"

I raise my eyebrows at him.

I slam the boot lid down. Getting rid of her; that was the easy part. Now I have to go tell the boss. I get in the car, ramming the key into the ignition. Some night this has been. I pull my seatbelt on. My eyes dart to the clock on the dashboard; five to one. I put the car in gear and begin to reverse round a shipping crate.

Three hooded figures approach, all in black. I freeze – big mistake.

The first guy reaches the window before I could take another breath. I almost choke on my heart as I see the Glock in his large, gloved hands. The others surround the vehicle. I stare at my fate.

"The boss wants you to have this."